# THE BOY IN THE MOON

KATE O'RIORDAN

# THE BOY
# IN THE MOON

Flamingo
*An Imprint of* HarperCollins*Publishers*

Flamingo
An Imprint of HarperCollins*Publishers*
77–85 Fulham Palace Road,
Hammersmith, London W6 8JB

Published by Flamingo 1997
1   3   5   7   9   8   6   4   2

A catalogue record for this book
is available from the British Library

ISBN 0 00 225555 3

Set in Meridien by
Rowland Phototypesetting Ltd, Bury St Edmunds, Suffolk

Printed and bound in Great Britain by
Caledonian International Book Manufacturing Ltd, Glasgow

# ACKNOWLEDGEMENTS

The author would like to express her gratitude to Kathleen O'Riordan and Michael Carroll for their kind assistance with historical data (*Where the Deer Ran Wild* by Michael Carroll).

And a very special thanks to Eoghan O'Riordan for all his invaluable assistance with the agricultural details.

For Mam

# ONE

# Is It Love?

Once, when he was nearly four, she found him outside in the garden staring up at the moon with his head cocked to one side. He was silent and very still. She crept up behind him, quietly, so as not to disturb his contemplation. It was a soft twilight in September – low-slung, grainy sky ballasting a swollen, somehow predatory moon. Her son appeared to be entranced. She turned from him and the strangeness of the evening to gaze back through the french windows to the normality of the living-room – soft light, sofas, cushions, padding. Everything as it should be, where it should be – touchstone suburbia, the reassurance of crystal and chintz.

He sensed or smelled her presence but still he did not move. She wondered at his thoughts and then he turned, slowly, widened brown eyes reflecting moonlight for an instant as his gaze settled on her. 'It's not a man in the moon,' he said.

'It isn't?'

'No. Look.' He pointed upwards. 'Look. It's a boy, and he's screaming.'

She followed the line of his finger, then shrugged. 'How so?' she asked.

'See – two eyes, and there's a squishy bit for a nose and look – look, mum, I said – there's the mouth and it's a bit to the side and it's open wide, like this – Look, look, like this . . .'

He held his head to the side at a slight angle, opened his eyes wide, pulled his mouth to the left and yawned it open as wide as he could. She looked up at the moon, then down at him again. He was right. It did look as if there was a boy screaming in the moon. 'I wonder why he's screaming,' she said.

Her son closed his mouth and gazed up again, but this time facing her so that he had to tilt his head backwards and spread his legs for balance. 'Because he's stuck there, of course,' he said.

It had darkened quickly and his headless form with just the triangle of jawline jutting up was in silhouette. She took a step closer. His shoulders began to move up and down.

'Shh,' she whispered, 'it's all right, darling. It's all right, Sammy, just your imagination. That's all it is. Trust me. There really isn't a screaming boy in the moon.'

He allowed her to hold him then and she rocked him for a while but he would not be consoled. She wondered at the intensity of his grief or pity, she could not be sure what strange emotion possessed him and when his sobs turned into hiccoughs, she put on her stern face – though she was trembling – and draped her voice in a cloak of impatience while urging him to bed. She knew her son and when he required her control and not her empathy.

When he finally acceded to her terse commands and trundled upstairs muttering under his breath, she felt that they were back in their own landscape. Their own familiar territory, where she led and he followed, albeit reluctantly at times, but followed none the less. And she could breathe again, spontaneously, and not with the forced shallow rasps he sometimes extracted from her when he led her into his strange and unfamiliar terrain.

When she looked up at the moon again, a slender tendril of cloud had snaked across the yawning mouth and she felt the sunken, staring eyes bear down upon her. She shivered and scurried back to the cushioned living-room.


'Darling?'

His head was under the bath water but he heard her call. He stayed below the water's surface and counted: one, two three, four . . .

'Dah-ling?'

He allowed his nose to break through the skin of water and bubbles. The nostrils dilated and contracted frantically. After ten years, the way she said 'dahling' still irritated him. Perhaps he was a bit too simple-minded but he thought terms of endearment should be just that – if, for that matter, they had to be used at all. Somehow they always sounded affected to him. He had heard other middle-class Englishwomen darling their husbands in the same fashion. They wielded the word, stretched it and sometimes brandished it. It was 'dahling' as a form of possession; it preceded an order, an accusation, as in: 'Dahling, can't you . . .' Never: 'can you', a reluctance on the part of the one addressed being taken for granted. 'Dahling, do you want to change Sam while I get the bottle ready?' It was a vocabulary rampant with vague, unspoken censures. A minefield. The only time he ever felt in any way sure-footed was after sex, and then the feeling did not last very long.

In Ireland, he noisily sucked his teeth whenever she said 'darling'. It was an oceanic distance from the barked 'Mrs' his father had used to summon his mother. Adult speculation had Brian wondering if his father had called her that in bed: 'Suck on this, Mrs . . .' No. Mrs, what he remembered of her, was born into the missionary position, horizontally inclined (in every respect), nothing doggy or foreign in the bedroom, certainly no saliva – ever. Now, Darling stood at the door of the bathroom, folding Sam's pyjamas against her chest. She looked pissed off. Ten years of looking pissed off – the wind must have changed on their wedding day. Brian winked at her – to piss her off some more.

'I've been calling you,' she said. 'Didn't you hear?'

'Have you?' He sat upright and reached for the soap. 'Sorry.'

'How much longer are you going to stay in there?'

'I'm nearly done. Did you want something?'

'Christmas Day – which suit do you want me to pack?'

'You're not packing for me, are you? Just do yourself and Sam. I'll do my own . . . in a minute.'

'I'm finished with us. Hours ago. Which suit?'

'The navy, I think. I don't know. What about last year's jacket with the grey trousers? Oh, I don't care. Anything. Pack anything. It's all the same.'

She pursed her mouth and tapped her foot. He hummed. 'The navy,' he said.

Sam called to her from his bedroom. She rolled her eyes and pretended to hesitate. Then she went to him.

Brian sank back into the bubbles once more. He raised his leg and studied it. Flexed the foot back and forth. In the steamy mirror ahead, he could just make out his features. He lowered the leg and turned his head from side to side. Good, blackish and moreover, loyal hair. He stuck his jaw out – not bad in a jowly, just-going-to-seed Irish politician

4

way. He pulled his lips back and gritted his teeth – still there anyway. He lifted his arm and flexed the muscles; they rose from their torpor obligingly enough. All in all, not bad for forty-three. Little satisfied tremor. In a couple of nights, he would be sitting on a stool under the corrugated iron roof of his favourite local, listening to the buckshot rain above, his tongue gliding greedily over a Guinness moustache.

The thought occurred to him that the thing about being Irish was the measuring out your life in Christmases, Easters and slivers of August. It was the same for the immigrant and for those who waited at home. Around the end of November every year, the pull was at its strongest. By December, he would be filled with a quiet anticipation, coupled with an underlayer of dread – on parole and elated for Christmas, an alien again throughout January and February.

The phone rang. He lifted his other leg to study it. Julia was remonstrating with Sam as she ran from his room to answer the phone. Brian listened. It was Julia's mother, Jennifer, another Darling. Calling to say goodbye and *bon voyage* and happy Christmas for the third time that day. He heard Julia impatiently say that she did not want to hear the weather forecast. Whatever horrors awaited them on the ferry would just have to be faced. Brian thought of cauliflowers.

Whenever he thought of Julia's mother he thought of cauliflowers. It was her hair. White and permed into fat florets which framed her plump cushion of a face. Her eyes were blue and discontented, like her daughter's. Richard, Julia's father, was a tortoise – slow, unenthusiastic gait and elongated neck – ready for the guillotine from the birth. The skin on his face seemed to droop too under bristled black eyebrows. Most of the time, Brian could not make out his

5

eyes, just two gleams of light beaming out hesitantly beneath their canopies. It was a habit of Brian's, to make vegetables or animals of people. He had done so since childhood. Julia had begun as a cat and metamorphosed over the years into a pineapple, although she had had her moments of bovine splendour too. He stretched and listened to her trying to get Jennifer off the phone, knowing from the sound of her voice that she was still folding clothes against her chest with the receiver cradled between her head and shoulder. 'We've managed to get to a phone on Christmas Day in the past, I don't see why it should be a problem this year,' Julia was saying. She stopped for a while and listened. 'Jennifer, please stop fussing,' she continued, addressing her mother by her Christian name, which meant that she was getting cross. Brian shifted up uneasily in the bath and watched the rivulets stream down the black dense hairs on his legs and forearms.

When he heard the click of the replaced receiver he placed both hands on either side of the bath as though he were just about to rise. But Julia was checking window locks downstairs, bolting the french doors to the garden, checking the various alarms while she cleared away any remaining debris from their dinner earlier. He could hear the musical clickety clack of her heels beating out across the tiled and wooden floors below. A swish of drapes closed, another, then another. Click clack back to the kitchen again.

He was in the main bathroom – he had thought she might need to use the *en suite*. But she would probably keep going for hours yet and shower just before bed, something he could never understand. More doors opened downstairs. The final final check. Julia, he thought, did not open doors so much as assault them. She wrenched handles and entered rooms with the door swinging on its hinges behind her, as if she expected resistance at every turn. She ran up and down stairs, one hand outstretched in vague deference to a banister rail she never touched. She reversed her car with a savagery that made him wince. And she pounced on ringing phones like a cheetah.

Sam wandered into the bathroom, scratching his head. He lifted the toilet seat and peed.

'Sam,' Brian said.

'Dad,' Sam said over his shoulder. He yawned.

'It's late. You should be asleep. We've a long day ahead of us tomorrow.'

'I know. I had to make a pee.'

'You packed all the toys you want to bring, then?'

'Mum did it.'

'So what did you choose in the end?'

'Just the usual stuff.'

'Books too?'

'Yeah.'

'Did Mum find room for the spaceship in the end?'

'No.'

'I'm sure I could squeeze it into the boot somewhere.'

'She says there're too many bits. They'll only get lost.'

'She might be right.'

Sam yawned again. He was standing motionless, still holding his penis over the toilet bowl.

'Sam? I think you're finished . . .'

'I know.'

'Well, what's keeping you then? Away with you to bed.'

'I'm thinking of a poo.'

'Have you got one?'

'I'm thinking of it.'

'Go and sit on our toilet.'

7

Sam shook a few last drops and flushed the toilet. 'It's gone back up,' he said.

'Hands,' Brian said.

Sam gingerly dipped his hands into the bath-water suds. His father leaned across to kiss his cheek. Sam wiped the wet cheek with his pyjama sleeve. 'Fly is a word without a vowel in it,' he said.

'What's that got to do with anything?'

'I'm only saying.'

'Bed. Now.'

'Your willy looks all squishy.' A final yawn and he was gone.

Brian looked down. He had not realized he had been in the bath that long. He sighed and lay back. Contemplated the knots and gnarls on his raised feet for a moment. Strange thing, the body. Lived in for a lifetime yet there were parts of it, the back of his head for instance, the middle of his back, his scalp, that he had never really seen except in an unsatisfactory fashion in the mirror. This was, of course, quite apart from all the internal bits. The ridiculousness of self was a thought that had often struck him, as a member of a large family, which in turn had led to the affirmation of self in the smallest and most curious of ways, like his pepper consumption. Even now, Brian could not eat his food unless it was practically concealed beneath a black frost of pepper. He wondered if Teresa, the youngest, still spat into her plate before she began to eat. Quite probably. They had all managed to devise ways to repel nimble, filching fingers from their dinner plates . . . Feet pounded the stairs, but they ravished the master bedroom. He was safe for a while yet.

*

8

In the en-suite bathroom, Julia quickly shunted out of her clothes and stepped under the shower. She decided against washing her hair, it was too late. She turned the shower off and grabbed a towel, checking the cabinet above the sink as she dried herself for any last forgotten items. The ladyrazor. And an anti-cellulite cream, brown gunge caked around the stopper, which wouldn't work now anyway even with a blessing from Rome.

She sucked her stomach in and turned sideways. Her breasts were still full enough, quite large and round with tight compact nipples. In the mirror, the left breast always looked larger but Brian pretended not to notice. She reached for the tweezers and plucked a couple of straying hairs around each nipple, then a couple more above her top lip. She lifted her eyebrows without raising her brow, to see what her eyes looked like without the sagging eyelid flaps. With everything sucked in, pulled up, and her eyes looking slightly surprised, she could see what she was like in her twenties. With a sigh, everything collapsed, thirty-eight again.

The skin was still good – cream with the odd curdle. Nothing special about the lips – they functioned; by contrast, the cheekbones were high and almost anachronistic. Blue eyes, just on the turn, a dulling around the cornea. Remortgaged blonde bob – a clone in the schoolyard and Sainsbury's. She thought about Brian resplendent in his bubbles for the past two hours and waited for the little spring of irritation to well up, but it didn't. Instead, something fell inside her, a weight, a charge, and she felt herself opening. It was strange how that could happen. Most of the time she felt irritated. And then, suddenly, unexpectedly, her cervix would widen and she would feel confused.

9

On a straight run approaching a green light, he braked in anticipation of a change; for the same reason, she pressed her foot to the floor. After ten years of marriage, this was the most significant difference she could cite if they ever had to face a divorce court. Not less than everything – she smiled ruefully at her own reflection, and wondered if she would know herself if she met herself in a crowded room. The features were familiar, of course. But expressions were entirely a different matter. What did she look like laughing? Crying? Sad? She had no idea. She was really a composite of someone else's perceptions. The thought saddened her for a moment. Then the thought of the two weeks ahead saddened her even more, stretching out like the concept of purgatory Brian had grown up with. A spartan fortnight full of everything her middle-class credenda told her was charac-ter-forming, wholesome and true, but which in reality inevi-tably proved to be wearisome, harsh and boring.

Sam was asleep when she tiptoed into his room with the towel around her. She could see his face from the crack of light which the landing offered, and his head: a miniature universe. Beside him lay the spaceship, contrived to tug at her heart, which was by Sam's and Brian's standards made of granite or something entirely extra-terrestrial, a Plutonic ice-ball. Sam snuffled in his sleep. Brian hummed from the bathroom. They were so entirely dependent on her. Awake, asleep, she ruled them. She gazed at the spaceship. It was full of tiny men and women. For a moment, she swelled like a god.

Sam's dark hair stood up, electrocuted. His long eyelashes cast spiky talons on his cheeks. He was plump, like Jennifer. Julia could see him, years from now, like some tiny Nero, all white curls and cherubic smiles, fiddling while London burned as she, maternal mentor, looked on approvingly. Sam snored. She went to him and stroked the demerara freckles along his cheekbone. He sighed. All softness and light and complicated layers which gave voice to the man he would become. A man. Sam. It was an impossibility. He was too innocent to belong to either sex. She bent to kiss him and his curled fist opened slightly to indicate that he knew she was there.

Thus far, a self-contained little boy, content in his singularity, with an adult vocabulary holding forth in a high-pitched squeak. The gusts of her anger sometimes pinning his ears back, making him blink before she uttered a word. His silent disapproval thereafter sending her panting to the fridge for comfort.

He resisted her embrace for a moment, as she knew he would. But then plump arms wound around her neck and he breathed sweet, unpolluted breath on her. She felt ashamed of her own scent. He tugged at her neck and inhaled deep within her hair.

Outside his room she stood for an instant recalling his first day at school. She had stood by the classroom door and watched him melt into an alien world of masculine declensions that she could never decipher for him. Nudges and back thumps and rushes for the door, each boy trying to outdo the other. The girls huddled in sinister little groups of twos and threes, the boy group swelling to encompass more and more until they heaved in one great throbbing caterpillar, chewing up the playground. She was excluded. After years of being there, the only thing, the only one, she had to be satisfied with nothing responses.

'What did you do today?'
'Nothing.'
'Who did you play with?'

'No one.'

'Where did you play?'

'Nowhere.'

She had found it extraordinary that he was already inculcated in the language of silence, of non-committance, of secrecy, at the age of five. What was there to hide at five? Everything, it appeared. Even more secrets now that he was seven. Sometimes, she felt envious of the silent vocabulary that passed between father and son.

'Sam.'

'Dad.'

Everything reasserted by the vocalizing of one another's name. Sometimes, she felt very alone, stretched out on a rack of inarticulacy. And then Sam would turn to her with one of his blistering, knowing smiles, the ones reserved for her alone, and she felt a renewed confidence. Confident enough to direct them again. For that was what they seemed to want of her.

Not so bad, really, she thought, forcing moisturizer into the parched pores of her forehead. On a good day, in her lemon suit, the grey nubuck pumps and seven deniers, she could still draw herself up, stretch herself out – so taut she could hear herself ping.

In the other bathroom, Brian was humming louder and louder which meant that he was expecting – no, inviting her intrusion any minute now. She pursed her lips and left him to it.


Brian wondered what he had been thinking about for the past half-hour – the blanks were growing longer these days. Nothing much most probably. Some old crap about his own reflection or his sense of self. It worried him mildly that he had succumbed so easily to the self-absorption of Julia's class – anomalous to his upbringing, he thought with satisfaction. There was grit and hard grind for you. He gave himself a flinty look in the mirror and pulled the towel between his legs, just rough enough to smart a bit. Now so.

He padded, still dripping, into the bedroom. The suitcases were stacked up neatly by the door. His clothes for the morning lay draped across one chair, Julia's across the other. She was already in bed, reading. Glasses perched on the end of her nose. 'You're wet,' she observed, turning a page with a licked thumb.

He stood by the end of the bed and slapped his palms against his chest. 'And yourself?' he asked hopefully.

'Dry as in Gobi, Sahara . . . Martini.'

'No change there then.'

She peered at him over the rim of her glasses. 'We have to be up at the crack of dawn,' she said.

'So?'

Julia sighed, allowed the book to drop to the floor, folded her glasses shut with a click. She studied him for a moment with her head cocked to the side. Is it love, she wondered? After so many years, she felt what she could only describe as 'shy' on occasion. There was something slightly embarrassing about making love with your partner. Snorting like a zebra one minute, rubbing Ariel Ultra into the skid marks on his underpants the next. The groping hands of night that would not dare to fondle by day. Waking from an erotic dream in the half-light of a winter's morning to grab your partner's frayed pyjama collar – 'You'll do.'

Middle-aged sex was nothing if not safe; no need for health exhortations there. It was comfortable and reliable, warmth

13

and familiarity tinged by a certain something unpleasant like the smell of your own sneaky fart under the bedcovers. And safe, God, safe as houses.

There had been moments. They had tried whispering obscenities or, in Brian's case, little affected grunts, nothing earthy or guttural, no uhhhs, and so patently out of sync that she had bopped him on the back of the head one night: 'Shut up.'

Understandably perhaps, he was very quiet for a long time after that. Not so much as a gruntlet to dilute the lonely sound of two bodies wearily shunting into each other in the dead of night.

She wondered if every marriage was as smelly underneath the perfume sprayed on for friends and family. Below the surface: strata of unresolved, residual odours – like decay – so that the simplest gesture or caress took on a thousand resonances, rekindled a thousand rancid grudges. Briefly dispelled by ropy buttocks pumping up and down in mechanical despair, beneath which slappy thighs spread just wide enough for entry. Tentative arms reaching out under as yet unsoiled sheets, always ready for rejection – as if it were the only thing that could be counted on. Keeping each other company in the end as if that were an end in itself. She often thought of all the miserable elderly couples out there keeping each other company. Now, for a brief moment, she wanted to cry. She felt that she should – for the passage of love, or what passed for love, or something like it.

'Tempt me,' she said.

'I thought that's what I was doing,' Brian responded plaintively. He whipped the towel off and grinned at her. Sometimes he harboured dark thoughts concerning his wife. Sodomy up an alley by a mad, defrocked priest with a club

14

foot – that would soften her cough. He fantasized doing it himself on occasion. On the premise that she was generally softer, a bit soporific, the day after sex – still vocal, of course, but less strident – he'd figured sodomy would buy him a week at least. However, although she was open to most things, the servants' entrance was most definitely bolted. He had got as far as accidentally on purpose losing his way one time. Just a little prod to see how she would react. Then a cheesy, shame-faced grin when she had craned around incredulously.

'Where do you think you're going? Piles, remember?'

Remembering her piles was not high on his daily agenda, in truth. But he never forgot them again.

Now, Brian began to rotate his hips in slow wide circles. He hummed a striptease tune and wriggled his backside. Fair play, I'm a tryer, he thought. Julia watched through slitted eyes; well, he's trying and I don't see anyone else there, she thought.

The journey in was always the same for Brian. He felt that he was travelling to a safe, familiar place. Nothing to harm him there, just a warm enfolding darkness where there was no need for the cutting quality of words. Where he could just be without having to worry about what or who it was that he should be. She was soft and fragrant as a pineapple inside. They fitted one another. It was as simple as that. They just fitted. He kissed her mouth, remembered a porn video they'd watched together and told her that he was seeing her stretched out on the bonnet of a car.

'Colour?'

'What? Oh, red.'

Julia twisted her mouth to the side. It would be red – high-gloss polish, perfect for rippling cellulite. She wondered who it was he really had over the bonnet. There were times when she had a genuine craving for him, but tonight was not one of them. She had to suppress a sneeze – always a martyr to her polite upbringing.

'I'm coming,' Brian gasped.

She thought: Don't let me stop you, dear.

He thought: I don't know why I don't just go down to the local abattoir and shag a dead sheep.

He blinked. She twitched. He yawned. She sneezed. He came. She didn't.

They curled up. She reached for a wad of tissues.

He thought: I could divorce her for less.

She thought: The sheets need changing anyway.

They thought: Not so bad. Must do that again some time soon.

'Sore pet?' he joked, a throwback to the days when they used to skin each other.

She thought: You'd have to pump a bit harder than that, buddy. 'Mmm,' she responded, because she might need him again.

She wrapped his arms around her waist and ground her buttocks back against his damp crotch. Nestling in for the night. He kissed her sweaty neck. The kindness of it, she thought, imagining her on the bonnet of a red car.

A high wind pulled up at the bathroom window, out of nowhere. Julia sighed. They were safe. Brian snored softly.

Oh yes, it was love all right. A build-up over the years, invisible most of the time, but always there, always returning, accreting like plaque on teeth. And just as ineradicable. Brian snored again, Julia elbowed his ribs. She fell asleep – contented.

*

16

Sam provided their wake-up call at dawn. He tried to burrow between them, prising their bodies apart. Brian reached bleary-eyed but frantic for his pyjama bottom. Julia wrapped the duvet around her naked buttocks. Sam burrowed deeper.

'Sam, you'll be on a psychiatrist's couch for life if you come any closer,' Julia managed. She flailed an arm backwards, connecting with Brian's nose.

'What's a – that thing you said?' Sam asked.

'A man you'll have to see for a long time if you touch your mummy's bottom.' Brian wriggled into the pyjamas.

'Like this, you mean?' Sam deftly slid pinching fingers under the covers.

Julia yelped and threw herself halfway across the room. 'Sam! You know better than that. What have I told you about touching bodies . . . other people's bodies, and allowing them to touch –' She broke off. Everything turned into a lesson one way or another.

'You're always squidging me,' Sam said.

'That's different. I get paid to squidge your bum.'

'I do yours for free.' Sam beamed.

'Do you want to reach eight?' Brian asked. 'Bugger off downstairs and I'll be down in a minute.'

'What's . . .' Sam was peering under the covers.

Julia couldn't think what Freudian nightmare lay waiting to be revealed. She grabbed at his hand. 'You heard your father. Bugger off. Do some drawing or something while you're waiting for us.'

'I'm bored of drawing.'

'Read then.'

'I'm bored of reading.'

'Just bugger off anyway.'

'I'm bored of buggering off.'

17

Brian raised his hand. 'Move – or I'll skelp you.'

Sam curled his top lip. 'Yeah, sure you will.'

'Come and give Mummy her morning kiss,' Julia wheedled. That should do it, she thought. 'Mwah, mwah, mwah,' she went to Sam's cheek, looking up to check if Brian was annoyed, as she intended. He was.

'God Almighty,' he exploded, 'I can't be up to ye're games. Sam, go now, before I boot you up the arse.'

Sam giggled and ran from the room. They were under his control again. Brian looked at Julia; she shrugged.

'He's a character,' Brian said proudly.

'He's a little shit,' Julia reciprocated and lowered her eyes to hide her own pride.

Brian hummed; he grabbed at his clothes, trying to conceal his excitement. Home.

'A bit excited, are we?' Julia teased.

'Don't start,' Brian said. He had to scowl to suppress the little shiver of delight which coursed through him.

Surprising herself, she hugged him. Ah, baby, she thought.

He yawned and stretched. Thought: Got you.

# TWO

# Pendulum Swings

Alarm bells were ringing. Julia swallowed a mouthful of bile and toothpaste and shouted downstairs: 'Brian? Are you deaf? Sam's got the alarm going again ... Turn it off and give him his breakfast.'

In the hall, Sam added to the cacophony. Arsenal vs. Manchester United: 'Goooal! Yes! Bergkamp has done it again. Yes! Yes!'

He was prostrate, punching the air with his fist when she flicked the alarm off and signalled him to the kitchen with a pointed finger, which he ignored. Brian was already there, crunching on toast while he read his horoscope in yesterday evening's paper. He remained standing, however, just in case she thought he was doing nothing to help. Julia shovelled Coco Pops into a bowl for Sam, thinking that they might at least lend a uniformity of colour when regurgitated later on the ferry.

'I don't know why we have an alarm anyway.' Brian flicked to the sports results. 'I mean, nothing ever happens when it goes off, and besides, there's nothing much to rob here, is there?'

Julia downed a glass of orange juice. 'I guess the alarm is to ensure that no one discovers that fact, don't you think?' she said in a levelled tone. Her thin smile said: Failing accidents and breast cancer, thirty maybe forty years to go.

In the hall the ball thumped against the front door. 'That's it! Arsenal have clinched it with a mag-nificent goal. Arsenal two hundred and twenty-three to Manchester's lousy two. And the crowd are going crazy . . .'

'Alarms, shutters, infra-red lights and the like, all to adver-tise what you don't have. It's a bit nuts, you have to admit,' Brian offered. He looked up. 'I'll bring the bags down, will I?'

Julia studied her fingernails. 'You do that,' she said. 'And Brian?'

'Yeah?'

'I have never wished you a slow, agonizing, horrible death. I just want you to know that.'

As the car pulled away from the house, Julia took one last lingering look back. Her gaze took in the bleached winter bones of the magnolia tree in the front garden and the mel-low red bricks of the double-fronted Edwardian house with its large white-framed, multipaned windows. The middle-class dilemma, she thought: more work, bigger house, more work, bigger house, more work, biggest house – death. Big house sold by son to pay for drug habit.

It really does sink, she realized, the heart; it was nearly in her stomach, on its way to her ankles. But there was no way out of it this Christmas – Brian's sisters would be home from Australia, the first visit in fifteen years. Besides, for some reason entirely unfathomable to her, Sam loved the place. She had refused to accompany them last summer. Off they went – Sam waving goodbye at Heathrow from his perch on Brian's shoulders – to the rain and wind and the absurdly contrasting stoical countenance of Brian's father and his equally stoical dog. As it happened, they returned wearing two well-entrenched tans while she was wan and pale from a fortnight's rain in London.

Sam was in a daze in the back. She craned her neck to check on him. He was staring out the window through bleary eyes. It was still a watery dawnlight. The streetlamps glowed orange against the pallid sky. Julia reached her hand back; Sam grazed it with his own, then contemplated the window again.

'How long more?' he asked.

'We've only just left,' Julia said. 'Hours to go yet. Play a game of football in your head.'

She watched him in the rearview mirror while he mouthed a running commentary, legs twitching, head jerking from side to side, as he headed the ball into the net. She wondered if any passing drivers would have sympathy for them and the mentally retarded paraplegic in the back.

They drove on through dark, sleepy suburbs. A preponderance of Indian restaurants in one area, followed by DIYs and bleak boarded-up shopfronts in another. Truck-drivers congregated in a caff on a corner, sipping from steamy mugs, staring out morosely at the infrequent passing cars. Julia wondered where they had come from, where they were going. What did they do when they got there? Turn around and do it all again? Not surprising then that they looked so baleful, slumped over their coffee cups. Brian fiddled with the radio dials. Sam fell asleep.

A light rain slanted against the windscreen. The M4 snaked ahead, its grey lanes empty and forlorn-looking. It suited her mood. She looked at Brian from the corner of her eye. He had that fixed quality to his stare which she sometimes found

21

a bit discomforting. He appeared to blank out for whole chunks of time. Since she had known him, there had been times when she'd felt that there was a vacuum deep within Brian, but the impenetrable glaze of nothingness in his eyes masked it entirely. A pie-chart with a slice taken, five minutes missing from a clockface. She attributed it to the fact that he was a surviving twin. Perhaps it was inevitable that there should be an enduring lacuna in the survivor. She couldn't say; certainly Brian said nothing. He had had a twin; he died; end of story. Fell over a cliff. Matter-of-fact, just like that. Julia had laughed. It wasn't intentional, but the way he'd said it was so perfectly in tune with her first introduction to Brian's spartan homeplace – here is the house, here is the field, here is the cliff at the end of the field, here is the cliff at the end of the field which Noel fell over – that she had almost expected him to mime 'here is Noel, falling over the cliff.' She simply could not help herself: 'Was he pushed or did he jump?' Brian had glowered at her all day after that.

'I'll have to stop at the next service station for petrol.' He cut across her thoughts.

'Why didn't you fill up last night?'

'Didn't think of it.'

'If we stop it will wake Sam up.'

'So he wakes up.'

She glared at him from the corner of her eye and silently mimicked his last statement with an exaggerated shrug. The shrug which had first attracted her to him. He was so casual. Nothing fazed him. Went into computers because he had had to put something down on the form to apply for the government student grant. Straight from the farm to bollocksing up other people's computers for them. Milking cows or suckers, what odds? Same shit in the end anyway. Easygoing, hard-working, dumb guy. She had liked that. Thought it was honest. Only he'd turned out to be neither dumb nor particularly hard-working – easygoing, certainly. So easygoing, she thought, that when he walked, one buttock had to wait a second or two for the other to align itself. Easy like treacle pudding, horrendously sweet at first but then you became immune to the taste. Even grew to like it – but only to a degree, of course. She figured now that the very reasons you chose a partner were the same reasons you divorced them. Brian chuckled. He had caught her mimicked shrug.

'What's so funny?'

'You.'

'What about me?'

'You're so sharp sometimes I wonder that you don't cut yourself.'

'Sometimes I do.' She smiled in response and settled back with her eyes closed.

She would make an effort, a real effort, she decided. She would just let them all get on with it. Even if the sisters from Australia proved as ghastly as she expected. They regularly sent Brian photographs of themselves and their families framed in cardboard hearts, with little printed notes: *G'day from Aussieland.* 'Oh God,' she sighed aloud.

It was while she was Speech Therapist attached to the North Middlesex, eleven years ago, that she had first met Brian. He was installing the brand-new top-of-the-range computer system into the hospital. The same computer that caused her colleagues' faces to redden and their fists to clench involuntarily over the next few years, every time it was mentioned. Brian swore that it had nothing to do with his inputting skills that the damn thing chose to offload its data in such an arbitrary fashion from time to time.

23

She had liked his smile, the way he chatted as amiably to the dinner women as he did to clerical staff. Liked the look of him too, the soft burr of his accent, the constant self-deprecation which usually conceals a healthy arrogance, but which in his case turned out to be warranted well enough. She had liked the fact that he had made a hundred assumptions about her too, felt inclined to prove to him that she was not the archetypical middle-class Hampshire lass he took her to be – even if she was. Moreover, she was a middle-class Hampshire lass (with thighs) fast approaching thirty, desperately busy, happy, ambitious, hectic, social – single. And single every Friday night with a skip of chips and a vat of Chianti.

Even back then, his lack of urgency, which she equated with lack of ambition, irritated her. There had been moments during the past ten years of marriage when the air around him irritated her simply because he was breathing it. Still, they had sort of stumbled into wedlock, though she had never quite figured out Brian's motivation. He said he loved her. There was no reason to suspect otherwise. She said it too, on occasion. I love you. I wuv you. I weally wuv you. What was that supposed to mean? Until she woke up one morning to find that after ten years of acute, possibly terminal irritation, she had fallen in wuv with her own husband. Now that was scary.

Brian chuckled to himself. He could see Cotter's spittle glistening quite clearly on the dangling rasher rind, while Cotter cast a slit-eyed glance around the schoolroom. Everyone kept their eyes and heads well down, except for Padraig in the back, of course. Brian was selected again.

24

'Oy, you, Donovan. Put that in the bin there for me.' Cotter sucked the rind into his mouth one more time, then wriggled it again. Brian opened one eye, holding on to the fleeting hope that maybe Cotter meant Edward this time. But the schoolteacher's whiskey eyes were fixed on him. Edward snickered behind him – Cathal too – as Brian stood up with an inward sigh. He promised himself that he would puck shit out of them later in the yard.

Cotter did his usual trick, holding on to the rind for a second so that Brian's fingers slid along the spittle before it was in his grip. Then Brian made a mistake: he turned his mouth down at the corners. He tried quickly to upturn it again, but he'd been caught.

'Oh, now,' Cotter said expansively, 'oh, now, what have we here at all?'

Brian threw the rind into the bin and returned to his desk, but Cotter was in no mind to continue with the morning's lessons anyhow, not with the hangover he had on him and now that he had some serious tormenting to do. Brian winced when he heard his name again.

'Oy, Donovan. Up here, boy. That's right . . . Stand here beside me and explain that little girly face you just did.' Cotter did an exaggerated moue of disgust for the class, and they sniggered obligingly.

Brian picked them out one by one in his head as he gazed up at his teacher, rounding his eyes innocently. 'I – I don't know what you mean, sir.' Just a little stutter for effect. Cotter liked stutters; mostly he laid off Edward for that reason. Stutters and stammers were suitably deferential, they showed a respectful hesitancy. All of Cotter's children were hesitant, respectful and speech-impaired.

Brian weighed up the odds: on the one hand, slow

25

crucifixion by whiskey withdrawal throughout the long day ahead of sums, catechism and English; on the other, instant gratification by means of extradition of torture into waiting repository of stupid boy who asked for it. Brian knew which one he would choose. He lowered his eyes humbly and awaited his fate. Cotter farted. That meant he was excited. Brian feared the worst. He looked up and followed Cotter's sadistic gaze to the back of the classroom where it fell on the grinning, rocking figure of Padraig, the class half-wit. Brian groaned.

'Oh, now,' Cotter began, farting again. 'Master Donovan, sir, you're telling me that your lips did not ... What way will I put it at all?' He craned forward. 'Ahh, twitch? Did they or did they not twwwitch when your, ahh, fingers encountered my, ahh, saliva?'

'They never twitched, sir. I swear it – on my brother's life, sir. I swear it.' Brian had time for a thundery glance in Edward's direction.

'So you're not a gedleen then?'

'Oh, no, sir.'

'I'm glad to hear it. I am. Because I won't have gedleens in this classroom and so I won't – except for the girls themselves, of course.'

The girls, including Brian's twin sisters, twittered appreciatively. The veins stood out on Cotter's nose; his eyes, of now indeterminate colour, filled with patriotic tears.

'Because' – he had to stop for a plaintive snort – 'because, one of these weekends, any day now, I'll be expecting you lads there to march by my side, to march like MEN, and what'll we do, lads?'

'We'll take back the North, sir,' resounded the chorus.

'Aris!' Cotter shrieked.

26

'We'll take back the North, sir.'

'Spoken like men.' Cotter dabbed his eyes. He reached under his desk flap and pulled out a Woodbine, fingers trembling poignantly as he struck the match. 'A bit of spit won't put us off now, will it, young Donovan?'

Brian shook his head. 'No sir.'

'You've a mind to share Padraig there's victuals with him so, I'm taking it?'

''T'wouldn't be fair to him, sir, but I've a mind to do it if it – if it would help the North, sir.' Brian's mind cast desperately around for a way out. He couldn't think fast enough. Maybe he should try a bit of cheek to incense Cotter into a strapping, but then he might end up taking the strap and the worst of all punishments anyway; there was no time, damn it, Cotter was farting with every draw on his cigarette which meant it was all over bar the shouting.

Brian turned his head. He gazed over the bowl-and-scissors haircuts, delighted to a lad that it was not them facing the worst of all possible fates: Victuals with Padraig. The same Padraig who came to school every morning resplendent in his one grey suit and navy blue tie, all of twenty-five if he was a day. But there was no place else to send him. So he came to school and rocked and beamed his way through every lesson, until Cotter rang the bell for break or victuals and then Padraig came into his own, unwrapping slices of lard, two Ginger Nut biscuits and a heel of white bread. This was washed down with a screwtop sauce bottle of milk, and that was the problem. Padraig never quite got the hang of his eating co-ordination. He licked his lard, stuffed the bread into his mouth, then shoved the bottle neck into the mixture – and chomped. While he chomped and sucked, he also beamed. Padraig was good-natured. He was compelled to

27

smile or laugh through every meal, which meant that his food was compelled down his chin. When that happened, his tongue was compelled after the food which had escaped it, so he ate and drank and beamed and retrieved, all simultaneously. Brian's heart sank. He knew what was expected of him. To the right, by the window beaded with slanting rain, Edward's eyes shone with belief. Brian had no great desire to disappoint his younger brother, but he felt aggrieved. He had done nothing so heinous as to merit this, the worst of all possibles. Cotter's eyes gleamed. He reached for and tolled the bell. Brian slouched to the back of the class and nudged Padraig sideways.

Padraig was already rifling through his small cardboard case for his lunch. He licked the slab of lard and offered it to Brian. Brian licked, then turned away. All heads craned back towards them. Padraig bit into his slice of bread. He chortled to himself happily. Nobody blinked as the bottle neck intruded into the hedonistic mess. Glug glug. A merry Padraig extruded the bottle, leaving a glutinous residue of lard and dough and milk encasing the top. Not a breath as Padraig extended the bottle toward Brian. Cotter released a resonant volley for Ireland from the forefront of the room. Brian held the bottle; he blinked rapidly; his hands trembled. He pursed his lips. He clamped them to the glass, shuddered for an instant, then drank with such fervour that the classroom erupted into cheers and roars of such approbation as to make Cotter keel sideways headlong into the bin harbouring his own beloved bacon rinds. He was so overcome by fervent love of his country that he called a halt to the rest of the day's lessons, and pronounced that from that day forward, 19 April 1966 would be remembered as the beginning of the South's incursion into the North's silent but awaiting bay. Brian stood for his bows. He was twelve. And triumphant.


'What are you laughing at, Dad?'

'Oh nothing. Nothing.'

'You must have been laughing at something,' Sam persisted.

'I've forgotten already.'

Sam grumbled to himself as Brian pulled into the service station. Julia was pretending to be asleep. He filled the tank and joined the motorway again.

'Are we there?' Sam asked.

'Not yet.'

'Mu-um . . . ?'

'Shh, she's sleeping.'

'How long more?'

'Couple of hours. Go back to sleep.'

'I wasn't really asleep. I just had my eyes closed.'

'Well, just close your eyes some more then.'

'Let's play something.'

'Like what?'

'I don't know. I Spy maybe?'

'All right. I spy with my little eye something beginning with M.'

'Em . . . Mum?'

'No. Motorway. Your turn.'

'You didn't give me a fair chance . . .' Sam was about to protest.

'Do you want me to take over?' Julia interrupted, shifting up on her seat.

'OK,' Brian said.

'Pull in.'

'I thought you meant with I Spy.'

'Pull in, pull in. I'll drive now.'

'You're not supposed to stop on the motorway.'

'Pull in.'

Brian sighed and stopped on the hard shoulder. They swapped seats. The rain was pelting down in fat crackling drops. Julia swerved out on to the motorway. She was nervous, he understood, about the journey, about the destination. He experienced a spasm of pity for her. And then he felt a spasm of pity for himself, because he would pay the price for her nervousness.

Halfway across the Severn Bridge, Brian turned to Sam. 'We're in Wales now, Sam.'

'How long more?'

'Oh, we're a few hours off Pembroke yet.'

Julia stopped at the next service station and they all got out. She stalked ahead to the Ladies with Brian and Sam following behind her. When she came out again, Brian was standing by the large rain-streaked windows, sipping coffee from a cardboard cup.

'Where's Sam?' Julia asked.

'Isn't he with you?'

'What do you mean?'

Brian held the cup in mid-air. 'He followed you.'

'No he didn't – I thought you were taking him to the Gents.'

'He ran off – after you.' Brian held his gaze steady and sipped from the cup. 'Check the Ladies, will you?'

'Jesus Christ.' Julia cast him a contemptuous look and whirled around. Her feet pounded the floor away from him. She returned within seconds, breaking into a run as she

30

approached. Brian frowned and sipped again; he knew he should be doing something but he was overcome by the peculiar sensation of being grounded that he experienced whenever Julia charged into action. 'He's not there.'

'Don't panic. He's probably in one of the shops.'

'Well? Are you going to stand there drinking coffee all morning or are you going to help me look?'

Brian drained the last of his coffee and observed over the rim the whitening of her face and the clenching of her left fist. 'Take it easy,' he said, deliberately drawing his words out slowly. 'C'mon, you check that one there' – he nodded toward the newsagents behind her – 'I'll check the Gents.'

As he headed for the Gents he saw her running up and down the aisles in the shop. They met by the window again. 'Not there,' he said with his mouth pursed, jerking his head back toward the male toilets.

'Jesus – Jesus Christ – Jesus Jesus Jesus.' Julia was frantically looking around her. 'Run around, quick,' she shouted over her shoulder.

'Julia, it's . . .' he called out, fixing a smile on his lips for the people who had begun to stare at them. He shoved a hand into a trouser pocket, formed his mouth into a whistle and broke into a trot after her.

'Sa-am!' Julia was calling. She stopped suddenly and turned. 'Not after me, you fool. You check upstairs.'

Brian veered toward the escalator; he took the steps two at a time. There were probably video games up there, that's where Sam would be. He started to run to the left, stopped, turned and walked to the right, his mouth still silently whistling. He checked the upstairs grill room, the toilets, the shops. His palms were sweaty by the time he returned to the escalators. Then he whistled aloud and descended with both hands in his pockets. There was no sign of Julia at the bottom. He raised his eyebrows and gazed around.

She came running from the area behind the shop. Her skin was stretched tightly over her face, her blue eyes opened wide and unblinking. She stopped stock-still when she saw him. Her mouth opened. 'You're sure he's not upstairs?' She panted.

Brian shrugged and his forehead creased into a frown. He gazed out toward the carpark.

'The carpark?' She was screaming now, people were beginning to stop and edge toward them, attracted perhaps by the almost palpable scent of her fear.

'Sam would never leave the building on his own,' Brian offered. He could feel the skin on his own face begin to tighten and stretch.

'On his own?' she shrieked. 'But what if someone told him that we were there?'

He fervently wished she had not said that. 'He's here somewhere, let's look together,' he said, brushing past her outstretched arm. 'Where are the video games in this place?' he called over her shoulder.

She ran after him. 'At the back there,' she pointed.

They looked around. A boy not much older than Sam pulled and hauled at a lever and stared into the flickering screen. 'He's not here.' Julia's voice sustained a quavery note that set Brian's teeth on edge. 'I'm going to the carpark – you stay here in case he appears,' she said.

He watched her from the glass doorway. Her hair was matted to her scalp by rain as she ran up and down the labyrinth of parked cars. He saw her stop for a moment to catch her breath with her torso bent forward and her hands resting on her knees. She glanced up and he could feel her eyes sear him from the distance. He looked around for a security guard. Julia burst through the doors, blinking rapidly. 'Jesus. *Jesus*,' she said.

'I've been looking for a security guard,' he said.

'And?' She looked around hopefully.

'Haven't seen one yet,' he said.

'He's got to be here,' she said. It was a question, he realized too late. She brushed past him and ran up the escalator.

'He's not –' he began but she was gone. Brian started to run around the downstairs shops and eateries. He ran in circles. Around and around. He kept ending up by the video games. That was where Sam should be. The boy was still there, staring at a blank screen now. He gazed up at Brian.

'A boy,' Brian gasped, 'about this high – dark wavy hair, freckles, brown eyes, red raincoat. Have you seen him?'

The boy looked around for his parents. He shrugged. Brian ran back to the escalators. Julia was pulling her wet hair back with two hands and shouting at some man in a uniform. Brian heaved a sigh of relief. A uniform. At last. But the uniform was not looking very reassuring; his face wore a decidedly worried expression as Julia gesticulated at it. Then the uniform turned and ran up the escalator, speaking into a radio at the same time. Brian's heart beat twice, then seemed to stop; he had to remember to breathe. Julia's expression was dazed when she turned to him. She staggered backwards with her hand over her mouth. Brian approached slowly but her other hand began to make a waving motion, a film clouded the blue of her eyes. Brian remembered to breathe again. He took another step but she ran sideways and crashed through the door of the Ladies.

\*

33

She was blacking out. Little sparks of light erupted then vanished on the periphery of her vision. Her heart felt like a huge dysfunctional machine within her chest. It hammered down on her ribcage. Beads of sweat solidified on her forehead. She ran to a sink and splashed cold water on her face. A long, slow moan erupted from the pit of her stomach; she felt it carry up, through her gut, into her lungs, strum silently on her vocal chords for a moment, until it broke free and the sound made her body shudder. She saw little fat legs kicking, she heard the muffled sound of his terrified screams, she saw his exposed, vulnerable white belly, she heard him call her name . . . She splashed water again. Her legs could not sustain her weight. They buckled. She hunkered down and from some unknown corner of her consciousness she saw, beneath the cubicle door which skirted the floor by a foot, a pair of white sneakers, standing perfectly still, perfectly aligned, and perfectly familiar. She dry heaved and called his name. The lock on the cubicle slid back. A brown eye peered through the crack.

'Mum?'

'Oh, Jesus. Jesus. Sam. Sam darling – Sam darling . . .'

He ran to her. She clutched at him. And had to turn her head away to stifle the dry heaves. Sam was crying. He shook her shoulders. 'I only went to the video things,' he said, 'then I couldn't see you or Dad so I came in here in case the bad men . . . like you told me . . .'

She had to swallow a mouthful of saliva. 'It's OK now. I'm here. Mummy's here. It's OK, darling . . .'

They rocked together for some minutes. A woman entered the toilet area and stood staring indecisively at them. A drunken mother perhaps? One of those drug addicts? Julia gazed up at her and laughed. She had to force her grip to loosen on Sam's shoulders. He would show bruises tomorrow. When his crying subsided, she staggered to her feet, reached down and scooped him up. He clung to her. She covered his face with kisses and carried him out to his father.

Brian was standing beside the security guard. As Julia approached with Sam's head nestled between her cocked head and her shoulder, a cry went up from the surrounding onlookers. She ignored them, she ignored the visible double take of the guard. She ignored the woman to her left who repeatedly made the sign of the cross over her breast. Gimlet-eyed, she approached Brian, who did not move, did not emit a sound or display a single, solitary show of emotion. He stood motionless, his hands by his sides, his face white and taut-looking. Sam turned and reached out his arms.

'Dad,' he said.

'Sam.'

Julia felt life itself drain from her arms as she surrendered her grail to the outstretched arms before her. People clapped. The security guard moved to disperse them just like on the television. Sam was nuzzling the side of Brian's face. Brian's eyes met hers for an instant, then he hooded them and whispered something to his son. Julia swung past the dispersing crowd, the newly officious security guard, the glass doors, and as she headed for the car, she felt her shoulder bag slap against her waist in a rhythmical, rain-drenched adagio. She reached the navy blue estate and slumped against it. Inside, she could see the meticulously packed suitcases, the crates of wine, the well-concealed Santa boxes – Sam's new bike, his puzzles, his stocking-fillers – and she felt entirely alone for a moment. As if in a way Sam had really been taken from her. She lifted her head and gazed at the approaching

35

sight of Brian with his arms wrapped protectively around Sam. Even at this distance, she could see the tremors still quake through Sam's otherwise limp body. She wrenched at the door, then remembered that Brian had taken the keys from her.

Julia was silent for so long that Brian instinctively knew that she was mouthing to herself first, the familiar litany of his past transgressions. He could feel little waves of sympathy emanate from Sam in the back. Brian stared blankly ahead. The trick with Julia was to keep apologizing, over and over again, in the same modulated tone and never to flinch or show her a wound, because if she saw a gash or suspected one, she would tear at it with her teeth. Brian cleared his throat, it was difficult to get the timing right in these matters. 'I'm very sorry,' he said.

He could see her shoulders stiffen. Her palms clapped together silently. 'It is one thing to try and bring up your son as best you can,' she began, enunciating each word as if speaking to someone learning English, 'but it is quite another to have to do so in direct competition with a father who would appear to have some sort of a death wish for his son . . .'

'I am really sorry,' Brian said.

'What is it with you? Is this a macho thing between fathers and sons that I haven't been told about – or are you just inconceivably stupid?'

'I thought he was with you.'

'Did you think he was with me the time you took him up the loft ladder in your arms?' She flexed her lips. 'You walked down that ladder – frontways – with a two-year-old child in your arms. A week later, you fell from that ladder yourself and broke your arm . . .' Her foot was tapping. 'Did you think he was with me the day I caught him running around the garden with a secateurs pointing up at his throat? Or the day I just happened upon you chopping wood in your father's shed with your three-year-old son behind you, swinging – swinging, I say – an axe over his head? Hmm? . . . I didn't hear you . . .'

Brian rubbed his jaw. This was a two-hour job, easily. He longed for Pembroke. Sam had covered his ears in the back.

'This is going to be a bad one,' Sam said.

'Of course I have only myself to blame really,' Julia continued. 'I mean, you'd think I'd know by now that I must not under any circumstances, not even for one lousy fucking second of the day, allow my son out of my sight when his kamifuckingkaze father is around –'

'Mum, you used the fu word. Twice,' Sam interjected.

'I know, Sam, and I apologize. Forget everything I've ever told you – you may, from now on, occasionally use the fu word. All right?'

'I do already in the playground sometimes,' Sam confessed soberly.

Brian observed from the corner of his eye the double tic of Julia's features as she digested that bit of information. He felt a sharp spasm of love for his son, aware of what he was trying to do. But Julia was in mid-flow and would not be appeased until she had tasted blood. She was working herself into a frenzy, fisting the glove compartment and crashing her knees together.

'. . . And another thing,' Julia continued. 'Sam is seven now. Old enough to notice things. I won't have your father drinking from his saucer like he does, do you hear me? He

37

can bloody well use a cup like the rest of us, at least while we're there . . . And that dog – that dog is not to come inside the house while I'm in it – filthy, flea-ridden creature . . .' She continued, without stopping for a breath, saying all the things she had vowed to herself that she would not say.

Brian adjusted the windscreen wipers to accommodate the sweeps of rain which made visibility almost negligible. He stuck his tongue in his cheek and tried to wander in his mind to a safer place. Instead, he thought of last Christmas. He had rarely been so miserable. A misery he could see etched on the faces of Julia's parents and her sister also. Carol, Julia's only sibling, younger by six years, had spent her time slipping into the kitchen after Brian, lighting surreptitious cigarettes and downing extra stiff measures of her Canadian rye so that she could fix a smile on her face before she returned to the living-room for yet another of Julia's party games. Charades, Happy Families, What's My Line . . . Evening after interminable evening. Julia had collapsed into bed each night, exhausted from entertaining. Brian had almost felt sorry for her, but he felt sorry for Richard and Jennifer too when he saw them put aside their newspapers with weary sighs and teeth-gritted smiles when Julia's exhortations for them to join in grew steadily sharper and more demanding. There was something so desperate about the way Julia entertained, as if, in a way, she were following a manual, some guide to happy families, only she had missed out on a whole slew of the rules and could not allow for a moment's silence.

It would not be such a bad thing, Brian always thought, to end up like Julia's parents. They were mild, easygoing people, comfortable in company, comfortable with one another. While they took on the forms of a cauliflower and a tortoise separately, together he saw them as a gentle sudsy lather, the kind his hands made when he rubbed them with those half-cleanser, half-moisturizer bars of soap. A dissonant note had struck him one evening when he tasted those suds in the bath. They looked so creamy, so enticing, but the reality was just like soap, bitter and harsh as any disinfectant.

Sometimes, he saw their eyes narrow in wonderment as they gazed at their eldest daughter, as if they could not quite figure out where she had come from. She was impatient with them. When her mother clapped her knees and said: 'Shall we have some tea?' Julia invariably snapped: 'You want tea? Then make it – Just make it. It's your decision.' And Jennifer would flush most miserably, move to rise but Julia would be in the kitchen already, flicking the kettle on and crashing cups on to saucers, in an access of guilt, Brian understood. Once, Jennifer had whispered to Brian: 'We should have called her Matilda,' but that was the closest she ever came to a direct criticism.

'Sometimes I think you do these things just to hurt me,' Julia was saying.

'Mum, leave Dad alone now, he's said he's sorry,' Sam said.

The gurgle was out. Brian bit his lower lip. But it was too late. She had caught it.

'What?' she spat. 'What did you say?'

'I didn't say a thing.'

'Yes, you did. You went "hmmph" – I heard you.'

'I feel sick,' Sam said.

Julia craned around. 'Sam, stop whingeing.'

'I'm not whingeing. I really do feel sick.'

'Do you want me to stop?' Brian asked.

'Roll your window down a bit and take deep breaths, Sam,' Julia ordered.

Sam fumbled with the window. He breathed in and out in an exaggerated fashion.

'Better now?' Julia asked. Her voice had softened.

Sam nodded his head. Brian looked in the rearview mirror. He met Sam's eyes and crinkled a smile with the corner of his own eyes. Sam beamed.

They drove on in silence for the rest of the journey, Julia pressing an imaginary accelerator to overtake other cars on the single-laned, winding road which took them the rest of the way to Pembroke. Theirs was the second last car on to the ferry. The roll of the vessel was almost immediate. Julia craned back to check on the sprawled, white-faced figures on the Pullman seats behind. Sam was moaning softly.

'The rest of my natural,' she cackled, just loud enough for Brian to hear.


They were going to break the journey in County Waterford to spend the night with Brian's brother, Edward: a two-and-a-half hour drive still ahead of them once the ferry docked.

It seemed to Brian that a million years had passed since they had left London by the time Julia indicated into the close of houses on the outskirts of the town where Edward lived. He had to admire the unerring way she had arrived there having only ever visited once before. She drew the car up to the correct house. Edward opened the front door. He had a brush and pan in his hands. Julia got out and hauled Sam from the back seat. Edward made for Brian's side of the car. Brian rolled the window down and they slapped one another on their forearms. Edward leaned against the car murmuring his greeting. His clothes were soaked in an instant. Julia lunged at the front door, prodding Sam in front of her. She called over her shoulder: 'It's raining, for Christ's sake . . .'

Brian and Edward followed her in. She was already by the fire in the living-room, stripping off Sam's vomit- and cola-stained clothes from the ferry trip. Sam hugged his body, his knees trembled, his teeth chattered.

'Hi, Edward,' Julia continued to address him over her shoulder, 'listen, run a hot bath for Sam, will you please? He's frozen . . . And Brian? Check the fridge – Sam needs something hot to eat, it doesn't matter what. Are there eggs? Fine. Scrambled eggs and toast. If there's any bacon there, bacon too –' She suddenly checked herself and cast Edward a cheek-splitting smile. 'Sorry, Edward, we've just had the most horrendous journey.'

Edward, who was looking slightly dazed, shrugged and moved a step closer to his older brother. 'No p-p-problem,' he said.

Julia's shoulders lifted. She'd forgotten his stutter. Brian thought that it should be inscribed on her tombstone the day she first met Edward and he asked her what she d-d-did and with a perfectly straight face, without so much as a blink, she had responded that she was a speech therapist.

Edward shot upstairs to run the bath. Brian headed for the kitchen. Sam began to slowly defrost by the fire. The welcome smell of frying bacon made him lick his lips in anticipation. Julia smiled and moved to help him to the bathroom.

'I can walk,' Sam said haughtily.

She squidged his naked bottom as he passed and he squealed. Brian smiled and began to hum in the kitchen. Edward rejoined him and opened a couple of beers. They talked about the rain, the journey, Edward's house, his new

41

job as an accountant for the local sugar factory. Although his clothes still stank and his hair still plastered itself across his scalp, Brian felt a warmth, an ease permeate through his sodden body. This was a nothing conversation in which he could participate. It carried no hidden messages, meandered toward no hidden agenda. It was complete in itself. A circle of nothingness yet within that circumference, somewhere in the vacuum, lay mutual childhoods, shared remembrances, secrets told in trust – lifetimes. For a moment, he felt happy and secure. He always felt like this around his siblings: Edward, younger by two years; the twins in Australia, who called every month and, despite a gap of fifteen years since he had seen them, Brian still felt that familiar sense of ease when one or other of the slightly Australianized accents greeted him on the phone. Then there was another brother, Cormac, the second youngest, in Edinburgh: Brian rarely met him these days but they stayed in touch; and finally the baby of the family, Teresa, married in Dublin with six children of her own. She had visited him in London a couple of times but did not care much for Julia, although she had never said as much. Two children had died apart from his twin Noel: a stillborn girl before Brian and an older boy, of meningitis, when Brian was three. A couple of miscarriages as well. Their mother had lasted long enough to bear the others and succumbed to breast cancer not long after Teresa was born. Now, Brian was the eldest. He saw the gleam of admiration in Edward's eyes as he watched his brother deftly flick the bacon over. Brian pointed at the fridge and Edward intuitively understood that butter was required.

Sam and Julia came downstairs. Julia still looked exhausted but Sam's cheeks glowed, his dark hair was slaked to the side and he looked renewed and cosy in his Batman pyjamas.

He sat by the table and held his fork and knife up. Brian dished out the food and rumpled Sam's hair. Julia was feeling guilty so she rattled on at length about the new kitchen decor, to make up for her earlier surliness. Edward stood with his hands by his sides, unsure where to place himself amidst this admiration. He showed her the new washing machine. She oohed appreciatively.

During the meal, Brian noticed that Edward never stuttered when he was addressing Sam. He inscribed the notation on a part of his brain, certain that Julia would comment on the same thing tomorrow. Sam was kind to Edward, Brian further noticed, in a way that children could be kind to elders who were somehow different. He felt proud of his son and, sitting there, mopping up the bacon grease from his plate with a swatch of bread, proud of his wife too. She looked so ethereal, so pale and almost vulnerable-looking. He longed to touch her. She lifted her gaze from her plate and cast him a smile. He could see the complex vein patterns stand out, throbbing and bluish on the sides of her smooth milky forehead. Instinctively, he reached out and wiped a speck of food from the corner of her mouth. He saw her smile again, and saw Edward's look of wonderment, and he realized, a little sadly, that his action had not been so instinctive after all.

Edward suggested that he might take them for a little tour in the morning, if they agreed, of course, and weather permitting, of course.

'We'd love to, wouldn't we?' Julia said, her gaze taking in Sam and Brian, 'but it's bound to be terrible, isn't it? . . . The weather I mean . . .'

Julia took Sam to bed. Brian had to go to the toilet upstairs. He stood outside Sam's bedroom door and listened to them. He loved the sound of Julia's voice when it crooned and coaxed Sam to sleep. She could be so gentle, so irresistible; he could feel his own lids heavying, his breathing decelerate.

'. . . Beyond all measure of space and time and . . .'

'. . . Everything.'

He heard.

'Sorry I was so cross with Daddy.'

''S'OK.'

'I'll be the nice mummy tomorrow, I promise.'

'OK.' A loud yawn.

'Sam?'

'What?'

'It's not *really* OK to use the fu word.'

'I know.'

'Am I a horrible mother?'

'No. You're lovely.'

Brian smiled and crept downstairs. Later, when Edward had gone to bed having poured two enormous brandies for his guests, Brian turned to Julia. 'You *are* lovely,' he said.

'Am I?' She flushed prettily.

'I'm sorry about . . . earlier today. And all the other times. You're quite right, I am careless with Sam sometimes.' He sighed and swallowed a mouthful of brandy. It left a pleasant little sting on his tonsils. 'It's just that – well – I just don't want him to be afraid all the time –' Brian broke off and smiled sheepishly. 'Maybe it's a father thing . . .'

'But why should he be afraid?'

'Like I say, maybe it's a . . .' Brian shrugged, he reached for her hand. 'Anyway . . . Forgiven?'

'Yes.' Julia smiled. She cast him a sidelong glance, unsure if she was picking up the right vibes. The steady gleam of his blue eyes told her that she was. He stared meaningfully at the rug beside the still blazing fire.

'Here? Now?' she asked, a giggle catching at the back of her throat.

Brian raised his eyebrows. Julia drained her glass and shunted toward him on her knees. As they made love with their ears straining for any creaks on the stairs, she thought about the absurd revolutions within an ordinary married day. The pendulum swings through every contrasting emotion – five minutes – the difference between anger and reconciliation, love and hate.

# THREE

# The Hide Man

Jeremiah preferred to do his own killing. That way, they got to use every scrap of the carcasses. He would slaughter up to twenty of the lambs at a session, sometimes a couple of aged ewes as well, if they were past breeding. The eviscerated bodies hung on hooks in an outhouse, awaiting collection by the local butcher's truck. For some reason, they always reminded Brian of a line of strung-up babies. He got the job of sifting through the offal, selecting the finer morsels – liver, heart, kidney – for the butcher, the lesser – intestines and stomach – for his mother to boil up in a film of stomach lining later. She stewed the heads too, in a large cauldron over the open fire in the kitchen, making a broth with carrots and parsnips. The air was filled with the high sweaty scent of mutton.

The blood dripped from Jeremiah's butcher's block into a channel which ran into a tiled pit. When this was full to overflowing, either Brian or Edward used a bucket to tip the blood into a large square vat where it half congealed beneath a canopy of buzzing flies until Brian's mother found the time to make black puddings. If they slaughtered a couple of heifers too, the contents of the vat could stand at nearly three feet deep. Occasionally, if the evening was warm and when all the work was done, Brian and Edward would squelch along the bloody channel in their bare feet, the soft, still-warm blood oozing between their toes like heavy cream.

Jeremiah's method of slaughter was quick and effective. He caught the wriggling lambs high up between his waist and the inside curve of his elbow – one fast jerk of his arm and the neck snapped with precision. While the animal cast about on the ground in its death throes, Cathal or one of the twins would swing him the next keening lamb by means of its hind leg. Brian tried his father's method once, but only succeeded in half wringing the creature's neck so that it lay paralysed on the ground, staring up at him with terrified, unblinking eyes. Then he heard his father's impatient growl as he swung the beast up to finish the job.

Cathal's posh cousin, Martina, from Dublin, liked to visit the farm to watch the lambs playing in the higher fields. 'Aren't they sweet?' she crooned.

'You mean to eat?' Brian said.

She cast him a disgusted look and flounced away in her pink petticoat. As Brian watched her take delicate faltering steps over the backyard, to protect her black patents, he had the curious thought that she was a bit like a little lamb herself. Sometimes after that, he would have erections as he watched the prinking babygirl steps of the lambs being led to slaughter. In later years, when he first heard of sheepshaggers, he remembered those eleven-year-old erections with a measure of discomfort. For all he knew, maybe that was how it started.

Apart from the one roast leg of lamb each Easter Sunday which the family could afford to keep back for themselves, the best thing about the slaughtering months was the hide man. Brian thought he was like a devil, appearing out of nowhere, twice yearly, to collect the animal hides. He was

47

a tall man from the Midlands somewhere, with an accent which sounded strange to Brian and the others.

'Talk some more,' Cormac would plead.

'Ahv no time for fooking tak and so ahant,' the hide man always responded and then talked for hours anyway, but they could understand little of what he said. He smoked constantly, a fag butt clamped perennially between his thin lips, yet Brian never saw him strike a match and the fag was always the same length, curling smoke directly into his nostrils and up into his eyes, which Brian never managed to get a good look at either, because they were always tightly squinched against the smoke. He wore a long tan coat, down to his ankles, streaked and stiff with dried blood. Brian could smell him coming from the top of the road. He smelled like the bowels of hell.

By the time he arrived, the pelts in their separate outhouse looked alive again as they writhed with rats. The hide man carried a thick blackthorn for that purpose. The children jostled for space in the doorway to watch him swing the stick like a hurley, batting the rats into every corner. On occasion, an extra large black male would stand his ground, staring and hissing balefully, a moment off striking. In that moment, the hide man would suck on his cigarette, draw the stick back with silent expertise and launch it like a javelin into the jaws of the enemy. 'Tak me on, woodyeh, yeh fooker yeh.' He never missed.

He gave Brian a penny once, blackened copper with red specks of meat on it.

'What's that for?' Brian asked.

'Fir bean a gude lahd, I sees dah.' The hide man tapped the side of his nose. 'Pu dah i yoor mout now, dasas whir Ah allus kipt me muneh.'

That was the same day the hide man saved five-year-old Cormac's life. Brian was down the fields about to bring the cows up for milking when he happened to glance up toward the outhouse where his father was still busy at work with the lambs. Two short skinny legs stuck up from the blood vat, kicking frantically in the air. Cormac had fallen in head first and could not lever himself out again. Brian broke into a run, desperately trying to estimate if he could cover the distance in time. He raced uphill, shouting at the top of his lungs to his father who he figured must have seen Cormac's legs by now but continued with his sheep-skinning anyway, when the hide man rushed out from the pelt outhouse and grabbed one flailing ankle, pulling a dripping, choking Cormac from the blood. The hide man shook him by the leg until Cormac's lungs could fill with air again and he let out one earsplitting scream which brought his mother crashing out from the kitchen, baby Teresa hanging off her remaining breast.

The hide man gently deposited Cormac beside his father, who did not look up. Brian could not be certain but he thought he detected a note of censure behind the hide man's jocose tone. 'Saf now, aher his thravels.'

Jeremiah darted a sideways glance at his wife to prevent her from moving to comfort her by now hysterical son. She stepped back obediently.

'He can travel away,' he said, indicating Cormac, 'we've plenty more where he came from, at home.'

Brian turned and went down the fields again to the cows. Later, he got his penny from the hide man.


'You were twitching in your sleep again,' Julia said drowsily.

'Was I?' Brian stretched and yawned. 'What time is it?'

'Nearly eight.' Julia looked from her watch to the window. She groaned. It was a sharp clear morning. Touring time.

Edward was already in the kitchen preparing breakfast. He cast her a shy smile and waited for her to greet him first. 'What sort of cereal does Sam like?' he asked.

'Oh, he eats anything. Anything at all. What have you got?'

Edward checked the cupboards; rows of unopened, newly purchased cereal boxes filled the shelves. A solitary rusted tin of tuna competed for space. 'Everything,' Edward said. 'I like cereal.'

Julia stood and pretended to study the cereals. She lifted them out and frowned. 'This one, I think,' she said, putting the Rice Krispies on the table.

'I like those too,' Edward said, pleased. She had chosen the only opened box.

She studied him from the corner of her eye as he made toast, buttering the slices with the seriousness he seemed to accord to everything. He had the same colouring as Brian, dark with blue eyes, but there the resemblance ended. Edward was tall and concave. His shoulder blades stood out, his stomach and back appeared almost as one, as if a ladle had scooped out the centre of him. His hands were white and very long; the flat-topped fingers flexed constantly, moving in and out like the delicate tentacles of a sea anemone. He wore black-rimmed, round spectacles, behind which his eyes sustained long-lashed nervous blinks for seconds at a time. Sometimes, he reminded her of a slender shaving of Brian.

Sam was about to say he hated Rice Krispies when she silenced him with a look. He finished his bowl obligingly and leaped up for the dreaded tour. Brian was doing his older

50

brother hearty act – she pinched her nose and forced an enthusiastic smile on to her lips.

They headed off in Edward's small hatchback so that Brian could check the engine out. He knew as much about engines as Julia knew about the sexual proclivities of greenfly, but that was not the point. She had often observed how Brian's family used material goods like trophies, so that they might praise one another indirectly. It was not the done thing to say 'you look good' or 'you must be doing well to afford such a big house', instead engines or brickwork or employment contracts were studied with great seriousness and sagacious noddings so that the nodder might take an active part in the acquisition, in the success. Thus, Edward's car was pronounced a 'right little runner', the perfect vehicle for the single man. Julia could see Edward visibly swell. He was seated in front with Brian driving. She had elected to sit in the back with Sam for reasons of her own.

Sam was in one of his dreams. His brown eyes stared out of the window in glazed fascination. She wished that she could tap his head open like an egg and crawl inside for a look around. When he inhabited his own little world like that she felt excluded. And she had to hold her breath sometimes to stop herself from clumsily treading with heavy footfalls into his own private space. It was difficult standing back observing. She was aware that she allowed him a leeway, a licence she could never countenance with her husband. But even at that, she still had to hold herself mentally back at times so that Sam might breathe, so that he might blossom into himself. The temptation to nip and tuck, to prune, was overwhelming.

Brian, or so it seemed to Julia, required nothing of or from Sam save that he be there; she, on the other hand, felt a profound sadness that she seemed to require not less than everything for the same reason.

There would not be another. Her womb had been in trouble even before Sam. She lived under a constant threat that the men in white coats would one day, and one day soon, whip it out to fling the empty redundant sac on to a waiting platter. She hated the idea of that barren space they would leave inside her.

Julia allowed her eyes to stray from Sam. Outside, a fretwork of colours drifted by. The fields to the right were irregular in shape and hue. They were not only green, she observed, but russet and brown and occasionally black. They stretched out over a gentle incline. Dark copses of trees clustered around gleaming homesteads: this was anglicized country. Neat, symmetrical, an undulating version of Surrey or Sussex. To the left, the land flattened and stretched, the unhurried waters of the Blackwater river carved a python conduit through the unusually prostrate landscape. The car followed the curves of the river, passing through rich, fertile farm country. They drove past mature escarpments of trees on the right bank, where large grey-flagged houses with unmistakably English bay windows looked out across the valley below. Houses accessed by long avenues of rhododendrons interspersed with gaunt Scots pines, their lower branches amputated or simply worn away by time. It was a solid landscape. Aged and sure of itself like an old Italian painting. Julia sighed with contentment. She was reminded of her home in Hampshire.

'Da-ad, tell me about the school again . . .' Sam was pleading.

'Sam, you don't want to know, believe me,' Edward laughed over his shoulder.

'Go on,' Sam urged.

Brian laughed. Julia could envisage his stretch. She clamped her lips together.

'Well, what do you want to know?' Brian was saying. 'That it was a two-mile walk with one room and one teacher who was a sadist?'

Edward threw his head back and guffawed.

'What's a sadist?' Sam asked.

'A person who enjoys inflicting pain on others.'

'Oh, that was old C-C-Cotter, for sure,' Edward said.

'Tell me about the day he beat you so bad, Dad – you know, the day you had to go to the hospital for the stitches.'

Julia's ears pricked; she had not heard that story before. She saw Edward's shoulders stiffen. 'T-t-that wasn't –' he began but Brian cut across him.

'You're turning into a right ghoul, Sam,' he said.

'What's a –'

'Sliced my ear open and half the side of my head that day he did,' Brian continued, 'with that bloody strap of his. I think the buckle caught me. It could have been my eye, mind you.'

'He hit you with . . .' Julia tried to access the conversation but Edward was guffawing again.

'Remember the rasher rinds?' He nudged Brian's arm and pulled an imaginary length of rind from his mouth. 'Hoy, you lad, put that in the trash . . .'

The way they were nestling their backsides into their seats augured a long trip down memory lane. Julia had no desire to accompany them. Then her gaze softened. Sam's eyes shone, he wanted to take it all in, the child laying claim to the adult's past. Quite understandable really. Their sugar-coated

53

past was a safe place for Sam. She remembered a day not long after he had started school: she had stood beside him while they waited in the playground for the bell to toll him into class; he stood still, gazing into space while other boys brushed against him and urged him into play with elbow nudges and little inoffensive kicks, and she had realized that he was pretending to daydream, pretending to be fixated on some distant bush or other, but his legs were trembling. This was his defence. He had caught her eye and his own widened, imperceptible to another, but she had caught the little flash – he was warning her off. Then suddenly, his body jerked into action. His legs carried him away to the boys amongst whom he wrestled, kicked, elbowed and asserted himself. And she had smiled to herself in confusion, glad that he was finding his way, glad too that he was able to interpret a language which was alien to her.

'I'm going to pull in up here,' Brian was saying. He pointed to a spot where the road widened and a castle stood on the left behind a smooth green park with trees protected by wooden slats arranged in circles.

'T-t-this is where I thought we might stop,' Edward said.

They got out and stood with the castle as a backdrop for photographs. Julia craned around and stared at the severely grey stone building. It was most definitely a castle, with square, serrated turrets, scratch-like windows scoring the bleached stone in linear sets of three, and narrow rectangular minarets with blunted tops scraping the blue-white sky behind. It stood on a hill, surrounded by evergreens and straw spires of naked poplars. It was at once ugly and beautiful. She sighed and felt glad that Edward had proposed this tour. She felt her body begin to relax. Her toes curled in her boots. She laid her cheek flat against Brian's shoulder for another picture. The air in her nostrils felt crisp and spicy, full of rotting leaves, river and implacable grey stone.

Brian and Sam found an empty can for a football. Julia strolled behind with Edward. 'Sam loves listening to you and Brian going on about your childhood,' she said.

'He d-does?'

'Brian makes it sound like some sort of childhood Eden,' Julia continued. 'Was it like that for you too?'

She had only been making idle conversation so the vehemence of his 'no' took her by surprise. Edward would not meet her eyes, his shoes scuffed the kerbside.

'I d-didn't mean to sound so . . .' His voice lowered, as though he were afraid that Brian might hear. 'S-some of it was OK, I s-suppose, but m-mostly I remember b-being c-cold and hungry and . . .' He shrugged, made to move on, but Julia's outstretched hand prevented him.

'And what?' she asked.

'Af-Afraid, I suppose.' Edward smiled self-deprecatingly. He looked ahead to Brian. 'He w-wasn't though.'

Julia was curious but her gaze had followed Edward's to where Brian was allowing Sam to cross the wide main road on his own. 'Brian . . . ?' She called and broke into a trot after them.

They all headed toward the stone hump-backed bridge which crossed the river, with Sam trotting in front. A sharp cathedral spire pierced the sky to the left. Julia bunched her fists and placed them on the stone ramparts of the bridge. Below, the Blackwater bisected the park in front of the castle. Willows, birch and drooping alders leaned their denuded branches down to the swirling waters. The valley stretched ahead, tree-filled, green, curvaceous. She sighed again. There were signs of life in the castle: mellowed light emanating through latticed panes from one wing only. The sight was somehow reassuring. Black crows circled overhead, but the River Blackwater was not black at all. It was multicoloured, purple and green and silver where the sunlight grazed across its eddying surface.

Edward leaned sideways across the stone wall to take a picture of the castle. He turned to her and she knew from the expression on his face that she was about to receive a discourse on local history. She quickly bypassed him and plunged her hands into her coat pockets. Edward signalled with a jerk of his head forward that they were to walk on across the river and up the winding road to the village. Julia turned to urge Brian along too. And her knees nearly gave way beneath her when she saw what he was doing. She opened her mouth to bark a command, then, fearful of momentarily distracting him, she swallowed the rocks in her throat and uttered her words in one strangulated gasp: 'Brian, for Christ's sake, Brian . . .'

Sam was standing on the bridge wall. Brian had one arm wrapped around his son's knees. Sam took a step forward, smiling at the horrified expression on Julia's face. She quickly glanced down at the river – it was at least a forty-foot drop – then up at Brian and Sam again. She wanted to jump forward, she wanted to scream, but she was terrified that any sudden movements, any sudden sounds might sway their concentration. 'Get – him – down,' she hissed.

'It's all right.' Brian waved his free arm. 'Look, I've got a hold of him . . .'

'Down. Now!' Her voice was rising inexorably, she was still too petrified to move.

Sam took another step forward. Brian was holding on to the leg of his son's jeans.

'Relax,' Brian urged. He cast a look toward his brother and she saw his eyes roll slightly backwards in their sockets. 'It's all right,' he repeated.

'Jesus, Brian,' a pale-faced Edward interjected, 'it's not all right, boy, it's not all right . . . Get him down, in the name of God . . .'

Julia took a tentative step forward. Sam giggled. He took another step. She raised her arms towards him. He took another step. Instinctively his arms widened in response to hers. Her fingertips tingled, they summoned him to her, she could feel his body already, her arms ached, she took another step.

At that moment, a van came across the bridge too quickly from the village side. The driver braked suddenly on his approach to the bridge but was forced to coast through on a wing and a prayer. Julia leaped forward. Brian blinked rapidly. Sam's arms were still outstretched. She saw him take a step backwards. She saw Brian's shocked face. She saw his hands grapple with air. She saw the pinchful of jeans between his thumb and forefinger which was all that remained of his hold on Sam. She saw Sam waver as the soles of his sneakers rocked back and forth for an instant against the stone of the bridge; his outstretched arms flapped wildly, pushing back the air behind him. She saw Brian's white bloodless thumb slide along denim until his fingers pinched together, holding – nothing. Sam's mouth formed a soundless O, his widened, terrified eyes held hers as he sailed back into empty space. He fell with his mouth open, looking up at her. He was silent. Until a sound, like no other, indicated that he had reached the end of his journey. Brian froze. Julia straddled the bridge and gazed below. Edward restrained her. Sam lay spreadeagled, his lifeless eyes gazing directly into hers, his mouth in a perfect circle, his legs already being pulled by the current of the river while his torso grazed the ground. A thin trickle of blood seeped out from behind his head where it had hit a jagged rock. The river tugged at him, pulled him to it. Inch by inch his body succumbed until, with arms outspread and his eyes and mouth still open, he was swept along, a bobbing, inconsequential twig.

And then, someone started screaming.

# FOUR

# Seeing Stars

Her thoughts naturally inclined toward gravity and the human propensity for making the inconceivably huge, small as – apples, say. The apple had represented falling for the longest time, from Adam and Eve's fall from grace to the apple which clunked Newton's crown, giving him gravity in the truest sense, to the decadence of the Big Apple.

The longer she pored over her books, the more it became apparent to her that the jargon for immensity had long been rendered vitiate by the scientists. Bereft of a language grand enough, they had had to resort to the terms of their childhood. Big bangs, black holes and superstrings. And when they gazed upwards, to their own galaxy, cerebral though they were, milk was what came to mind.

She, of course, was looking for Sam, in stars, in milk, in language.

Although she understood little of what she read, she could not put the books down. Sometimes, in the early hours of the morning, she would find herself staring at a series of complicated equations which made no sense to her, but she liked the fact that they made sense to someone.

At times it seemed as if anything was indeed possible. The passage of a particle from A to B had to be allowed what was called a sum of histories, so that from the possible, theorists might extrapolate the probable. It was even possible that in an infinite meta-universe anything that is possible will happen an infinite number of times in an infinite number of places. It was also possible, if not entirely probable, that everything she saw in the night sky was there for no other reason than to sustain life on a tiny blue planet orbiting an insignificant star near the inner edge of one of the spiral arms within the Milky Way galaxy.

It was possible that there were other universes, other dimensions which existed within these universes and consequently other laws of physics which would be comprehensible only to intelligent life observing these laws. And she wondered if in some contractionary state of the universe, in some inexplicable dimension, if there might not be a moment, a moment which would occur infinitely, when, in a reversal of time, Sam would swoop upwards to land on a stone bridge and fall into her outstretched, waiting arms.

Jennifer could not understand why Julia was so adamant about going to Ireland. Five months on, it was time to put away the books and face the harsh reality of his non-existence. Julia could neither summon the energy nor the inclination to explain to her mother that she had to be where Sam was buried, a place he loved – but more importantly, a place where she might find him. She could not see him in Hampshire.

He had fallen from her, succumbed to gravity, aptly named she considered, being in effect its own open grave.


The force of the wind made her take a step back. It blew from the west, from the horizon, straight at her from the expanses of the Atlantic. She stood on the crest of a high peninsula which trailed into the sea like a crooked finger separating two bays. Ahead of her, across the quartering sea, another mountainous peninsula dipped into the waters, hidden in part by the hummocked back of an island. Below, small fields with grey dry-stone borders gradually declined in terraces to the ocean. Her gaze moved slightly to the right. The house, whitewashed over dry stone, faced the west at an angle so that its narrow gable end caught the worst of the gales. Behind it, the long rusted corrugated-iron shed was sheltered to some degree by the house. Sheep plucked at the stubby grass in a field to the right of the shed and stone outhouses. A few threadbare pines stood in an emaciated line, offering little protection. Other farmhouses spread out widely spaced and equally exposed along the decline. The scent of turf fires coupled with the pure salty air was a heady combination. Julia breathed in deeply and coughed. Her lungs were not used to such purity.

Above, the garish white sky with patches of milky blue raced inland, casting shadows over the landscape one moment, bathing it in a flat white light within seconds. She watched a spool of light unwind from behind a low dark cloud over the middle of the bay; where the light fell on to the grey sea, it made turquoise circles on the water's surface.

She returned to her car and drove down the narrow winding track, indicating left at the second turning downwards. The dog, a black-and-white collie or what remained from the fleas, circled the car and barked half-heartedly. She pushed him away and stood by the door with her hand on the latch, then she decided to knock.

He had a tea-towel over his shoulder and the sleeves of his striped, brushed-cotton shirt rolled up to just above the elbows. He stared at her for a moment as if trying to remember who she was, then, with an almost imperceptible nod of his head, gestured her inside. She ignored him and returned to the car to pull her suitcases out; at the door again she stood in front of him and lifted her eyebrows. He did not reach for the suitcases.

'You're staying,' he said. It was not a question.

'Is that all right?' she asked.

He did not respond but inclined his head slightly again. She followed him in, dragging the suitcases after her. He made directly for the stairs which led off the downstairs kitchen, which was in effect the lower half of the house. At the top, he opened the door of the bedroom where she and Brian used to sleep. Nothing had changed. The same nylon flowery quilt covered the small bed, two walnut lockers on either side, an oak wardrobe, bare floorboards and the drawn orange sateen curtains casting an eerie rufescent glow around the room. It smelled of must, salt, an accumulation of dust and something sweet too, something sugary like the grainy scent of stewing blackberries. She shook her head. 'No,' she said, 'the other.' She jerked her head back toward the door behind her. He opened it without a comment.

It was Sam's room. A tiny cell, eight by eight, a single bed along a narrow window that faced directly on to the sea, a highbacked chair and hooks forced into the stone walls to carry clothes hangers. A lamp without a lampshade on the chair. That was it. She nodded. 'Thank you.'

'D'you want tea?' he asked. The way he said 'tea' sounded like 'tay'.

'Please,' she responded. 'That would be nice.'

He returned downstairs again. She gazed around the room. Seagulls gyrated just beyond the window panes. They called then swooped then called again in rapid staccato shrieks as they soared up on a lift of wind. She thought that they must surely make the loneliest sound in the world, but she remained untouched. The bed was hard when she sat on it. The horsehair mattress had a deep indent in the middle. She ran her finger around the circle.

Downstairs, she watched him scald the battered aluminium teapot. He allowed the hot water from the kettle to lap around three times, discarded it into the basin of dirty dishes in the sink and scooped up three tablespoons of loose black pungent tea-leaves from a tin.

'Will you want milk?' he asked over his shoulder.

'Yes, please.'

'There's none,' he said. 'Today,' he added.

'That's all right. Black is fine.'

They sat in silence and sipped from chipped mugs without saucers. He sifted a huge amount of sugar into his cup directly from the packet on the table. The cup looked awkward in his hand, he sat the base of it in his curled palm and forced his head low enough to meet the rim. She figured the rarely made gesture of not using the saucer for his tea was in her honour. She almost wished he had, she had never seen anything quite so clumsy-looking.

The dog scratched at the door outside. Julia moved to let him in.

'Lev him out,' Jeremiah said, without looking up.

The dog ran in anyway. He made for Jeremiah and performed an intricate series of circles with his tail tucked between his hind legs and his top lip moving up and down over his teeth in an ingratiating obeisance. Jeremiah lashed out with his leg and sent the whimpering creature sprawling toward the door of the back kitchen.

'Maybe he's hungry,' Julia offered tentatively.

63

'He's always hungry.'

'When do you feed him?'

Jeremiah looked surprised, if a slight lift of his eyebrows might be interpreted as such. 'There's no especial time,' he said after a while.

He bent forward and sipped. Julia blew on her hot tea and studied him from under her lashes. He was a tall man, taller than Edward and leaner. His face was a mesh of deep grooves, so dark some of them that she had wondered in the past if her nail would be impregnated by dirt if she slid it along one of the deeply etched lines. His eyes were an electric blue, like Brian's, under thick white eyebrows. The full head of hair was white also, standing on his crown in cropped thickets. The dog looked on from his chosen corner and thumped what was left of a tail against the wall behind him. Julia thought him an incredibly stupid beast to be so endlessly and pointlessly hopeful.

She lifted the teapot and filled both their cups to the brim again. Jeremiah ignored his full cup and scraped his chair back. He left the room for the outside yard with the dog rubbing against his black wellington boots with the rolled-down tops. Julia sipped the now tepid tea and stared into the ash-strewn open fireplace. It dominated one wall of the room with an oak settle to the side of it and two armchairs with lumpy cushions of indeterminate colours facing into the hearth, two dingy crocheted blankets draped over the backs of both chairs. That was the living area. She was seated in the kitchen area, with a tall dresser to her back dotted with woodworm holes, and the handmade trestle table with four rush-seated chairs in front of her. To the left a few makeshift cupboards led to a belfast sink which sat under an uncurtained sash window.

Beyond the sink stood a few shelves, a curiously ornate leather armchair and a grandfather clock with a sallow face which appeared to be in good condition. Just behind the clock a door led to the back kitchen which contained a grimy stove; a gleaming white fridge, which Julia had purchased herself some years past; a tiny angular cubicle with a shower and toilet, which she had insisted on installing at the same time as the fridge, not feeling well disposed toward using the outside toilet; and a mat with a blanket along one wall which was Jeremiah's bed. He had not slept in the third upstairs bedroom since the death of his wife.

Her feet scraped back and forth over the stone floor rolling bits of grit beneath the soles of her shoes. She held the cup suspended in mid-air while her unblinking eyes slowly roved around her surroundings.

The door opened behind her letting in a swirl of un-seasonally cold May air. Jeremiah approached the hearth with lumps of turf pressed against his chest. He allowed his hands to drop and the rich brown peat fell to the floor. His head inclined toward the fire and then he left again. Julia reached down to pick up a block. It was rectangular in shape, the outside bone dry and wispy, reminding her of loose tobacco. When she broke the block in two, the inside was dark and shiny smooth like treacly fudge and smelled of wet bog. She crumbled the dry outside texture with her fingers, allowing the matted strands to drop to the floor. Then she decided to finish her cold tea before she set about making the fire.

Hours passed. The sky was darkening outside. Julia sat by the table cradling the untouched tea in the cup of her hands. She stared blankly at the lumps of turf on the floor. A mouse, like a tiny dark missile, shot across the room and disappeared under the door to the back kitchen. Her eyes darted after it for a second then returned once more to the turf. Around her, the furniture dissolved into an inky formless mass. An occasional gust of wind rattled the window panes, the grandfather clock ticked into the otherwise silent room.

Thus far, her reception was wholly reminiscent of the first time she had ever set foot in this house. Jeremiah had not attended their small wedding in London and, on their first visit as a couple, had greeted his newly-wed son with some barked order or other. In his haste to comply, Brian had entirely forgotten to introduce Julia, who was left staring around the kitchen with a steadily sinking heart. She had extended her hand but Jeremiah had turned away, with just a nod of his head acknowledging her presence. She had thought then that he was singularly the rudest, most ignorant man she had ever met. She had wished that Brian might at least have had the decency to forewarn her, even a little. As the nightmarish week continued, she came to realize that Brian saw nothing wrong with his father's behaviour. He just wasn't 'much of a talker', Brian's phrase to counter her furious nightly whispers.

Julia had wondered if she was especially unwelcome because she was not Irish, not Catholic. But in truth, she came to figure that it didn't much matter one way or the other. Once they crossed his threshold, Jeremiah gave people things to do, as if, in a way, they could have no other reason for being there in the first place. He had even tried it with Julia – handing her a mop and bucket one day, his eyes grazing the floor meaningfully. 'Not one hello, or welcome, or how are you,' she had hissed to Brian later in bed, 'but a bloody bucket thrust into my hand.' Brian had laughed. That meant she was accepted, he had tried to explain. Shared work – a communion of sorts. Julia had remained sceptical, but she did wash the floor, for Brian's sake.

Over the years, she had built up a barrier of indifference to Jeremiah. Resigned to visits when she had forced herself to tick off the days, and sometimes minutes too, until they could return to civilization again. Resentment growing again once Sam was also of an age to follow Jeremiah's terse commands with an eagerness she had never encountered at home.

And now the strangest thing. Here she was, hoping to stay for an indeterminate time with this least comforting of men. Yet, the last few months had brought about a hasty resketching of Jeremiah in her mind. She had come to wonder if his own griefs throughout the years had made him so diamond hard. There was something in that she could identify with, something familiar amid all the estrangement of recent days. Perhaps it was a longing for his silence which had drawn her here so inexorably. At a time when everyone was trying to find some words of consolation, she had known instinctively that he would offer none. Perhaps, in his own taciturn way, he understood.

When Jeremiah returned he was carrying a small tin pail. He switched on the single, shadeless light overhead. Its wattage was low, serving only to illuminate the immediate area in a shadowy, orange light. He quickly set about the fire, soaking balls of paper in petrol first and heaping the turf on to the flames. As the warmth hit her face, Julia shivered and realized that she was quite frozen.

Jeremiah moved about behind her. She heard him wash his hands. Then he washed the dirty dishes within the sink. After a while she detected the acrid smell of lard melting on the stove in the back kitchen followed by the unmistakable odour of frying fish. The dank, dark kitchen seemed to come alive with the scent. She transferred her attention from the turf to the perfumed air around her. She had had no idea that fish could smell like that. By the time Jeremiah emerged carrying two plates, Julia's mouth was full of saliva. She had not eaten for nearly two days. The time it took to load up her car and travel here.

He cut slabs from a crusty batch of bread, lathered them with butter and laid them directly on the table. There was a herring and one potato cake for each of them on the plates. He put two forks beside the plates, sat down and began to eat. Without looking at her he nodded toward the tin pail by the sink. 'Goat's. She gave a bit if you want it.'

Julia stood and went to the pail. It had a foul odour and the colour was none too enticing either. She poured a little into a cup and sipped. It tasted as foul as she expected but she drank the meagre contents of the pail anyway – her throat felt parched. Then she ate her fish and potato and two hunks of bread. The dog whined outside.

A number of times, she sensed his fleeting glance but when she looked up, he was busy chewing, eyes firmly fixed on the table. She felt that she ought to say something. Offer some explanation for being there, but she couldn't think of anything that might make sense to him. It was Jeremiah who broke the silence finally. 'Brian,' he said.

Julia's head shot up. It was impossible to tell if there was a question in the flat rendition of the name. She wondered how much he knew about the last five months.

'I saw him yesterday . . . well, not "saw" exactly . . . but he was there – at the house, when I went to get the car and my stuff.' She spoke in a rush, her cheeks suffusing with hot blood at the memory. A long, uncomfortable silence followed while he nodded.

'He'll not be coming then?'

Julia screwed up her eyes, trying to read the impassive features. 'No,' she responded and was about to leave it at that when she felt a spurt of anger at what appeared to be a deliberate coyness on his part. 'Brian and I . . . well, you must know, surely . . . ?' Her voice trailed off, waiting for a signal from him to let her know that she need not continue, but he continued chewing. 'We haven't been together since – since the bridge . . .' She could not bring herself to utter Sam's name in his presence just yet. 'But you must have heard –'

'Nothing.' He cut across her. 'I heard nothing from no one.'

'But Edward . . .'

'Pah! Edward.' He clicked his tongue, sending her a sour look.

Julia picked at her cuticles. He was so patently in the dark, she felt sorry for her earlier irritation. Evidently, Brian had not been in contact. She pulled at a long sliver of transparent skin, leaving a little bloody track in its wake by the nail curve. 'They took us to the hospital . . .' She looked at him; he nodded her on, his lips pursed into a tight moue. 'Of course, pretending all the while that there was a remote chance of resuscitation or whatever.' She smiled bitterly. 'Maybe they feel they have to do that until they can get you sedated . . . Brian just kept screaming. A terrible sound. Like an animal caught in a vice . . .' She had to draw blood from another cuticle to force her voice to continue. 'They sedated him pretty quickly. I wouldn't let them near me though. I remember I wasn't even crying . . . I just sat there while everyone rushed around as if something might still be done to . . . Anyway, long before I saw the doctor and the priest

69

moving along the corridor toward me and Edward, I had told him to call my parents to come and get me.' She stopped and pulled at a ridge of skin with her teeth. 'A nice call to get, huh? "Your grandson is dead, come and get your daughter." Still. Maybe they were glad of something to do. I don't know . . . But they arrived hours later.' She looked up searching for his eyes but he remained intent on the table. 'And I flew back with them. I've been there ever since . . . Edward called a few times. He said that Brian was kept in the hospital for a few weeks. Then Edward took him back to London in the car. That's all I know.' Julia stopped abruptly, glad of the pain in her fingertips to concentrate on. Now, she waited for him to ask why she had come here, and she wondered how she would respond to that. 'Thank you for arranging the funeral and . . . and things,' she added quickly – to get it over with.

''Twas Edward did it.'

'I must thank him.' She did not mean to sound so bitter, softening her tone to add, 'A pretty strange funeral, without either parent –'

'Every funeral's strange,' he interposed.

Yes, she thought, he would know that only too well, having buried a wife and three small children, one of them, Noel, the same age as Sam. Perhaps his thoughts had been of Noel as he stood over the disturbed earth – peeled back this time in readiness for her son. They remained silent for a long while again, and Julia wondered if this strange, adamantine creature was beginning to harbour similar feelings of kinship toward her. Certainly, the mask gave nothing away. And yet she felt all the – unspoken – pulsate in the air between them. Like the constant tick of the grandfather clock behind her: she did not have to hear the sound to know that time was passing. Neither did Jeremiah have to speak of feelings to confirm their existence. She felt that she had misjudged him greatly in the past.

Reminded of the clock, she craned her head around to check the time. It registered half past ten and the sky beyond the window was a deep shade of navy blue, not quite full black yet. Jeremiah clattered the plates into the sink, then sat on one of the chairs by the fire with his back to her, pulling from the cushion beneath him a weekly local newspaper. From under the chair he extracted a pipe, a tin of tobacco and a box of matches. Julia had not observed them earlier. When the pipe was smoking to his satisfaction, he reached down, pulled out a small flat naggon of whiskey and poured a small tot into a tin cup also extracted from the Sesame cavern beneath the chair. He puffed at the pipe three times to keep it alight and turned to her with the bottle raised, lifting his eyebrows. She shook her head.

By now the room was full of smells. Sweet burning turf, pipesmoke, residual food odours and a slight waft of cheap possibly stale whiskey. Julia continued to sit in her chair shifting her gaze between the high-flamed fire and the back of Jeremiah's rectangular white head as he pulled the newspaper nearer and nearer to his squinted gaze. With a grunt and a puff of smoke he reached under the chair again, this time producing a pair of steel-rimmed spectacles. He read on as she watched. The sky outside was true black. The dog continued to whine.

At half past eleven, he tapped his pipe against the arm of the chair, replaced each item beneath it, folded the newspaper in three movements of his flattened palms and reached under yet again, from the other side this time, drawing out a black wooden rosary. His right hand dextrously clicked the

71

beads forward one at a time until his thumb and forefinger reached a slightly larger single bead, there was a pause in his hand movements, an inclination of his head and then his fingers continued the forward clicking motion for the next ten beads. When he reached the next hiatus in the form of the solitary larger bead, he stopped, made the sign of the cross, kissed the silver crucifix at the bottom and replaced the rosary.

Then he leaned toward the fire. He separated the burning blocks with a poker, spreading them out across the hearth. The flames immediately died down. He rose and went to the sink where he washed his hands and arms to his elbows, lathered his face with soap then dried each finger separately on a dishcloth. 'I'm away,' he said.

'Thanks for dinner.'

'Dinner's at one o'clock.'

He had turned about, heading for the door to the back kitchen when he stopped. She waited for the inevitable questions then, but that was not his intention.

'Will you be wanting the . . .' His head inclined forward, she understood that he meant the toilet.

'I suppose I'd better.'

He stood aside and waited until she returned then quickly brushed past her and closed the door behind him. Alone in the kitchen, Julia looked around once more. She switched the light off and climbed upstairs in the dim glow offered by the dying fire. In her room she sat in the darkness on the edge of the bed, staring out of the window. The sky had cleared and she had never seen so many stars. It was as if a whole layer of sky was missing here, so that the firmament hung lower than usual and each individual star radiated a crisper light. She pulled down the window and stuck her head out, the force of the wind making her gasp. Out to the west, along the horizon the illuminated sky came to a sudden sharp end at the curve of the earth. The sea below picked out an arbitrary selection of stars to mirror, with large pockets of blackness in between where she could only vaguely make out ripples of soft grey mist rising from that darkness. She closed the window again, sat back, and knew instinctively that it was precisely midnight. Sam's birthday. He would have been eight.

Julia continued to sit on the edge of the bed for an hour as the wind flung itself at the window panes. Salty air seeped through cracks in the wooden frames. She pressed her nose to the hollow in the mattress to see if she could smell Sam, but there was only musty horsehair. Her hands rested limply across her lap; she studied their shape in the gloomy light.

She thought of Jennifer's face yesterday evening as she stood beside Richard in the driveway, waving her daughter goodbye. For the briefest moment, Julia had sensed her mother's guilty relief, which was perfectly understandable, because Julia knew herself what a dark, brooding presence she had become in their home, causing subtle inflections to the light as she passed through rooms.

She had not meant to thrust herself upon them for a five-month duration, but days had drifted into weeks as she holed up in her bedroom with a collection of books. She had felt increasingly sorry for them but was unable to do anything about it until the decision to go to Ireland had hit her so forcefully late one afternoon. Jennifer had thought the notion was crazy. Fanciful. Just another way of opting out, of not facing up to Sam's death. Julia had listened to her on the phone to Carol in Toronto later that night. 'What are we to do with her?' she'd cried.

73

Her parents had taken to calling Carol every night. It was as if the curled flex of the telephone represented some sort of umbilical cord and they dared not move far from its ambit. Nightly, Julia listened to her mother's agitated tone and the steady thrum thrum of her father's baritone which pitched upwards from time to time in a freakish altisonant note. They pleaded with Carol to come home again, to 'do' something with Julia. Her visit after the funeral had been so brief. Maybe she could get through to her sister now. Get her to go back to work. Get her to leave that bloody room and those bloody books. The relief in their voices was palpable when Carol apparently agreed. Carol would come. Carol who was light as sifted flour, floral perfume drifting in swathes across rooms, molten-sugar-haired, unambiguous, undemanding and smilingly grateful – a sweet sponge of a daughter.

That was over a week ago. And Julia had pre-empted her sister's visit by taking the ferry last night. The journey itself, a merciful relief after the longest day of arguing with Jennifer, travelling up to London, saying goodbyes – and, of course, Brian.

It had started early in the morning with Jennifer's refusal at first, to call Brian to let him know that Julia would be there later for her car and various things. Julia had made a list and could not get Jennifer to hold it, never mind read it. Jennifer kept shaking her head, didn't Julia realize that Carol would be here in a few days? Julia could not explain that Carol's presence in itself did not promise the same salving effect for her as it might for her parents. She had gazed sadly at her mother's profile. The frayed silver perm, glazed, pink-rimmed eyes, clenched lips, a dusting of powder across the bridge of her perfect little sausage nose. A face adrift in such incomprehensible pain.

74

They were strangers to one another. It had always been so. A lifetime's silence shivered between them.

'I'm sorry . . . Really, I am,' Julia said. 'You've both been so kind and patient . . . But I want to go. I *must* go.' She was struck by the formality of her tone.

'It's called running away, Julia,' Jennifer said flatly.

'Maybe. Will you please call Brian and read him the list?'

Jennifer nodded in defeat. At the door, a cough, a pat of her chest, a watery smile and blue eye searching for blue eye. But they had chosen to blink at the same moment and Jennifer left with a shrug.

Julia quickly dressed and stood by the window. Richard was on his knees patting fertilizer around the rose bushes. He straightened and placed a hand to the small of his back from time to time. Then, intense concentration again. She watched him use both hands gently to cup a new yellow rose-bud. A tender smile played on his lips. Beyond the wisteriaed pergola, crisp white and pink blossoms still clung to the apple and cherry trees. A wooden swing suspended by blackened rope hung from an outstretched branch. Bluebells around the base of the trunks.

She turned and gazed around the room. Large, light-filled, with butter-yellow walls, cowslip-patterned bed-linen, mahogany dressing table, matching wardrobe. Exactly as it was throughout her childhood when she would spend hours by the window, listening to Carol downstairs – the tinkle of her laughter drifting upstairs from the kitchen, the perfumed scent of newly baked fairy cakes. Front door closing behind him, the shwoosh shwoosh of his feet on the door mat – her father, in from the garden; Carol's laugh sounding nearer when he opened the kitchen door. Jennifer's voice, contented, in charge, asking about the garden. Door opening again as Jennifer followed Richard out to inspect his evening's work. The two of them strolling, hands clasped behind their backs, a scuffing of feet by the sweet peas, a holding of scented buds to the nose. Down to the pergola, winding stray vines around the white frame. Nostrils dilating by the lilacs. A surreptitious glance up towards the changeling daughter's window, fleeting mystified frowns that she could not be part of such ungrazed perfection. Little guilty half-raised hands, her finger-curl response, then back to her books again. Carol humming in the kitchen. Evening banks of cloud lining up to the east.

Downstairs, as she shunted into her jacket, Jennifer tried to persuade her to let Richard drive her up to London. But Julia insisted on taking the train. She felt a spasm of remorse again as a mixture of hurt and anger knotted her mother's features.

'At least to the train station then,' Jennifer protested.

'But I want to walk,' Julia said, moving a few steps forward.

Jennifer wiped her hands on a dishcloth. She called after Julia. 'Julia! Sometimes I think you are a most deliberately – contrary girl.'

Julia gritted her teeth and hummed all the way to the station platform. At Waterloo, she took the Northern line, getting out again at Camden to wait for the right tube. Beside her, a young man bit into an apple. Minute speckles of spit and juice sprayed out where his teeth had punctured the red skin. The pungent scent drifted over the dusty air, laying an invisible apple carpet over the entire platform, sending jumbled childhood memories coursing in a free-for-all through her head. She closed her eyes, but within moments she found herself inspecting people around her again. It was as if her eyes were hungry for information after the long seclusion.

76

A woman stood nearby with her young son beside her. She had a young, hard face, long split-ended hair, ripples of sagged skin beneath distant eyes. The boy was fashionably dressed: clean, new sneakers; a padded tartan jacket. Any age from eight to eleven. It was hard to tell. His serious expression, and motionless diffident stance caught Julia's eye. Little mattered to the boy. He did not look around him. No natural curiosity there. For minutes she watched them. They did not address one another. For that matter, they did not move. Never even checked the overhead train listing. Still and silent, they might not have been together at all.

Julia felt an irrational, inexplicable craving swell within her. As she waited for the train, it became of paramount importance that the woman should touch the boy. That a word, just one would suffice, should pass between mother and son. Julia began to rock gently back on her heels.

Minutes passed. No sound. No movement. The boy un-aware of Julia's eyes searing the back of his tartan jacket. A light in the tunnel up ahead. The train trundled alongside. Doors slid open, bodies belching out. Still no movement. Then just as Julia was about to give up hope, the mother's arms snaked out, encircling her son's shoulders, gently pressing him forward. Inside the tube, her hand remained on his shoulder. Julia found a seat and closed her eyes for the rest of the journey, and when she got out at Highgate, the pair were gone.

On the long walk to the house in sweeps of misty rain nothing seemed remotely familiar – not the houses, the butchered plane trees, the long wooden barricade holding back Highgate Woods, the tall red-bricked houses. As if, in a way, she had stepped into the past of a stranger and walked along claiming nothing for her present.

Outside the house, she kept her head down in case a neighbour should see her. The set of spare keys fell from her hands on to the doormat. She picked them up with trembling fingers. Mentally praying that Brian had had the decency – no, the humanity, to abide by her exhortation that he should not be there.

In the cool hallway she stood for a moment, watching the light shift and fall through the stained-glass side windows. A steady hum from the fridge in the kitchen, the ticking from the carriage clock on the hall table, her heels clacking against tessellated tile. In the living-room, half-drawn drapes, plumped cushions, a skin of dust on wooden surfaces – and, strangely, *Playdays* on the television.

She climbed the stairs slowly. Hauling herself upwards by means of the banister rail. All the doors off the landing were slightly ajar. Except Sam's. She stopped for a moment with her fingers curled around the doorknob. Then a violent push – it swung open and she gasped aloud, a hand instinctively reaching for the doorframe to steady herself. Every inch of wall was covered in pictures of Sam. Smiling, grinning, crying, staring sleepily into the lens for yet another photograph; turning to feed the ducks; red-cheeked and sweaty, blinking from his cot in the first light of morning. The room, a cubed catalogue of a seven-and-a-half year span. On every surface, framed photographs. Sam's first step, his first visit to Santa, his first Arsenal kit, his last visit to Santa. On the floor, heaped piles of Brian's clothing. This was where he slept. Crumbs strewn around the carpet. This was where he ate.

'Julia.'

She could not move. He was behind her. Had stepped from the bathroom and now stood so close she could feel his breath on the raised hair down at the back of her neck.

78

'Oh, Julia.'

A funny sound struggled to break free from her vocal chords. A tiny mewl escaped. Sam's glistening eyes – filled with mischief, with unwavering trust, with life – beamed at her from a photograph. She wanted to tear at the papier mâché frame with her claws – that it should assume that privilege of containing him. Instead she wrapped her other arm around the doorframe also, and hung on for dear life. Over her shoulder, she hissed: 'How can you live?'

Moments passed after the intake of his breath. He bent forward, placing something on the ground. Then a slipping away of his body like a night tide drawing back from the rocks, a fleeting impression from the corner of her eye of a dark human paring in the crack of a doorway. She reached for the bag he had packed for her, plunged the car keys on top into her pocket, swept through Sam's room with her eyes tightly shut, reaching for his spaceship, and turned for the stairs, feet barely touching the treads as she fled.

Later, Richard sat in the passenger seat for a moment as Julia put the heavily laden car into gear. He didn't know which way to look. Jennifer stood by the front door, clenching and unclenching her fists. She refused to catch Julia's eye.

'Thanks, Dad, for . . . everything,' Julia said hesitantly.

'Dad'. A curious little user-friendly word. Not an appellation she had often used, even as a child. He was 'Father' or 'Richard'. This big, remote man with dense eyebrows and drooping folds of skin in his beige Burberry windcheater. He had always seemed a little bemused by fatherhood. Playing the role as if by rote. Saying things like: 'This is a teenage thing, I suppose.' Summoning a specious anger when demanded by Jennifer, but never with any degree of conviction. Scuttling out to the sanctuary of the garden. Yellow roses, if they could speak, could attest to the tenderness of his touch in a way that Julia suspected Jennifer never could.

She wanted to touch him, but found the prospect daunting, in a toe-curling sort of way. She gingerly extended four splayed fingers, drawing them down, millimetres from his face. A shy, crooked smile raised the flesh over his cheek-bones, making fleeting contact with her middle finger. She withdrew as though singed but twisted her mouth into the semblance of a smile, matching his. She recalled the passage of summer evenings, weeding the garden with him in companionable silence. Both of them estranged from the happy chatter of the kitchen. Jennifer and Carol, working in tandem, the rise and fall of their voices, melodious, in perfect pitch. Forever contented in one another's company. A pair.

She wondered if deaths always sent people scrabbling back to childhood, as if making sense of the past might make sense of the present. For the first time in years, she remembered the quiet hours she had spent with Richard after Carol's birth, when Jennifer had gone a bit funny for a while, wanting only her newborn's company. And she remembered how envious she had been of Carol and her baby gurgles that sent her mother into raptures. Julia wondered if she had chosen speech therapy so that she too might know that easy articulation. Certainly, with Brian, she had rarely been short of a word or two, and for a strange moment she missed him, instead of Sam.

Richard clapped his thighs. He said, 'Right,' and got out of the car with a sideways, apologetic look. There were things he should be saying. She understood, only too well.

They stood together, Jennifer and Richard, raised hands

mimicking each other's wave as she turned once to smile back at them. But the boxes in the car obscured their vision, and they did not return her smile.

Now, looking around the room in shadowy starlight, she wondered where she was going to put all that stuff. Maybe her books could be stacked in an outhouse or something. She pulled the spaceship to her stomach, listening to the tiny figures rattle about within. She wished that she had permitted Sam to take it with him at Christmas, and she wished that her parents had seen her smile.

The window looked like a sheath of black velvet with a sprinkled diamanté crust. When she closed her eyes, she could still see stars.

# FIVE

# Lining Up

Brian and Edward had a fit of the skits. It was the first time they had laughed since the death of their mother over a month ago. Brian was twelve and a half. But he hoped he looked older.

He felt his father's body stiffen beside them and knew that there would be trouble later. Teresa, the baby, was up in arms, squawking at the priest who spouted mass in Latin in front of the marble altar. The twins, Mary Ann and Pat, stood shivering with cold in their gingham Sunday frocks beside Cormac who kept his hands pressed piously together in front of him, from time to time casting surreptitious eyes up in his father's direction.

It was Cathal's fault. He had turned his head from a pew in front of them and indicated the visitors over to the right. Brian and Edward had been doing their best to ignore them, but it was difficult. Three girls from London, in mini-skirts higher than anything they'd seen on the Eurovision Song Contest on Cathal's telly, and none of them wearing so much as a lace mantilla on their heads. The girls were bored with the mass and pulled faces at their aunt, whom they were visiting, when she frantically nudged them to be silent. She was clearly mortified by their behaviour. Their older brother, about thirteen, chewed bubble-gum. Brian was a little shocked but fascinated too by the narrow trouser legs, pointed shoes and slicked-back hair of the mortal sinner. He vowed to himself that he would go to London, as soon as was possible, to wear shoes like that and chew bubble-gum in mass. Then one of the girls bent over to pick something up and he saw a flash of polka-dot knickers. Edward caught it too and they snickered. The girl looked back and blew a cheeky kiss at Brian. He flushed to the roots and saw his father's fist bunch around Teresa's calico dress.

Brian was overcome with a terrible sense of guilt for the rest of mass. He tried to conjure up an image of his mother's face, but as usual, he thought of an unbaked apple pie. Blanched, taut skin stretched out like pastry over protruding bones. Too tired to raise a hand against them, too tired to even raise her voice. The wisps of hair matting over her forehead as she mechanically rubbed nappies – skeins of sallow cotton strips – up and down the washboard long past midnight. The little trip of her steps as she ran to place her husband's dinner on the table.

One minute she was there, washing nappies, the next she was gone. Neighbours had watched with keen eyes as the children had filed past the father to place sterile kisses on her waxy purple lips. Women keening. The low thrum of men in little groups of twos and threes, their eyes slanting toward Jeremiah for a sign of grief, which was denied them. Brian and the others stood in awe when they saw the array of food and drink laid out on the table beside the coffin. Jeremiah's sister, Jude, a spinster from twenty miles east, with a face like a parsnip and a stinging slap always ready in her palms, had come to help him host the wake.

There was sherry and Taylor Keith lemonade for the women, whiskey for the men, and each of the children got their own bottle of Sinalco which they sipped then spat half a mouthful back, to make it last longer. The music continued until the early hours of the morning and when the last body – Cotter's, the teacher – finally reeled away from the house, Brian had found himself alone with his father, staring at the pallid body in the coffin. And for a moment, Brian had wanted to cry, because she was his mother. Then he saw Jeremiah pinch his own nostrils together before he sighed deeply and bade his son goodnight. That was the first night he slept on a mat in the back kitchen. And Brian cried, very quietly, so as not to disturb him.

And only last week, the sight of his father, silhouetted against a winter's evening, nodding to the man, Cathal's father, who had paid in cash for his cows and pigs and silage. No longer able to sustain the meagre living extracted from the farm without wifely assistance, with six small children to care for, he had finally, after years of refusal, sold the bulk of his land and livestock. To a neighbour who had a truck instead of a bicycle. And money, it seemed, to buy the universe. Leastways, Jeremiah's world. Brian flushed again as he remembered the turn of his father's head, the flickering of his shadowed eyes as he gazed at his eldest who looked on, uselessly, from the kitchen window, as the last beast trundled up the ramp of his neighbour's van. And the night coming down in indigo swathes around the slender form of a man who had just lost everything.

'*Ite missa est*,' the priest was saying, just as Brian had managed to conjure up an image of his mother in heaven, drying nappies.

His father was silent as they walked the three miles home from the chapel. They stopped to stick a bottle into Teresa's wailing mouth. All of them lined up along the ditch as

Jeremiah thrust the infant into one of the twins' arms before he stalked into the next field to find a suitable switch. He beat their backs together, Brian's and Edward's, until the veins stood out on the side of his temples and beads of sweat ran down his cheeks. Brian knew enough to remain silent and still, but Edward whimpered when his glasses fell down his nose and splintered into pieces on the ground. He got ten more whacks for allowing that to happen. And Brian had to glance sideways when he saw blood seep through his brother's shirt, because he hadn't been ready yet for his older brother's hand-me-down jacket.

Usually, being the eldest worked against him. Like when he needed new shoes for instance. There was no one above him to pass them down, so he had to wait until there was enough money. When Noel was alive, they spent every summer barefoot. A couple of times, he had had to make do with his father's old boots which were a hundred sizes too big, even when stuffed all around with brown paper. Apart from the inconvenience, it was a bit embarrassing. Cathal had given him a spare pair last winter, but Jeremiah had made him return them the following day. The same day, for the first time ever, Brian realized that his father had been lying all those years when he rose from the dinner table to light his pipe by the fire, saying he wasn't hungry. Brian had always thought that when Jeremiah checked the stewpot on the table before every meal, he was just wondering about the content and not the quantity. During some winter months, he forsook more meals than he ate, and Brian felt deeply ashamed for having taken the boots from Cathal.

'Bastard,' Edward now hissed behind him, through clenched teeth. They all followed in single file, taking three steps to every stride of the thin black-clad figure of Jeremiah, holding Teresa inside his jacket to shield her from the cutting wind. 'Bastarding, shitty, pissy f-fucker,' Edward continued in a whisper, trying to summon every swear word he could think of. He took care that only Brian should hear him. The others might tell.

'Shh,' Brian urged. 'I'll put calamine on your back later. Shh now or he'll hear you.' He craned around quickly to give Edward a smile of encouragement. Edward was in a bit of a mess all right. Behind his splintered glasses, his eyes blinked rapidly, a muscle in his cheek had gone into a constant tic, he was twitching from head to foot and his nose was running. 'Come here, you beautiful hound you, and give us a kiss,' Brian said, the old joke, to cheer him up.

'I'm going to cut his throat in his sleep one night. B-bastard.' Edward glowered.

Jeremiah turned around at the crest of the hill. The wind wrapped his suit around his body and sent his dark hair streaming behind. Cormac was lagging by now, his short legs had trouble with the uphill part of the journey, but he burst into a canter when his father stopped. Jeremiah signalled for them all to hurry up and as Brian reached the spot where his father stood, he felt the blue eyes graze the back of his head for an instant, and he realized what he had long suspected, that everything was all his fault.


Brian cried with his head turned into the pillow so that Sam in the photos might not see. He was in Sam's bed, had slept there – or not, more accurately – since his return from Ireland three months ago. They had kept him in the hospital for nearly seven weeks, ostensibly to treat him for shock – pills, pills and more pills – but in reality because Edward and the twins were paying. They were afraid that he might do harm to himself, or that was how they put it. Brian, who mostly remained silent throughout their visits, did not feel inclined to remind them that there was no greater harm he could do to himself any longer. If thoughts of suicide were troubling them, then they had no concept of the addictive qualities of guilt.

Now, he padded downstairs and switched the television on to *Playdays*. For a moment, he wondered who was sitting at his office desk. Some bright young thing no doubt. Hungry for any vacant chair. It had only been a matter of time in any case. They had been very polite, granting him leave of absence for as long as he needed. A lifetime? Sure, no problem – here, and take this crate of money with you as a mark of our, well, gratitude for all the years you put in when we didn't fire you because you had such a nice smile and the boss liked you. Only it wasn't quite like that. No crate. No gratitude. Just silence after a couple of months and an implicit understanding that his job was, well, gone. They didn't have to spell it out. A small severance cheque which arrived in the post did that with great eloquence.

He remembered that Postman Pat was on the other channel at this time and flicked over. Postman Pat, Postman Pat, Postman Pat and his black and white cat – Early in the morning, just as day is dawning, he picks up . . .

The doorbell chimed. Brian scuttled to the side of the sofa and hunkered down, squeezing himself behind a table so that the estate agent would not see him if he looked through the window. The bell chimed again. He heard the mumble of voices. A rap on a pane of glass. Brian held his breath. They went away.

When he stood again, his pyjama top clung to the sweat

on his back. Julia would be here soon. He made a mental inventory of the items on the list Jennifer had called out to him over the phone earlier. Her voice cold, sharply pointed, like a stalagtite. The first communication since his return. Hoary steam, or so it seemed, rising from the phone once he'd replaced the receiver.

The bag was packed now, awaiting collection in the upstairs bathroom. He had added a few things too, like the form for her signature agreeing to the sale of the house. And Sam's Arsenal away kit. He dreaded seeing her, and in another way, he wanted to prolong the moment. Maybe they would talk. And maybe, for that moment, they would hold on to a remnant of their past lives together. No – it would be better if he left temporarily, as Jennifer had demanded. He moved around the sofa, awaiting instructions from the TV.

It was a lovely day in Glendale. Postman Pat and Jess had just finished their early-morning round. Postman Pat turned to Jess and said, 'I don't know about you, Jess, but I can't take much more of this fucking life business. It's that hard and so it is.' Brian flicked back to *Playdays*. Just as the Playdays bus stopped for the Lollipop Lady, he heard the jangle of keys outside the front door. He ran into the hall, heard the keys drop to the ground and a woman's muttered expletive as she bent to retrieve them. Through the stained-glass side panels, he could see a familiar, if more slender form. Julia. He turned and took the stairs two at a time as the key turned in the lock.

From the bathroom, he could hear her slow approach up the stairs. The creak of the banister rail as she pulled on it for support. He remembered how he used to wonder at the way she always appeared to glide up in one fluid movement.

Like some sort of heavenly ascension. He could hear her, muttering under her breath, as if she had to coax herself on, until she stopped, silent, outside Sam's room.

Through a crack in the door, he watched the way her shoulders went up and down for a while. A curling of her hands around the doorframe. She was staring at the photographs he had placed around the room. And he realized, too late, how shockingly potent those reminders would be to her – he had, after all, lived with them for months now. So he went to her.

She was rigid for a while, once she'd heard the whisper of her name. Her jacket sloped off shoulders too thin for it now. Black roots by her scalp and long trailing split ends matted against the nape of her neck. The neck so white and vulnerable-looking, he reached out instinctively.

'Oh, Julia.'

And then, before she mobilized into frenzied activity, she asked that question. The one he had asked himself a million times. He slipped back to the bathroom and watched her through a crack in the doorframe as she flung herself down the stairs, swinging the bag he had packed for her, Sam's spaceship pressed tight against her chest.


The rest of the day passed uneventfully. Brian thought about that phrase as he watched television through the afternoon. No one ever said the day passed eventfully. There should be an additional clause for cases like his, he thought: the day passed – eventually.

He sat through *Grange Hill*, *Countdown* and the early evening *News*, ignoring the persistent messages on the answerphone from the estate agent. Then, Edward's voice on the machine. Brian half rose to interrupt, but sank back into the sofa again. He would get around to returning Edward's calls, one of these days.

The light in the room turned blue from the flickering screen as night closed in. Brian made toast and went upstairs again to Sam's room. His mother flitted in and out all night.

It was strange how she had sort of seeped into his memories throughout the past few weeks. For the longest time, she had remained a shadowy figure, her contours blurred, in contrast to the sharply delineated image of his father. Perhaps that was because she had always appeared, even to his child's eye, as a grey little adjunct to Jeremiah. He recalled now the way she scuttled in tiny shuffling steps, not too dissimilar to Chinese women with bound feet, he'd seen in later years. Her constantly drooping eyelids. The way her face made little twists from the pain in her final months.

She seemed to slip away entirely after Noel's death. He was her favourite, perhaps because she sensed her own weakness in him. For a while, Brian would be aware of her gaze, as if she were studying him, measuring the dead twin's progress. They did not speak of Noel in the house and now Brian wondered if the not speaking had in some way precipitated her illness.

Insubstantial, desultory images of her came into his mind. The way her eyes hastily skimmed back and forth across the supper table, checking that each child was behaving in accordance with Jeremiah's dining rules. Grace before meals, then silence while eating. The girls washed up while the boys finished their evening chores around the farm. A decade of the Holy Rosary on their knees by the fire before bed.

She kept a journal. A small leather-bound book which she called her 'recipe book'. She wrote in it every evening after rosary. Brian had a quick look once; it was almost impossible to read the tiny handwriting compacted into such little space. Apart from recipes – endless variations of the same stew – she kept a ledger, outlining her exact expenditure for the week to the last penny. She even listed every item individually. A few pages contained written prayers – sometimes with a line missing, as if she were recalling them from her own childhood and couldn't quite remember all of the words. He had been surprised to find also her meticulous detailing of the daily tasks on the farm. Season to season, she outlined every calving, every harvest, every crop lost to rain. She listed each field by name and the crop rotation in that field for the season. She even listed how many potatoes she had boiled for the evening's supper. Hurriedly skimming through it, vaguely aware even then that he was intruding, Brian found the births of his siblings listed in a similar fashion. The date, the sex, the time of birth, the weight, the state of health. Nothing of her own health.

He had been rushing his way through, anxious to get to her inscription of Noel's death, when he had heard her coming in with a bucket of rainwater for washing the nappies. She always collected rainwater in a tank by one gable end of the roof; it softened the cloth, she had been led to believe by her own mother. Mary Ann and Pat were with her, baby Teresa was swaddled in a box by the fire beside Brian. He had tried to shove the book back under her seat where she always kept it, but she had seen his movement from the corner of her eye. Mary Ann said, 'Look, Ma, he's at your book.'

Brian was about to protest. But he closed his mouth again when his mother shot him a sad, accusatory look.

'I seen him,' she said flatly.

Brian didn't know why he felt such a hot shame glowing

inside him. It was only a stupid book. Boring anyway. He said as much in a voice he hoped was as manly as his father's. She just nodded. She was used to that tone from men. Brian's shame deepened. He had the uncomfortable feeling that Noel would not have spoken to her like that. As he brushed past them on his way out to the yard, he gave Mary Ann a quick sideways dig in the ribs with his elbow. She howled obligingly. Brian did not attempt to look at her book again and only remembered it the night of her wake as he knelt by her coffin in the kitchen. The same night his father had retired for the first time to the back kitchen.

When Brian reached under her seat, the book was gone. He had wanted it as a keepsake; without it, his memory of her had grown increasingly grey. Just a scuttling shadow throughout his adult life until now, so many years on, he'd found traces of her again in Sam's room, as he waited for another night to pass, eventually.

# SIX

# Small Good Things

The dog keened softly in the yard, throughout the early hours of the morning. Like Julia, he appeared to have dispensed with sleep. In a curious way, she figured that they were both hungry, but his hunger could be sated with a bone. Grief was not so entirely dissimilar. It gnawed constantly, reaching crescendos at certain points of the day, then subsided for stretches of time so that the mechanics of living might be maintained – eating, sleeping, shitting. She endeavoured to keep Sam in her mind at all times, so that she wouldn't be suddenly plunged into awareness in the middle of a straying thought. Those were the worst moments. The mind was selfish, it instinctively sought solace, it demanded breaks, and then in an access of guilt, it rejected a moment's comfort. She had been surprised from the outset by her composure. It had nothing to do with some profound inner strength and everything to do with a quiet, desperate acknowledgement that there was nothing worse than this. Julia had grown accustomed to dry weeps. No tears. Just body shudders and heaves, then calm emptiness again. And an enduring ache that was slow and almost exquisite, in an unbearable sort of way, like a prolonged strain from a violin.

It was still dark out by the horizon but directly above the sky had lightened to a milky navy blue. The stars were fading.

Outside, it sounded as though another animal had joined the whining collie. She heard low rumbling growls, a snarl, then a moment's silence before the distinctive high-pitched yap of pain, followed by another. She crept downstairs in the dim, nascent light.

The wind almost blew her backwards when she opened the door. The collie shot past her knees, little specks of blood dripping from his hind leg. Another dog, a huge creature with black and tan markings, stood a little distance from her. He had arched his back on seeing her, a purfle of tiny hairs stood erect around his neck. Folds of skin drew back along his snout to reveal long, glistening canines. His growl was low, resonating from the pit of his stomach to thrum on his vocal chords. He held Julia's gaze for an instant, unblinking yellow eyes too close together in his skull. Feral eyes. The black thong of his tail stood rigid and motionless. Julia quickly closed the door and followed the collie to the kitchen where he had curled himself into a ball by the still warm ashes of the fire. He glanced up at her and continued to lick the grazed hind leg. She unwrapped the leftover bread from its swaddle of damp dishcloth and pulled it into bite-size pieces. The dog's tail thumped twice, hopefully. She laid the chunks by his head. He gazed up at her. Afraid, perhaps. He looked at the bread, then up at her again. She lifted a piece and held it to his mouth. Gingerly, with the extreme caution of a beast unaccustomed to kindness, he allowed his teeth to pinch a corner of the bread, then swallowed it whole. A gulp as it reached the back of his throat, another suspicious glance, another swallow of the next piece she offered. He chewed only the final three morsels.

When he had finished, Julia bent forward to examine his leg. He whimpered slightly when she lifted it. A ring of bite marks but nothing serious. She wet a cloth and dabbed at the already drying blood. She could discern older marks beneath the matted hairs there and on the other legs when she examined them, and along his hindquarters. The strange black and tan made regular forays, it appeared.

By now, streaks of sepia light stretched in bands across the sky to the west, beyond the kitchen window. Large grey-black crows settled on the fields beyond the window. They flexed their ragged wings and charged at one another in curious hopping motions. Black beads for eyes, sizing up the competition. Funereal comics. Dingy sheep with muddy twigs for legs stood still, as the wind inflated their pelts, puffing them up so that they looked like they might fly. The tethered goat massaged her curled horns sleepily against a plank of wood while down below, by the corrugated shed, a solitary Friesian sat like a sphinx, staring into the distance, a twitch of an ear from time to time signalling that she was, in a fashion, still alive.

Julia sat by the hearth and closed her eyes. She did not intend to sleep, there were chapters to read yet, but an intense weariness stole up on her. When she awoke with a start, Jeremiah was raking the fire ashes, fully clothed in a frayed black suit as creased as his face – Sunday mass, she remembered – and the kettle simmered behind him. The dog was gone.

'You gev him the bread.' He did not look at her.

'Yes, I did.' Julia blinked and shifted up on the chair. 'Sorry about that, but he'd been attacked by another dog . . . seemed to me it's happened more than once.'

He hawked and spat into the ashes, wiping his mouth with his shirt sleeve. A double dismissive hitch of his shoulders.

'Who owns that dog? He looked pretty savage to –'

'East a ways.' His head gestured in that direction. 'Connie Sullivan's. All his dogs got a strain in them.'

He set about making the tea and waved two bony fingers at the fire. She interpreted and knelt down to soak balls of old newspaper in petrol. He put two boiled eggs on saucers, a pinch of salt on the table's surface, two dry crackers.

'There's no bread,' he said sourly. Hard gums ground his food, little knots of muscle standing out on his cheeks. No back teeth. He spat out a sliver of eggshell and rose from the table. An afterthought stopped him by the door. He turned awkwardly. 'I'm away to mass in a while. D'you want to be taken to the grave?'

It was so blunt and sudden the way he'd said it, Julia almost choked on a shard of cracker. Doubtless, this was the reasonable conclusion he had reached for her being there. 'I'd rather wait a bit, if you don't mind . . .' she began.

'Suit yourself.' The door slammed behind him.

Outside, the wind curled around his gaunt, black frame; she saw the sea between his bony thighs as he walked at an angle to the gale and kept his head erect, every step a battle which he won.

Her gaze carried upstairs, seeing in her mind the three tiny bedrooms. She still found it hard to believe that so many children could cram themselves into so little space. Especially once Jeremiah had locked his bedroom after his wife's death. Brian had explained to her how the twins and Teresa had managed to squeeze into the bed she used now, taking it in turns to 'top and toe'. When they could no longer sustain this arrangement without someone falling over the side at least once a night, a narrow hessian mat was placed on the floor and they took turns on that. All the boys made do with the other room which had a single cot forced between the double bed and the window. Brian had laughed at the disbelief on her face. It had kept them warm, at any rate, she supposed, and wondered what he was doing this morning.

Remembering him standing there behind her yesterday, it was clear to her now that she had been moments from turning into his arms. It was almost laughable really, the insane desire to draw comfort from the person who had caused the need in the first place. She wondered if Jeremiah had also put in his fair share of time at this kitchen table, wishing his wife back, his children back. The thing about grief was how utterly complete and self-contained it was. Nothing escaped, neither the past nor the future, because now she could never know the end of the story. Sam's story. Grief sent you everywhere but the present. And she wondered if it was Jeremiah's sense of loss for his wife that had compelled him to the mat in the back kitchen, or egotistical show, or penitence because he had not loved her.

The day ahead seemed endless. Now that she was here, she had no idea how she might pass the time. Running away was no help in the end, it only gave you something to do while you were running. And you had to know what it was that you were running toward.

She reached for the mug of cold tea and leaned forward to rest her elbows on her knees. She forgot the mug and it clattered to the ground, smashing into three pieces. The sound startled her and she stared down in confusion, wondering how she had forgotten that she was holding it in the first place. One minute it was there, tightly in her grip, the next it had fallen, losing its shape, its purpose, a mug no longer. Just useless debris.

A memory came to her of Carol's face bent over Sam's crib when he was a newborn. There was wonder and excitement in her crisp blue eyes, but a trace of envy too, which Carol had chosen not to conceal. And Julia had felt an inordinate sense of gratitude to her sister for giving her that. They had awkwardly squeezed one another's hand until Julia had gently loosened her grip. It was too neat. She had realized at that moment the depth of the anger she still bore toward Carol, for all the years she had taken their mother for herself. Behind their smiles and tinkling talk of babies, they had kept their eyes hooded, because there was more in a glance, a flickering look, than all the speech in the world. A thousand accusations and counter-accusations in the blink of an eye, simple greetings throbbing with recrimination. Perhaps all families were like that, Julia thought. The unspoken, festering like cancer beneath a wordy epidermis.

Down past the rugged sloping fields, the Atlantic ocean yawned and stretched between the two peninsulas. Grey on grey. Jeremiah kicked the cow to her feet.


Some time after he had left for mass on his bicycle, Julia decided to look for an outhouse for her books. She could have put them in her old room, she supposed, but somehow she had the feeling that Jeremiah might not take to that. It might appear a little cheeky.

She cleared up the pieces of broken mug, made a fresh pot of tea and wandered outside nursing a fresh mug between her palms. The dog eyed her from a distance. He made a half-hearted foray toward her, then retreated again. She clicked him over with her tongue, but he kept a gap between them. Kicking distance, she thought. A white transparent light fused sea and sky at the horizon. She shivered more from tiredness than the cold.

The nearest stone building housed the hens. Beyond that lay what was once the piggery, empty now except for rotted straw and the remainder of a wooden door of some kind. A smell of damp within and walls still shiny black from recent rain. Useless for storage. There was a ten-cow tie-up byre to the right of the pigsty, also empty with half the roof missing. The nearby hayshed held the most promise, with a lean-to machine shed propped up precariously against it. Inside the shed, Jeremiah's equipment, mostly rusted and obsolete from lack of use: a plough, hay-turner, hayrake, scythe and a large axe for splitting timber – quite recently used, she figured, with tiny splinters of sawdust clinging to the honed edge.

The hayshed proved to be a disappointment, large holes in the corrugated roof mirroring rusty pools of rainwater on the floor below. At the back, where the roof provided some measure of protection, Jeremiah stored his turf. Little pyramids of still wet black fudge. Behind those again, she came across some items carefully pinned into the stone wall by long black nails. She didn't know the name for everything but she knew they had to do with horses. She recognized a bridle, two winkers – polished, she thought – and a straddle. Evidently, Jeremiah liked to keep the memory of his horses alive. She returned to the yard and stood there for a moment, trying to imagine the place alive with beasts. It was difficult amid such desolation. She wondered what had happened. Brian had never spoken much about the farm. His home. And she had never asked. She wished now that she had, if only to supplement the growing collage she was forming of Jeremiah, his history, in her mind.

Back in the house, she decided to try his old room upstairs. Just on the off chance that perhaps he didn't keep it locked any more. The doorknob turned easily enough in her hand.

She winced guiltily as she stepped through, feet creaking on ancient floorboards. The curtains were drawn. The air suffocating, full of stagnant dust, an underlayer of damp mould.

She quickly crossed the tiny room and hauled at the faded chintz, allowing the first light in years to fall bleakly on an oak bedstead, candlewick cover, single wardrobe and walnut chest of drawers. A gloomy picture of Christ pointing to his wounded heart hung above the bed. Her ears strained to catch any signal of Jeremiah's return. She knew instinctively that he would not be at all happy with the idea of her prying eyes. There was nothing to see in any case; quite what she had expected she couldn't figure out. Something of his earlier married life, she supposed. Hitherto, the closed door had never incited in her the slightest hint of curiosity.

She pulled at a drawer in the chest. Dingy grey nylons and a salmon-pink corset – never worn, Julia suspected. Another drawer revealed woollen socks, darned at each big toe, two slips and, underneath, long strips of cotton streaked with dried-in blood which had not been removed by boiling. There was something extraordinarily intimate about looking at another woman's erstwhile sanitary pads. As if the ghostly creature became vulnerable flesh for a moment.

The bottom drawer held more promise. Julia rummaged through yellowed, squashed shoeboxes, pulling out a handful of sepia dog-eared photographs. She sat back on her haunches by the window, sifting through the hoard.

Most of them were of Holy Communions, she figured. Perhaps one of the rare occasions when a camera was provided by a neighbour. One strained family portrait, Jeremiah staring beadily into the lens, towering above a gaunt, exhausted-looking woman with scraped back hair and surprisingly big, ungainly hands resting on the shoulders of her eldest son Brian – Julia recognized the smile. She figured that his mother could only have been a matter of months away from her death in that picture. She couldn't resist a smile at Brian's manly pose – he was holding baby Teresa wrapped in a swaddling blanket. The christening perhaps.

At the back of every photograph, the names of each member of the family were written in black ink. Small neat letters, so fastidious that Julia was reminded of the early attempts of a child at joined-up writing. She drew one photo nearer to the light. A very faded picture of Brian and Noel together after their Holy Communion. The familiar prayer pose, palms together in front of their chests. One front tooth missing to both cheesy grins. She was struck immediately by how different they looked – for identical twins. Brian was slightly taller, considerably broader in aspect. Something brazen in his expression as he faced the camera. Noel was easily the weaker of the two, yet his was the more adult gaze. The eyes were darker too, the lustre duller than Brian's. One beat behind in everything, it seemed, making Julia think that there was a sad yet serene quality to his fixed stare. It suddenly reminded her of Sam.

She quickly turned her attention to another portrait, this time of Jeremiah and the boys only, but instead of Edward standing beside Brian and Noel, it was their friend Cathal, his arm craning up to reach around Brian's shoulders as their sunburned faces laughed into the lens. They were holding pitchforks, Noel standing slightly apart, gazing out beyond the camera. There was something awkward about the composition. Julia couldn't quite put her finger on it at first, then she realized what it was: Noel looked extraneous somehow. She read the inscription on the back, then flipped the photo over to study it again. There was something else vaguely strange about the whole tableau, but she couldn't for the life of her work out what it was. She screwed up her eyes and put the photo against a pane of glass on the window. Light filtered through the smiling faces, but Noel's expression took on a sadder aspect, making Julia shake her head in frustration. She had the discomforting feeling that she was looking at something she could not see.

With a sigh, she returned the photographs to their shoebox. A small leather-bound book caught her eye. She idly flicked through the pages. A journal of some sort. The tiny black handwriting barely decipherable. Recipes and prayers. Julia shuffled over to the window again, carefully turning the leaves which were parchment-dry and brittle, browned at the corners. Her immediate hopes of some enlightenment on Jeremiah and his wife were quickly dispelled. She felt that she was reading a book of lists. Shopping lists, daily chore lists, prayer lists. After a few pages her head was spinning. The grammar was dodgy but the spelling was immaculate; the writing cramped and invested into the tiniest of spaces. It struck Julia that this was the journal of one who had precious little to say, but that it was also the diary, for want of a better word, of a woman who was conscious of that fact, and who had felt some strange, untypical compulsion to make her mark in any case. She read on through at least a dozen stews and half-finished prayer rhymes. The nothingness of the contents had their own addictive, almost trancelike effect on the reader. She had read through the birth and death of the first stillborn, recounted in terms as dry and dusty as old cake, so that Julia felt nothing for this arid scribe, when the sound of the yard door creaking open thrust her into a panic and she hastily bundled everything back into the drawers, running on tiptoes to the stairs. She held her breath as she creaked her way down, a guilty flush across her cheeks.

It wasn't Jeremiah as she'd feared. Cathal was putting some scones on the kitchen table and jumped visibly when he saw her. 'Julia.'

'Hello, Cathal. How are you?'

'Grand. I'm grand. But . . . when did you . . . ?'

'Yesterday.'

She watched him struggle with words for a moment. Clearly looking for the thing he should be saying. Or, at the very least, trying to say.

'It's all right, Cathal,' she said to put him out of his misery. She approached and leaned forward to kiss his cheek, remembering too late that he was not comfortable with such greetings. 'I know. I mean – I understand how you . . . What you want to . . .'

He looked at his shoes. 'It was a terrible thing,' he said. 'A fine lad. A really fine lad. Anne and myself, we're so sorry for your troubles.'

'Thank you, I got her note.' Julia fingered a scone. 'Will you tell her I was very grateful to her for telling me about the funeral? It was thoughtful of her.'

'She reckoned you'd like to know,' he said quietly. 'Are you all right?' he added, his head pushing a little closer to hers.

Julia swallowed hard. 'Today I am,' she said after a while. Adding in a brisker tone: 'Jeremiah's gone to mass, if you were looking for him . . . ?'

'Ah well, I figured that. He always goes to the twelve o'clock. Only Anne was baking last night so I thought I'd . . .' His voice trailed away. He scratched at the side of his neck.

103

Julia studied him from the corner of her eye. He was a couple of years younger than Brian – about forty, forty-one at most. Edward's age. A big, red, square face to match his hands, folds of flesh under grey eyes and around his full lips, a good head of wavy dark brown hair above a deeply grooved forehead. He had the kind of face that at once appeared to be familiar, as if you had always known it.

She had never spoken much with Cathal during her visits, but she had observed how he appeared to turn up every day, on the pretext of doing something or other for Jeremiah. Without the use of Cathal's tractor, and his freely dispersed nitrogen fertilizer, not to mention his freely offered time, Jeremiah's already tenuous existence might not have survived thus far. She remarked as much to Brian one time but he'd just shrugged – that was Cathal for you.

Cathal's wife ran the local sub post office which also doubled as a little shop, about a mile and a half along the main road. Between the shop and his relatively large farm, Cathal laboured every night until bedtime but he always fitted in his daily trip to Jeremiah. Yet Julia had never heard one word of gratitude from the latter. Never observed one complicitous gesture between the men. But Cathal didn't appear to be looking for thanks.

'Is Brian . . . ?' he said now, glancing around.

'No. I'm on my own,' Julia responded quickly.

'I see.'

'Cathal, I'm not sure why I came here, to be perfectly honest with you,' she blurted out in a rush. 'Jeremiah probably thinks that I've come to visit the grave . . .'

'Anne will go with you if you want,' he interjected.

'Yes – I mean – no.' Julia picked furiously at her cuticles. 'The thing is, Cathal, I'm not sure if that is what I want just yet. All I know is that I want to be here. Somehow, it just feels right. Does that sound crazy to you?'

He pulled at his ear, probably afraid that she might start crying or something. Julia blinked rapidly and pulled her face into a tight mask.

'Whatever helps,' he said.

'D'you think Jeremiah will let me stay for a while?'

'God, you're asking me?' His mouth pulled down at the corners.

'Well, it just seems to me that if anyone knows him, you do.'

He thought about that for a while, a surprised expression on his face. 'Sure no one knows Jeremiah,' he said, 'only himself.'

He seemed relieved at the prospect of extricating himself from this conversation, when the sound of the door latch signalled Jeremiah's return.

Jeremiah lifted his eyebrows slightly as he passed Cathal. The mutual grunt of the men reminded Julia of Sam and his schoolyard silent vocabulary. He heaped a pile of turf on to the fire, filled the kettle from the tap and, with an almost imperceptible flick of one forefinger, gestured toward the scones. Cathal had already reached for the butter knife when he realized, as did Julia, that the silent order had been directed at her. Cathal handed her the knife and she began to butter the scones, catching Cathal's reassuring smile from the corner of her eye. He was confirming her own conclusion – that she could stay. She had been put to work.


Life on Cathal's telly was very different to Brian's. Everyone seemed to have so much of everything, even the people on the ads, and they were selling stuff. To Brian, only people who had very little had to sell.

When Brian and Edward walked the mile and a half to Cathal's on Wednesday evenings, they pretended that they were going to do homework with their friend. Cathal watched everything, even the boring news, because his father liked to keep him up for the company, possibly because he became a father and a widower on the same evening. The brothers felt a bit sorry for Cathal for that. But they thought having a telly was some compensation. Jeremiah hated television, though he had only ever seen one, and would never have permitted them to watch *Voyage to the Bottom of the Sea*, Brian's favourite programme, which he re-enacted, scene by scene, on the way home afterwards with Edward, who never got to do the echoing submarine sound effects – boc boc – because of his stutter.

Sometimes, they got to see *The Virginian* too on Saturday nights, but they stopped playing that when Cathal, as Trampas in a rodeo, fell off the donkey in the backyard and needed seven stitches in his crown. Cathal's father told them that he didn't want them mooching around the place after that. Didn't they have any home to go to – hah! Brian hated the way Cathal's father always finished everything he said to them with a 'hah': 'How's himself, lads? Dead yet from bitterness – hah!' Forever the same question about their father, and that smug little coda, just to let them know how inferior they were.

Mr Regan, they called him to his face, Corny, short for Cornelius, behind his back. He was a small, fat man with big opinions, a small store-cum-post office and land backing down to where Jeremiah's sixty acres began. He wanted it all. Mostly, because it was Jeremiah's. The men despised each other. They had been best friends once, when they were growing up together, farm by farm, but something had happened to turn childhood fondness into adult hate. Brian only knew that Cathal was always welcome or tolerated at home, but mention of his father made Jeremiah seethe. Brian figured it was because everything seemed to come so easily to Corny, like the twenty-five acres he had managed to acquire of Jeremiah's land when the first set of boy twins were born, and the only option was to sell or starve.

Brian only knew about that sale when, years later, Corny sold the parcel of scrub and rock to a German for at least ten times the sum he had paid Jeremiah. It was then that he had come looking for more, loath as he was to part with any segment of his own two hundred or so acres. Corny was ahead of his time. He could see what his neighbours could not, namely the pending influx of English and Europeans, who, priced out of their own markets, were hungry for soil and for acreage with sea views and clean air. And wild, desolate sites on which to build their cottage industries, candle- or cheese- or pottery-making. While most of Corny's land was higher up and relatively fertile, Jeremiah's backed down to the sea and was rough and rocky, suitable in the main only for sheep. But Corny could see its desirability to foreigners.

Brian had a hazy recollection of Noel standing beside him, both of them pretending not to listen, as Corny turned up one evening to taunt Jeremiah with the sale of the twenty-five acres. Brian couldn't prevent his own eyes from widening when Corny casually mentioned the sum involved. And he felt a sharp sense of pride when he surreptitiously glanced up at his father's face which had not registered so much as a tic. He just nodded, as if the men were discussing the weather. Corny was a bit annoyed about that, because Cathal was there too, to witness his moment of triumph. Cathal kept his head down, a hand nervously rubbing the back of his neck. Brian could see the deep flush of embarrassment on his friend's cheeks and he felt a bit sorry for him for having such an eedjit of a father. Even at five and a half, Cathal knew that.

Corny, in his high-handed way, was telling Jeremiah that he'd take another fifteen acres of the scrub to the east of the farm off his hands, if Jeremiah had a mind to sell. As blunt as that; Brian and Noel were shocked. The disrespect – no circling conversations about what was wanted and what might be available, allowing a man to make the decision to sell with dignity and a huge show of reluctance. The implication being that Jeremiah *needed* to sell. The boys, including Cathal, waited for the explosion. But Jeremiah remained quiet and lit his pipe, having politely offered a pinch of tobacco to his neighbour first. He thanked Corny for his offer but he was not of a mind to sell. What was left would ultimately belong to a son. Corny had turned then, to stare pointedly at the twins. The boys understood that he was signalling to the fact that there were two of them, and land enough for one, if that. But they couldn't understand why he suddenly flushed redder than fresh blood and bunched his fists under the weight of Jeremiah's soundless, piercing stare. Corny had left then, poking Cathal in the back ahead of him. And Brian had nudged Noel to look at the expression on Jeremiah's face. He wasn't angry at all – a sketch of a smile played on his lips.

These days, it was Brian and Edward who were taunted, their ears burning when Corny repeatedly told whoever would listen about the time back in the early fifties, when the electric finally reached down to Jeremiah's peninsula, and how Brian's mother had continued to light the paraffins every night with a bulb shining above her head. And how she'd only learned to write from watching her young sons do their lessons. Hah! Country ignorance for you. The ruination of the country. As if the brothers were not standing there at all, mentally vowing, despite their downcast heads, to kick seven kinds of shite out of Cathal later when they got him alone. They rarely did, however, because Cathal was all right, he was just as embarrassed by his father as they were, and besides, he had a telly. Which was denied to them for a few months after the donkey incident, though then they managed to creep back in during the World Cup. But that was when they made their mistake.

They were playing the final in the yard at twilight. Brian was England, of course, splicing a wad of rolled-up newspapers into the back of the bucket, making Geoff Hurst's hattrick. He fisted the air triumphantly: 'They think it's all over, it is now . . .' when he saw Edward's face freeze.

'What's that ye're doing?' Jeremiah leaned against the doorframe, a stream of pipesmoke blowing from the side of his mouth.

'Oh, just a game.' Brian tried to force a suitably casual note into his voice. But Edward was letting the side down with his guilty expression. Brian frowned at him.

'What game is that?' Jeremiah said levelly.

Brian couldn't think fast enough, he couldn't be sure how much Jeremiah had observed – perhaps sufficient to let him know that they weren't playing Gaelic.

'Soccer.' Brian turned slowly to meet his father's measured gaze.

'And where have ye seen that?'

'Ah – we play it in school sometimes,' Brian answered truthfully. Then his teeth crunched down on his lower lip. He'd forgotten Cotter – they had to hide their soccer playing from him too. Jeremiah's eyes narrowed. 'Indeed.' He had registered the slip and now tapped the bowl of his pipe against the door. Brian quickly pulled a face at Edward. 'So Cotter's allowing Sassenach games in his schoolyard now, is that what you're telling me?'

Edward's agitation was pitiful, his knees were buckling. Brian desperately cast around in his mind to see if there was a way he could take his beating for him as well as his own. 'No,' he said quietly. 'I saw the World Cup Final on Cathal's telly and I was telling Edward all about it.'

There was always a curious moment, before his father's anger was unleashed in full, when Brian almost enjoyed a sense of peace; as if, in a way, he spent his days in dread, so that when he was actually plunging toward it, facing it head on, there was no more to fear. It was all over bar the strapping. He never understood why his father was so angry, sometimes he figured that all righteous men must incline toward wrath, the world around them being so decadent. Years ago, when Noel was alive, he had thought that it might have something to do with them being twins. Now it was just a fact of life, as incomprehensible as the feelings he had towards Cathal's cousin, Martina, when she mocked his patched trousers and he wanted to slap her and kiss her at the same time.

Jeremiah's left hand had curled into a fist. His long legs were jiggling. The weight of his stare was thrust at Edward, who looked as if he might swoon at any minute. Brian had backed him into a corner; if he admitted to watching the television, then Brian would get extra lashes for lying; if he

110

denied it, then he would have to endure the sight of Brian getting his share anyway. In spite of his own trepidation, Brian felt a pang of pity for his brother, who was never as weak as Noel had been, nor as willing to forgo his punishment at the expense of Brian.

'So, you didn't clap eyes on that infernal machine, is that right, boy?' Jeremiah was addressing Edward.

Brian shot him a glance, telling him to agree. 'I-I clapped eyes on it, sir, b-b-but I never l-l-looked at it.' Edward hung his head.

'But your brother here, he looked at it?'

'Yes.' A whisper. This was getting worse. As Jeremiah began to unbuckle his belt, signalling with his eyes for Brian to remove his shirt, Edward could endure the torment no longer. 'Sh-sh-shite,' he bawled.

Brian nearly laughed. Jeremiah's back stiffened. He could hardly believe his ears. Edward began to unbutton his shirt with trembling fingers. Brian cast him a furtive smile. Then an image of Noel falling back against barbed wire came into his head. The loosened stake giving way under the pressure – a stake which Brian should have checked for him. And he doubled over for his beating.

The doorbell again, for the fourth ring. Somebody was insistent. Brian sighed, switched off *Disney Club* and loped to the hall. He fixed his face for the estate agent but it crumpled instantly when he opened the door and saw Richard standing there. 'Richard.'

'Hello, Brian.' His stoop seemed more pronounced than ever. The elongated neck a straining reluctant bough, bearing his great head. Little white winglets curled up from his dense

111

eyebrows. Brian could barely detect the gleams of his eyes beneath the twin hedges. His feet scuffed the ground as he waited for Brian to invite him in. Brian took a startled step backwards. 'Come in. Come in.'

Richard patted a zipped leather holdall under his arm which he carried everywhere. Just in case a zipped leather holdall might be needed. 'Julia was up yesterday . . . ?' Richard's voice faded as they entered the living-room.

'Yes, yes.' Brian forced a cheery note to his voice. 'We didn't actually, ahh . . .'

'She said.' Richard patted the holdall again. 'She's gone to Ireland, you know.'

'Oh?'

'Last night on the ferry. Just – went.' The winged eyebrows went up and down, then remained firmly down, shielding his eyes. 'We don't know for how long, really.'

They sat on the edge of two armchairs, facing each other. Richard cleared his throat. 'Any luck so far with the sale?' He looked around, indicating the house.

'A few interested, but you know how it is.' Brian hesitated before adding, 'Did Julia say anything about it? I mean, do you think she's agreeable to . . .'

'Oh, yes. She thinks it's for the best. All round. For everyone. And work . . . ? Edward's sort of kept us posted on you, so to speak,' Richard added tentatively.

'Several interviews coming up. Good prospects, all of them,' Brian responded hastily, hoping he wouldn't have to compound the lie with descriptions of non-existent vacancies. 'Whiskey?'

'You've twisted my arm.' Richard studied his fingernails. Brian noticed the tremble of his hands.

I've twisted your heart, Brian thought, as he poured two

112

stiff measures. He patted Richard's shoulder, from force of habit as he handed the tumbler, and Richard froze.

'I always wanted to be a fireman,' Richard uttered in a muffled cry.

'Did you?' was all Brian could think of to say.

'I don't know why I said that.'

Brian nodded, stepped backwards toward his chair. Richard clamped his jaw and stared out the window over Brian's shoulder.

'Actually,' he said, 'the reason I'm here . . . Well, Jennifer felt very badly about the way she spoke to you on the phone yesterday. She asked me to come here and tell you that. We'd like it if you'd come and visit now that Julia . . . Jennifer would like to see you, Brian.'

'She would?' Brian craned around following Richard's gaze to the window. He was touched immeasurably by their kindness.

'So nice to see the magnolia still in bloom,' Richard said. He looked meaningfully at Brian. 'I've found for my own part, these past few months, that there are still a few small good things to be found in the garden . . . So you'll come . . . next Sunday say?' he added before draining his glass.

'I'll come.'

Brian filled their glasses again and they sipped in silence for a while as diffused late afternoon light filtered through the magnolia blossoms and muslin drapes, filling the room with soft, diaphanous light. It felt good to be in company again, after the long months of solitude. He felt intensely grateful to Richard, for his humanity, for not mentioning Sam, for not making him feel afraid. And for the first time in his life, he acknowledged that he had always been afraid.

113

But he had managed to cover it so well, that he had even fooled Julia and, not least, himself.

'Thank you,' he found himself saying as Richard rose to leave.

Richard nodded, he slapped his palms against his thighs, gazed around the room as if to check his bearings. A man surprised to be anywhere. 'Be brave,' Richard said at the door, because he thought it was the manly thing to say.

Brian understood and gave him a watery smile. Back in the living-room, he wondered why people had to be brave. There were no dirges to cowards. Sam had been brave – before he lost him.

He fixed another whiskey and sat in the deepening gloom of the afternoon, waiting for night, for sleeplessness, for morning, for the same thing again tomorrow. He wondered vaguely which spectral companion would invade his consciousness later.

He thought of Noel and his fear of heights. The unspeakable terror on his face that day when his father suspended him by the ankle, over the edge of the cliff.

# SEVEN

# Passing Time

'Shove over, gev me that,' Jeremiah barked. With his shoulder he hoisted Julia to the side as his hand reached out to cusp the goat's teat. After three weeks, she still had trouble coaxing the milk out. Jeremiah blew on his other hand to warm it, tweaked the teat between his thumb and forefinger and a rewarding stream hit the back of the bucket. 'Now try,' he said.

A few drops dribbled down the enamel pail. Julia gritted her teeth with frustration.

'You're squeezing too hard, woman.' Jeremiah hawked and spat with disgust.

Julia wanted to say 'at least she's not shitting herself' but refrained. Instead, she murmured softly to the skittish creature and a long yellowish stream hit the target. Julia beamed, looked up for his approval, but Jeremiah was already moving along to the next chore of the morning. The dog fretted his ankles and received a sideways kick head on. Julia clicked him over to her. He approached these days within kicking distance and she felt pleased about that. 'You'll never learn, will you?' she whispered to his eager face.

The milking of the goat was a milestone. She was able for all the other daily tasks except for that and now watching the steady spray landing in a froth inside the bucket she felt curiously elated. The strange yellow eyes with their black vertical line of pupil used to fill with terror at her approach. Goats could eat and shit at the same time, she had discovered. In fact, there was nothing they couldn't do without shitting. Shortly now, Jeremiah might even permit her access to the cow, seeing as she'd mastered milking the goat. She hummed in time to the pshtt pshtt hitting the bucket.

In the last few weeks, she had fallen into a steady routine with Jeremiah. Rising with the first crow of the yard cockerel to fix breakfast for both of them, then out to the henhouse to collect eggs. After that, an hour of turning the handle on an old Pierce pulper, six beets at a time, until the ball and socket joint of her shoulder felt swollen and disjointed as she tipped the resultant mush into a trough for the cow. The sheep took most of the natural grazing so the Friesian had supplementary fodder of beets and mangolds, Jeremiah had explained.

He had walked the land with her, or the fifteen or so acres which remained. Tersely explaining, as they walked, the crop rotation in each field, turnips for the sheep, an acre of fodder beet and mangolds for the Friesian, the eighth of an acre for Kerr Pinks, a ridge of carrots and parsnips beside them, a bank of cabbage and lettuce grown under a cloche made from an old window frame by the side of the house in an area he called the haggard. She had learned to strain the milk from the cow, separating the yellow cream from the duck-egg blue underneath. Her stomach was still growing accustomed to the rich buttery taste of untreated milk.

Jeremiah appeared to live on a diet of fatty boiled bacon, which he called 'mate', with potatoes and cabbage, which

116

they ate at midday, then fish or a lump of cheese for supper. Julia's palate had quickly wearied of the stodgy fare and she had tentatively tried to introduce a few changes, adding salads or fresh fruit from the nearby town, then freshly baked soda bread, which Cathal's wife, Anne, had shown her how to make with buttermilk. Jeremiah said nothing the first evening she'd presented this new diet, but a tacit agreement had passed between them, which resulted in Julia preparing all the meals from then on. Jeremiah, she had discovered, was partial to an apple, but he would never buy them. Julia had arranged for Jennifer to forward the contents of her personal savings account, and it would amply provide for her car and groceries for some months to come. She had also prevailed on Jennifer to forward the signed documents for the sale of the house to Brian. Once the mortgage was cleared, there would be precious little left, but he was welcome to any surplus, so far as she was concerned. She never wanted to see that house again.

The subject of her tenure here was not discussed. As long as she was doing something, it seemed to Julia, then she would be tolerated. Moreover, she was finding herself so worn out by evening that she slept the sleep of the dead until first cockerel crow. Her books remained unread in the main, piled up in the hayshed beside the pyramids of turf. Every day, she worked until she felt like dropping, just to enjoy the reward of uninterrupted sleep.

Whenever a chance presented, she crept into Jeremiah's old bedroom to absorb another few pages of his dead wife's journal. The monotonous lists of chores and tasks mirrored her own life so perfectly that she derived a strange comfort from the sameness, the predictability itself. It was as if her life had been taken out of her own hands entirely, and now ran along alien tracks, with Jeremiah electing the stops and starts according to his design. She had wondered if his wife had ever felt like that and, at that moment, she'd realized that she didn't even know her Christian name. Brian, if he referred to her at all, simply called her 'Ma'. Seeing as she was now so sneakily intimate with the woman's diary, she decided to try and prise a little information from Jeremiah, if that were at all possible.

She untethered the goat for a while, thinking it might enjoy a few moments' freedom, put the bucket to the side and swept the black buckshot droppings into a corner for Jeremiah to gather up, when the mound was sufficiently high, for fertilizer. Nothing was wasted.

He was thinning fodder beet with two cut-up jute bags wrapped around the bony knees pressed into the soil. Julia sidled over, the dog keeping a little distance from her. Jeremiah didn't look up but he registered her presence by indicating a hoe behind his ankles. Julia nodded. She was to continue weeding the earth around the mangolds, so that he would have a cleared space for replanting the thinned crop. Later, in the afternoon, he'd said that they would sow turnip seeds broadcast, over a very fine tilth, harrowed by Cathal a couple of days ago. The black, spongy soil of the tilled field spread down in a narrow strip to where Jeremiah's land came to an abrupt end, plunging in an almost vertical cliff to the sea below.

Julia leaned on her hoe for a moment, her eyes sweeping over the various fields, prepared in varying degrees for the different crops. A small, curiously barren patch caught her eye up by the western gable of the house. 'What's that spot for?' she asked.

Jeremiah leaned back on his haunches, eyes squinting as

he followed the line of her outstretched finger. His shoulders hitched dismissively. ''Twas meant for flowers or some such,' he said.

A vision of Jeremiah planting tulips didn't spring readily to mind, so Julia assumed he meant his wife. 'Did she have any luck?'

'With our wind?' he asked incredulously, applying his attention to the beets again.

Julia continued hoeing but her eyes constantly drifted up to the hopeless little patch by the haggard. She felt a pang of sympathy for the woman who might have had a touch of colour introduced into her drab life, had her husband thought to erect a windscreen for her. She determined to have a try herself. She was going into town with Anne in a couple of hours in any case, so she could buy some seeds and a few strips of calico with stakes then. Maybe a few perennials and some wind-hardy shrubs as well, to bear the brunt of the gales. In her mind's eye, she was already laying out the various bands of colour. It occurred to her that she should check with Jeremiah first. In case he had plans this year for the erstwhile flower patch. 'Would you mind if I had a go – with the flowers I mean?'

'Suit yourself. But you'll be wasting your time,' he said sourly.

'What was your wife's name?' Julia asked casually over her shoulder. Now was as good a time as any.

'What's that?'

'Your wife – I was just wondering what she was called.'

'Margaret.'

She allowed a beat to pass, hoping that he might offer something else, but his knees shunted forward on the jute bags as his hands rapidly pulled at the smaller beets.

119

'Margaret,' she repeated, as if they were engaged in conversation.

She jumped when Jeremiah let out a loud holler. He was scrambling to his feet, a bony finger stabbing the air accusingly. Julia turned quickly. The goat was knee deep in the cabbage patch. 'What you lev her loose for?' Jeremiah roared.

'God, I'm sorry . . .' Julia dropped the hoe and ran up toward the house.

She grimaced to herself as she led the euphoric, almost swooning goat back to its rope. A long trail of droppings followed behind them. 'Another fine mess you've got me into,' she chuckled as she tethered the rope with a double knot. A reciprocal chuckle from behind made her swing around guiltily.

Edward was leaning by the side of the house. He wore an Aran sweater at least three sizes too big, giving his already slender frame a somewhat childlike appearance. His hands were plunged deep into the pockets of his faded denims. They moved awkwardly toward one another, arms encircling in a feeble embrace at first until they both intensified the pressure before pulling apart. The terrible memory of the last time they had been in one another's company was a palpable thing between them. Edward smiled shyly. 'Your mother told me you w-were here,' he said. 'I ph-phoned last week, and she asked me check how you . . . She sounded worried about you,' he added, taking his glasses off to rub his sweater sleeve along the lens. The blue eyes were more like Brian's than she had remembered. 'So you're a f-farmer now, eh?'

'It's what I've always wanted,' she said jokingly, but the little rasp to her accompanying laugh set her own teeth on edge. 'I'm OK – sort of,' she added quickly, pre-empting the question on his face.

Edward nodded, understanding. He reached out and gave her hand a little squeeze. Their hands fell away at the same time.

'C'mon,' she said, striding past him into the house. 'It's time for a tea-break anyhow.'

On impulse, she turned at the door and caught the dark, glowering look on Edward's face as he stared down the fields at the approaching figure of Jeremiah. For a split second, she thought she saw real hate there, but then his expression softened again as he followed her into the kitchen, and she thought she must have been mistaken.

He scalded the teapot as she cut thick slices of spongy white bread, lathered butter on top and set out milk and sugar. She put mugs on the table for herself and Edward, a saucer for Jeremiah. He liked to soak the strips of bread in his tea, sprinkling a crust of sugar along the top, as he scooped up the flaccid mouthfuls with his fingers.

Edward watched her preparations with a wry smile on his face. 'Looks like you know the l-lie of the land by now,' he said.

'Keeps me busy,' she responded truthfully.

Jeremiah barged in. 'Did you tie up that bleddy creature?' he demanded of Julia, entirely ignoring Edward, who remained by the window with his rigid back to his father.

'I did. Sorry about that. It won't happen again.' Julia filled his saucer with tea. He humphed and sat to the table, rubbing his palms along his flannel pants.

As Julia sipped her tea, blowing over the top to cool it, she eyed father and son with growing bemusement. Not so much as a grunt of recognition passed between them. It was as if Edward were not sitting there at all. She decided to go along with it for now.

When Jeremiah scraped back his chair to return outside again, she told him that she would leave an Irish stew simmering on the backstove for later.

'Where're you going?' He frowned. 'We've the sowing in a while yet.'

'I remember,' Julia said. 'I should be back in plenty of time. It's just that I want to get a few things in town – with Anne.'

He nodded as if giving her permission and left again without so much as a backward glance. Julia began to clear the table, conscious of Edward's eyes watching her keenly. She scraped some carrots and peeled a few onions, putting the back of her hand against her nose to stem the sting of tears.

'Don't . . .' she said to Edward, sensing his questions.

'I'll f-finish that for you if you want,' he said, indicating the stewpot. So much gentleness in his smile that she had to look away again.

'It won't take me a second,' she responded, her voice over-bright.

A curious thing in women, she thought, this instinct to serve when nothing else made sense. She patted Edward's shoulder on her way upstairs. Anne always dressed for town, so Julia felt that she should make an effort too. She swapped her dung-streaked jeans for a paisley skirt and plain white shirt, sweeping her hair up into a topknot to hide the dark roots. A touch of vaseline to her chapped lips and she was ready. Before she left the room, she trailed a finger along the contours of the spaceship, which occupied the corner opposite to her bed so that it would be the first thing she saw each morning. She had been dreaming of Sam this past week, which was something she had been dreading, but somehow it wasn't as awful as she had anticipated. In the dreams, she could smell him: the faint tang of urine and sweat of his pyjamas in the mornings; toothpaste breath as he kissed her goodbye before school. And for brief moments, he was alive again, even though a voice constantly reminded her that she was only dreaming.

Edward gave her blouse and skirt a bright smile as she was leaving, as though he approved. And she felt curiously pleased about that. She returned his smile and asked how long he would be staying. When he said a few days or so, her smile broadened. There was something pleasant about the prospect of having Edward's friendly face around in the evenings.

That was when time moved most slowly. When too tired to read, but not yet ready for sleep, she sat by the fireside with Jeremiah, watching his pipe, newspaper, rosary beads routine. They rarely spoke. Sometimes, she wondered if Brian was praying these days. Her thoughts concerning him were so dark on occasion that she had to leave the kitchen abruptly to walk down the fields, inhaling deep gulps of exorcising wind and salty night air. Edward's presence might relieve her of those thoughts for a while.

Outside, the day was so far maintaining a brightness, with huge granite-bottomed cumuli wrestling with patches of blue sky. She elected to walk the mile and a half to Anne's; they could take her car. At the top of the track leading to Jeremiah's, she turned left and followed the high, narrow, winding main road, which was protected from the declining fields and sea by skeins of barbed wire. Marked sheep culled whatever they could from the roadside verges. Out by the horizon, a searing golden light divided sky from sea and drifts of blue-black cloud sifted down, marbling the gold with dark veins. The wind whipped through the folds of her skirt. She was breathless and a little giddy from fresh air by the time the bell clanged, signalling a customer at Anne and Cathal's store-cum-post-office-cum-home-cum-farm.

The shop was little more than a front room with dry goods stacked on bracketed shelves, a small deep freezer filled in the main with boxes of fish fingers, and the sub post office accoutrements – brass scales, stamps and lottery tickets. A corner was devoted to the display of Anne's dried-flower arrangements, which did not sell very well.

'Is that you, Julia? Come through . . .' Anne with an 'e' called from the parlour behind the shop. She was very adamant about that 'e', for some reason.

Anne was putting away her knitting when Julia walked through. She cast Julia a welcoming beam. That was one of the things Julia was growing to like about this place, the way that people didn't wait to show their hand. They displayed their wares instantly – no cagey, half-suspicious 'I will, if you will' greetings. Anne was an emaciated creature, so thin that Julia wondered if her stomach was transparent. The only rotund things about her were her ruddy cox's orange pippin cheeks. Even her scalp seemed to glow through the matted yellow strands of hair.

'I was just giving up on you,' Anne said affably.

'Sorry,' Julia responded. 'I waited to make their tea – Edward's come home for a few days – then I walked.'

'Edward's home?' Anne sounded surprised.

'Tell me,' Julia said, 'are they always like that with one another? So – hostile, is the word, I suppose.'

'Hostile?' Anne snorted. 'That's one word for it.' She

applied lipstick in a mirror over a walnut dresser. 'Look it,' she said to Julia's reflection, 'we haven't time to go into it now – I've a suit for a wedding on my mind. Let's go.' She turned, adding, 'To the shops, the shops, girl,' to Julia's fazed expression.

'Oh yes.' Julia tried to motivate herself. She took a few obliging steps then stood still again. Beyond the ambit of the farm she felt ill at ease and disoriented once more. After any period of time, she could feel herself slip back into that almost catatonic state which had exasperated Jennifer so much. The thought of Jennifer saddened her suddenly. While she could understand her mother's genuine concern – prevailing on Edward to visit like that – she still couldn't bring herself to use Anne's phone, as she knew she should. She would write again, later that night. Another nothing letter, guaranteed to send Jennifer into a frenzy of frustration. Anne was waiting by the door, her foot tapping impatiently on the shop's lino. Julia made to move again, but her legs felt heavy.

She gazed around the sanitized room, where every piece of china sparkled as if buffed just a moment ago, and lace antimacassars were draped over every armchair. Cathal was in the yard attending to his tractor. Something was wrong; his brow had furrowed into one long crease. Behind him, a large white satellite dish sat incongruously amidst the cow slurry. Polished, no doubt, by Anne every day because there wasn't a streak on it. Anne and Cathal had every mod. con. imaginable. Cathal had even acquired a radio he could take into the shower.

'He works hard,' Julia said, indicating Cathal with her head.

'Too bloody hard, if you ask me.' Anne smacked her thin lips. 'As if he doesn't have enough to do around here . . .' she

125

added in reference to the hours that Cathal spent attending to Jeremiah. Julia had gathered that this was a constant source of irritation to Anne.

'He's very good to Jeremiah,' she said now, to set the cat amongst the pigeons.

The telltale mercury barometer rose and fell along Anne's face. She turned her sour laugh into a light giggle. Julia joined her, returning Anne's droll glance. They pretty much shared the same sense of sly humour, Julia had realized over the past few weeks. Laughing at uncomfortable things in order to accommodate them. While Anne played the country bumpkin when it suited her, she had a knowing, devilish glint to her grey eyes at times.

'We'll stop off on the way home for a jar,' she said, winking.

Julia was about to agree with gladness when she remembered the turnip field. 'I would,' she said with a groan that sounded over the top to her own ears. 'But we have to do the turnip field later today.'

Anne's eyes widened mockingly. 'Oh "we" have to do the turnips, do we? Would that be before or after "we've" stuck a broom up our arse to sweep the yard out?'

Julia smiled, conceding the point. 'Well, at least Cathal won't have to do it. Think of it that way,' she responded amiably.

'You mean I'll get Cathal all to myself for one whole evening?' Anne said in mock horror. 'God, what'll I say to him?' She cast Julia a dry look over her shoulder. 'C'mon, let's go, or the shops'll be shut.'

They drove in relative silence for the fifteen miles into town, except for Anne's constant twiddling with the radio dial. She finally rested on some country-and-western station,

126

sending Julia a sideways apologetic glance. 'I'm a sucker for broken marriages and the . . .' Her voice trailed off as she flushed. 'Sorry,' she added and turned to the news.

They stopped off at a few clothes shops for Anne to get her suit for the wedding. Julia nodded or turned her mouth to the side to indicate her approval or not. Anne, now patently nervous, spent the entire time asphyxiated by embarrassment that anyone might know her, or know of her, or know her husband. It was a problem she had when she went to town. Julia could not really understand. You liked the dress, so you bought the dress; you didn't worry if the shopgirl wondered how you had the money or not. But Anne did. Anne worried about everything. When they stopped for a coffee, she thought that everyone was looking at them. Even the bag containing the suit she'd finally settled on caused her embarrassment as she tucked it like a thief under the table.

The town housed no more than four or five thousand at best but evidently town and country was a case of 'never the twain', at least for Anne's generation. Julia felt sorry for her as she watched Anne self-consciously dab her mouth, having managed to ingest a whole lettuce leaf in front of the eyes she imagined watching everywhere.

Julia bought some apples and oranges for Jeremiah and they walked along the pavements, stopping at windows to stare at things they did not want to buy. Julia was amazed by how the town had changed even since her first visit over ten years ago. Video shops and estate agents on every corner, craft shops tumbling over one another, cafés with awnings and real cappuccino. The Square she had always known as a carpark was now a paved piazza replete with fountains and exotic shrubs. Even the supermarket had signs in German and French and, outside, Mercedes and little nifty sports cars that somehow didn't seem to fit in. She felt herself longing to return to Jeremiah and the goat.

They drove out of town to the nearest nursery where Julia took advice for her shrubbery. She bought sea buckthorn, escallonia, oleasters and some griselinia to create further screening behind her windshield. Then some cotton lavenders, heathers and rock roses for the next layer and a few autumnal-flowering crocus bulbs, potted geraniums and peonies for the border. An image of the barren patch, transforming slowly, oasis-like, came into her mind and she was forced to stop buying when Anne said that the car was already full to capacity, and would Julia care to walk home or what? Julia felt as though she had stepped over some invisible demarcation line as they headed back in the flowery car. She had shopped.

As they headed out of town, she turned to Anne. 'So tell me,' she said, 'have you any idea why Edward seems to hate his father so much?'

'Edward's not the only one,' Anne responded, brushing a straying vine from her face. 'Didn't you ever notice?'

'Well, no. Not really.' Julia considered for a moment. 'I mean, Brian . . .'

'Oh, Brian's always seen the old man differently. The twins barely talk to him; Cormac's never been home, not once, since he left; and Teresa . . . She has time enough for him, I suppose. Maybe he was softer with her being the baby he had to bring up by himself.' She shrugged. 'I don't know. He's not an easy man to like, God knows.'

'Cathal seems to.'

'Pssh, Cathal . . .' Anne clicked her tongue. 'My own reckoning is that he still feels guilty about the time his da took the rest of Jeremiah's land off him, after the mother died. The men couldn't stand each other.' She was going to leave it at that until she saw Julia's quizzical look, encouraging her to continue. 'Cathal's mother, you see, she married Corny instead of Jeremiah and brought nearly a hundred acres with her. She and Jeremiah had been doing a line for years, then she chose Corny and Jeremiah had a marriage arranged for him. Cathal says it made him bitter. But I think he was always a twisted old bollocks. I mean, we all got a good thrashing when we deserved it, but the marks those kids had on them coming to school sometimes, especially your Brian . . .' Her voice drifted away.

'What was Brian like, Anne? I mean as a young boy.'

Anne gazed ahead through the windscreen, the corners of her eyes crinkling at some memory or other. 'Oh, he was the leader of the gang. Always the one to think up the games in the schoolyard. All us girls had the biggest crush on him. Edward and Cathal were like his right-hand men. You hardly ever saw one without the other two.'

'What about Noel?'

'The twin?' Anne frowned. 'He was before my time, really. I hadn't started school yet, when he was there. But Cathal remembers him a bit. Says he was fierce quiet. Brian was always sticking up for him.'

Julia studied her fingernails. 'Funny, isn't it? How different our child and adult selves can be . . .'

'Brian, you mean?' Anne cast her a shrewd glance. Julia nodded. 'All I know is, Cathal hasn't changed one iota,' Anne said, pulling a mock-rueful face, which Julia didn't swallow for an instant. She had rarely come across a more devoted couple. 'He's the same today as he ever was . . . up and down to that bloody Jeremiah. If people could be drugs, I'd say

129

that Jeremiah was a drug. And Cathal has to have his fix every day. I can't even get him to go on holiday with me, for fear he'd let Jeremiah down.'

Julia thought about that for a moment. Yes, she could see some truth in Anne's analogy. Over the past few weeks she had made subtle adaptations to her own behaviour, subconsciously reckoning in advance what would please Jeremiah, what might incur his disapprobation. Trying to second-guess his every requirement. Making sure that there were always apples in the kitchen, because she had caught a glint of pleasure in his eyes that one time. He hadn't effected a very obvious, striking change to her pattern of thought, it was just that he was somehow – insinuated, behind every thought. A presence.

'I wonder how he has that effect on people?' she asked now, more to herself than Anne.

'Because he has a will of iron,' Anne said. She gave Julia a quick, sideways glance. 'Because he never, not for one second, considers anyone but himself . . .'

Julia opened her mouth to protest that she thought there was some measure of kindness in Jeremiah's hospitality toward her at the very least, but Anne continued: '. . . and that's a pretty heady combination to a person who might be a bit – vulnerable, like. Leastways, that's how it is for Cathal. Jeremiah does his thinking for him, sets out the day for him. We all want someone to do our thinking for us sometimes.' She stopped and shot Julia a direct glance. 'Don't we, Julia?'

'I'm not sure that I . . .' Julia folded her hands on her lap. 'Maybe you're right there,' she added quietly.

Tammy Wynette was standing by her man on the radio. Julia gazed out of the window, a very different picture forming in her mind of Brian's childhood, from the 'poor but

130

happy' scenario he had always presented. She wondered why Brian and not the others found it so necessary to revise the past, and how much did other couples keep back for themselves. She felt a pang of remorse for all the times she had knowingly lacerated him with her tongue, intentionally tried to make him feel small, because as long as he was still smiling that infuriatingly easygoing smile, then her barbs could not be hitting their target. Perhaps she had been scoring bullseyes every time, but Brian had no way of telling her that. Then her face tightened again. If such was the case, then he had certainly punished her, stratospherically beyond the degree of her crimes.

Anne was studying her from the corner of her eye. She was chewing her lower lip, evidently turning something over in her mind. Julia had a feeling that she knew what was coming. A film of sweat broke out across her forehead. She cast Anne a sideways pleading look but Anne was already indicating to the right and pulled up outside a small grey-stoned chapel. She turned the key in the ignition and stared straight ahead. Her voice was gentle and encouraging. 'I think it's time, Julia, don't you?'

Julia began to tremble. She put her face in her hands. 'I can't . . . I can't, Anne. Not yet. Not today . . .'

Anne leaned across Julia and opened the car door. She gave her shoulder a pat, then silently motioned for Julia to step out. Julia put one foot on the ground and was about to pull it back in again when Anne motioned once more. 'Go on,' she said. 'Try.'

Julia nodded and heaved herself out in one sudden movement. Her legs were shaking so much as she walked away from the car that she almost sank to her knees a number of times.

To the side of the church, lines of crosses and marble head-stones stretched out in a horseshoe shape. Battered poplars bent in the direction of the prevailing wind; behind them, a few mature, squat Irish yews offered a ridge of shelter to the small deserted graveyard.

'At the back of the church, to your left,' Anne called after her.

The granite steps were pockmarked from weathering. Little pools of last night's rain still settled into grooves and conduits. Overhead, the sky had turned the colour of ancient linen, shot through with loose threads of long dark cloud. Wind, intimate as an X-ray, lasered through her body and out the other side; it swooped on the poplars and sent them fizzing to the side. Seagulls circled overhead, calling melancholically to one another. A short line of crows stood like black, tattered nuns along one gable of the church. They cawed but did not move, despite the wind.

At the top of the steps, Julia paused and filled her lungs with the rain-filled air. She made it halfway around the church then stopped abruptly, leaning her head sideways into the cold stone; she breathed in lichen and rain and eternity, then clawed her way back to the car.

'All right?' Anne whispered.

'I – I couldn't,' Julia gasped. A mist of rain coated her face. She had to remember to breathe. 'I couldn't.'

Anne waited for a moment then slipped her hand over Julia's and gave a hurried little squeeze. 'All in good time,' she said.

'His eyes,' Julia choked. 'Looking at me . . .' She buried her face in her hands again. 'If I could have reached him . . . Held on to him . . . Jesus Christ, if I could hold him now . . .'

She was crying then. Rocking back and forth, her mouth

issuing long racking sobs with seconds passing in between. And Anne reached across, drawing Julia into her skeletal embrace, holding her there, for hours.

# EIGHT

# High Places

Noel was screaming his head off, real terror in the cries which sent Brian careering from the yard and down the fields to see what was up. Jeremiah had Noel swinging by one ankle, dangling his upside-down body over the cliff's edge. To cure his fear of heights. Noel was babbling incoherently by now, but he called Brian's name when he saw him. A dark lock of hair danced on Jeremiah's forehead, his cheek muscles had knotted with rage. Noel would take his turn checking the barbed-wire stakes at the end of the field, just like everybody else. A man could lose his sheep in a trice. Not to mention the possibility of finally conceding to weakness on the part of one of his eldest sons. His blue eyes flashed Brian a warning: this time, he would not tolerate any intercessions on behalf of his six-and-a-half-year-old brother. The torment continued for another five minutes, until Noel stopped wriggling, possibly aware of the strain on his father's wrist; his cries had receded into mewled whimpers. Brian watched without blinking, silently willing his father to place Noel here on the grass, beside him. His hands clenched tightly, holding Noel's ankle. After a final shake, it was over. Noel sailed back through space and hurled himself into Brian's waiting arms.

'No more of that,' Jeremiah barked as Noel began to sob hysterically once again. Noel bit down on his lip, but his shoulders heaved uncontrollably. Jeremiah stared pointedly at the mallet by his feet, signalling for Noel to continue with the task in hand: namely, the hammering of each stake in turn, until all were secure against the wind once more.

When Jeremiah had stalked up the fields again, Brian lifted the mallet and began to swing. It would take hours because the wood was so heavy, and by the final stakes he would feel like his arms could drop off. The mallet was nearly as tall as himself. Noel sobbed gratefully and remained at a distance from the edge. His fear of heights had not been cured, much less his fear of his father. And Brian made a mental note to add the stakes to the miscellany of tasks he had to perform secretly for his brother. Sometimes, he hated Noel for not being strong enough. For being so afraid. But he felt a fierce protectiveness toward him too. It was very confusing and most of the time he felt all mixed up inside.

Like the times their playful tussles spilled over into something darker and then they would kick and lash out at one another, not contented until one of them drew blood – usually Noel's, but occasionally he could hold his own with Brian, if his temper really got going. They did not fight that often, but when they did, Jeremiah encouraged them. It might start in the kitchen – a nudge to get at the plate of bread first – then Jeremiah would signal for them to spill out on to the yard, calling out to them as they locked on to each other, rolling down the fields. If one of them managed to gain a foothold, Jeremiah would call to the other to 'put out the leg, put out the leg'. A final trip over an extended leg usually signalled the end of the fight. Generally, it was Noel who went flying and Jeremiah would cast him a look of disgust as he walked away, hitching his shoulders as if to purge himself of his son's weakness.

But for every fight, there was a time when Brian took a beating for Noel too. Admitted to things he had not done so that he would not have to smell his brother's fear. A smell he slept beside every night when they curled around one another, listening to the screams of the wind outside, safe for the rest of the night at least.

Brian pulled into the hard shoulder off the North Circular. It was hot and he had to mop his brow. His eyes were stinging from drops of sweat which had filtered through his eyebrows. In the last few weeks, since Richard's visit, it had got so that he couldn't tell between eyeblinks where or with whom he would find himself. It was as if the past was waylaying him, preventing his participation in the present, so that, the previous two Sundays, he had set out for Hampshire but ended up sitting for hours in the stationary car, before slipping back into the house to call Richard and say that he would try again, the following week. He was determined to make it today, now that Noel had managed to slip into his thoughts more forcefully. He felt certain that Noel was leading him somewhere, a place he did not want to go.

Outside, a furious summer had arrived, laying waste to newly planted window boxes, making trees sigh from exhaustion. Brian stuck his head out of the window. Little warm gusts of wind carried mingled scents of dust motes, petrol and Sunday afternoon barbecues. He put the car in gear and drove off.

Past the Devil's Punchbowl he stopped again and left the car. He was suffocating. He stood by a concrete fence, staring across the endless fields of oily, neon-yellow rape, severed here and there by smooth ploughed green straits and the gravid contours of wych elm hedgerows. The rape smelled of dog's piss. Then the colours began to dissolve into the chiaroscuro half-tones that surrounded him of late, as if everything lay beneath a dusting of pepper. Not grey exactly, more a frayed, rotting shade of dun.

He thought of Julia and he remembered her smiling. She hadn't often smiled at him in the last few years, but when she did, he felt as if a great weight had been lifted from his shoulders. And he realized that he had been afraid with her too, afraid of losing her. The constant fear of her disapproval, so like his father's, that made him wilful like a child, forcing her to disapprove even when she wanted to be nice, so that he could face the unfaceable, instead of dreading the inevitability of it.

He remembered her on holiday some time – her throaty laugh as she beckoned him closer. He had thought for a moment that he would never love her so much again. And told her so. She had been soft and pliant, half-cut from too much wine and sun, and she had smiled that lazy way she had and told him that she didn't want to be loved at that moment, she wanted to be ravished. She had reached out for him then, but he had cracked open a can of beer and, chuckling, told her that she should have thought of that before she'd chewed his balls off.

For a moment, he wanted to touch her so badly his arms ached. But she was with Jeremiah. Appropriate that, in a strange sort of way. Jeremiah had taken everything else.

He turned for the car, stopped and passed a hand over his face. Why should he suddenly think that of his own father? A man who might be in a position to offer some crumb of comfort to Julia. Truly, Brian considered, there were no depths he would not plumb.

137

He drove on past manicured hedgerows and fine strong limbs of ivy-less tree trunks. Narrow, straight roads, perfectly paved; mellow red brick, squinting window panes behind wooden gates and evergreen arches. Sunday Supplement country.

The scent of roast beef filled the hallway. Brian walked through to the living-room where Richard sat behind his opened *Telegraph*, flicking a corner down at Brian's approach.

'Well, well,' Richard smiled, 'you made it. And early too.'

'Such a fine day . . .' Brian allowed his voice to trail away. That was the nice thing about Richard, he thought, you could say nothing all day and leave with the impression that things were said.

'Jennifer!' Richard called over his shoulder, 'Brian's here.'

Brian perched on the edge of an armchair. He inhaled a deep breath, waiting for Jennifer. She trotted in from the kitchen, bustling in an exaggerated way, her eyes over-bright, a practised curve of a smile on her lips. Her hands rubbed against a dishcloth so that she wouldn't have to embrace him when she leaned forward to peck his cheek. She smelled of gardenias.

'Brian.' And all her rage and grief was held there, sus-pended on a word. His name.

Brian exhaled. He looked toward Richard, unable to meet Jennifer's brittle gaze. She danced around the room, fixing drinks, filling an ice-bucket, picking up imaginary loose threads from the Chinese rug.

'Traffic?' Richard asked.

'Not too bad.' Brian stood. He didn't know which way to look; he patted the car keys in his pocket. 'Look . . . Maybe I should . . . Maybe it would be better if I . . .'

'Whiskey?' Jennifer handed him a glass, indicating with a

nod of her head that he should sit again. He slumped back. 'Any news on the sale of the house?' she asked, sipping a sherry. Her voice had a tinny quality, metal tapped against fine china.

'Not yet,' Brian said. And wondered how long it took to drown in guilt.

Richard slapped his knees before he stood. 'I just want to have a quick check to see if that stuff worked on the slugs,' he said, his eyes already raking the garden. 'Lunch is still a little ways off, isn't it, Jen?'

She nodded, granting him permission to leave. They sipped in silence for a while. Jennifer exhaled a huge sigh. 'Houses don't sell the way they used to,' she said.

Brian grunted in agreement. He kept his eyes fixed firmly on his shoes. He felt for her, the little wounded cauliflower, she was making such a brave effort. He wanted to tell her that it was all right, really, he was not worth such a herculean endeavour.

Jennifer rose, filled her sherry glass again and stood by the french windows. Her gaze was compassionate as she stared at Richard shuffling through his rose bushes. Brian thought they had both aged greatly since he had last seen them together.

'It's laughably simple in the end,' Jennifer was saying.

'It is?' He waited for her to continue.

'Yes, it is.' Her lips trembled, unused to the nakedness of the speech they were uttering. 'You just wonder if you've been loved. If you've loved enough . . . I was never really certain that I loved Richard. I'm still uncertain . . . but I think so.' She nodded. 'I think so.'

Brian turned to return her watery smile. His gaze took in the little pearly teeth, the quick frilly dilations of her perfect

139

nostrils and he wondered if Julia had always been uncertain about him too. Perhaps all love had to have a measure of inconstancy in order to survive, in order to adapt – except for the love of children.

Later, throughout lunch, her spirits appeared to have lifted a little. They spoke of the garden and Richard's enduring battle against the slugs. The likelihood of another long hot summer. Brian tasted nothing. Mechanically chewing three times to the left, three times to the right, a swallow, gone. Richard cleared the plates away as Jennifer brought a glass bowl of trifle to the table. She was ladling voluminous quantities into pretty china dishes when the spoon suddenly fell from her grip and clattered to the floor. Her fingers flew up, fluttering wildly in mid-air.

'How could you?' she gasped, clutching her own throat, desperately trying to restrain herself but the words insisted. 'How could you have put him on that wall, Brian?'

'Jen, darling . . .' Richard interjected.

Brian's head hung low on his chest. His hands were folded on his lap.

Jennifer began to cry. 'No one thinks of the grandparents. I loved that little boy. His dear, sweet little face . . . Where is my daughter?' She spun around, looking distractedly across the room, hoping for ghosts. 'Where is she?'

'You know she's in Ireland, dear,' Richard said softly. He tried to reach for her but she careered around the room, kicking out at furniture, sending her china display crashing to the ground.

'In her mind, I mean,' she cried. 'Where is she in her mind? I don't know. I never knew. She was such a strange little girl. I want to help her. If I could just help her . . . It might – it might help me . . . Oh God, oh God. I just want to wake up and for everything to be the way it was. I want Sam back. I want Julia back,' she added angrily before collapsing into a chair. 'I just want them back,' she repeated hopelessly.

She uttered a cry and slumped forward, making a frenzied washing motion with her hands through her hair. When she looked up again, her eyes were distant, fixed on another time, another place. The usually immaculate perm stood on end, mad curls billowing all over her head. Two red spots glowed hotly along the line of her cheekbones. She looked like a demented clown, and Brian blinked rapidly. It seemed so out of character, so callous of Richard to be laughing like that. He wished he would stop. But Richard's mouth had set into a thin line, so how was he producing that loud sound?

They were both staring at him now. Jennifer's jaw had slackened. Brian looked around; the laugh continued. He realized that his own shoulders were heaving up and down. His hand flew to his mouth – Yes, it was open, he was the culprit. Still, he couldn't stop.

Richard snorted. He threw his head back and began to bray, stopping abruptly mid-bray with a guilty expression on his face, then he continued to honk with his handkerchief stuffed against his mouth.

Jennifer's eyes darted back and forth between them. Her lips parted to berate them – and she chuckled. Just a light cack cack sound at first, leading into a full-throated howl. Her arms reached out to grip the armrests. 'Oh my God,' she gasped. 'Oh my God.' She laughed with abandonment. 'What's this? What's this?' she hollered, wiping her streaming eyes.

Brian couldn't answer her, he was wheezing and spluttering between the gales. The three of them laughed for several minutes. Jennifer rose suddenly and swooped at Brian, she caught his head in a fierce grip and pressed him against her chest. Brian wanted to stay like that for ever.

'I am so completely and utterly – sorry,' his muffled voice addressed her left breast. 'So completely . . .'

'Shh now,' Jennifer was saying. She stroked his head. 'I won't say that it's all right, that everything is going to be all right, but – we've had a laugh. We've managed to get through another day. And we've had a laugh.'

Brian wanted to tell her that she was the finest woman who ever lived – next to her daughter. He wanted to tell her that he had never, not once, been uncertain about his love for Julia. He felt she would like to know that. He wanted to tell her about all the nights he'd lain, sleepless, in Sam's bed and thought about the possibility of killing himself; he wanted to tell her that he would do it, right now, this very minute, if it would in any way ease her pain; that he had not done so already, because he felt that he did not deserve the release. He had to take his beating.

So he began to talk about Sam. They pulled their chairs up close and listened, interrupting from time to time with an anecdote of their own. Their eyes shining with remembered happiness, their hands formed shapes in the air, indicating his height at a certain age, motioning the way he ran from the car to greet them . . . the way he said goodbye.

Much later, as Brian left the buttered squares of Hampshire window panes, the anthracite sky a blanket draped over shingled roofs, he thought about Julia again. And for the rest of the journey home, he pretended that she was sleeping in the passenger seat beside him with Sam lightly snoring in the back.

When he reached home, he went immediately to Sam's

142

room and curled up on the bed, fully clothed. For the first time in nearly six months, he sank into a deep black sleep almost immediately. But even there, Noel managed to find him.

Julia felt a little frisson of excitement. She read the same lines over and over again.

> Noel was keeping on crying. He had me worried so. Jeremiah is not afraid of nothing but me and Noel hate high places. I told him me too. I told him I am feared every time when I go up for the rain tank. He stopped crying soon after and went to sleep. Thank God.

Julia hastily reread the preceding pages, looking for some reference to the incident which had caused Noel's tears, but there was none, which made these little renegade lines all the more unique. She was now halfway through the journal and this was the first note that could be deemed in any way personal. She felt hungry for more, but the next few pages drifted back into the same familiar monotony of recounted chores, meals, evening prayers. The woman must have been deeply troubled by her son's tears to have felt compelled to include them in her little history of lists. 'Margaret,' Julia said aloud, rolling the name around her tongue. A face forming in her mind at last, to suit the name.

Julia sighed deeply and shoved the book back into its drawer. She crept quietly from the bedroom and went downstairs to prepare the midday dinner. Jeremiah had cycled to the local Co-op earlier for a bag of hen grain. He had been surly with her all morning, because she hadn't returned in time for the turnip-sowing yesterday. She decided to bake an apple tart to make it up to him.

She was rolling the flattened pastry around a floured bottle when the long matchstick figure of Edward in the distance caught her eye. He strolled by the cliff's edge with a book tucked under his arm. Some tome on geology, she surmised. Edward studied rocks. From time to time, he stopped, rubbed his glasses and stared out to sea, as if something had attracted his eye, then he continued down to the eastern bluffs. She thought he cut a solitary, lonesome figure and wondered again why he had never married.

She slammed a chicken in the oven and stuck the apple tart in the fridge until she could bake it after the chicken. Then she skimmed the cream to go with the tart from a bucket with a layer of muslin on top. Jeremiah always left the separating to her these days. Woman's work, she supposed.

She had a little time on her hands, so she decided to make a start on her shrubbery. The plants she had bought yesterday were lined up along the barren patch, watered, ready to go down. She had turned the soil and spread compost late last night, after Jeremiah and Edward had retired.

The dog was worrying the goat again, nipping at its ankles and circling around with a self-important air of menace. Julia dropped her trowel for a moment and sat back on her haunches. She understood that the dog was harmless but the goat was shitting herself anyway, not that it took that much to release a volley of pellets in any case.

'Dog,' she called because he didn't have a name.

He left the goat and came bounding past her, as if someone had called to him from the fields below. His flank brushed against her lowered buttocks on the way. She had noticed the way he had taken to doing that: just a quick, furtive rub against her, signalling complicity – no movement in the tail to suggest anything further, but fur straining to press against flesh all the same.

'Leave the damn goat alone,' she called after him.

She decided to stop planting for a while to concentrate on erecting the windshield. Her face grew purple with the effort of hammering the stakes into the earth, but she succeeded in forming a horseshoe shape around the patch. Wrapping the calico around the stakes was quite a different matter – the wind kept getting in the way. It rushed at the cloth, blowing bubbles between the stakes. She was thinking of giving in when she heard Edward behind her.

'You need something p-p-permeable,' he said. 'Something that'll let a bit of wind through.'

'I was trying to keep the wind out,' Julia said, turning, her cheeks streaked with sweat and dirt. She passed the back of her hand over her forehead.

Edward grinned. He had forsaken his usual Aran for a long baggy T-shirt, the bony shoulders sticking up like knuckles under the flimsy cloth. 'You'll never manage that,' he said, 'you have to ack-ack –'

Julia waited as he wrestled with the word stuck in his throat. Her mind urged him to slow down, draw the word out, enunciate each syllable separately – sing it if necessary. But she said nothing, because Edward had never asked for advice and she felt she would embarrass him by offering.

'Acknowledge it,' he said finally. 'Hang on a sec, and I'll get you something.' He moved away and disappeared into one of the stone outhouses. He returned with a green roll of plastic tucked under his arm. 'T-t-there,' he said. 'Plastic fencing – tiny airholes, see? To let the wind through. D'you want me to . . . ?' He didn't wait for her reply and set about fixing her stakes more securely, then he wrapped the plastic around them, tying it tightly at both ends.

Julia remained on her haunches; she was exhausted from the morning's work and the inauspicious start to her shrubbery. She studied Edward from the corner of her eye. He worked quickly, the long, graceful fingers manipulating cord with an articulation lacking in the speech and body. It appeared as if his slender frame could not contain the nervous energy which flowed through it; it jerked and twitched from time to time, the hands always miles ahead of the rest of him. The long spidery lashes behind the dark-rimmed glasses gave the cobalt-blue eyes a childlike, intense concentration. He was an attractive man, in spite of his nervous afflictions, or perhaps because of them, she thought now. He became aware of her silent study and a slow flush crept up the back of his neck. Julia looked out to sea.

'What are you t-t-trying to do, anyway?' he asked over his shoulder.

'Jeremiah told me that your mother tried to grow things on this patch – you know, flowers and stuff, but the wind . . .' Her voice trailed off.

Edward nodded. He looked up toward the kitchen window. 'Now that you mention it,' he said, leaning on a post for a moment, 'I can remember her, down here, on her knees, p-planting things.' A little perplexed frown, 'I remember thinking that she looked ha-ha-happy.'

'She didn't often look happy then?' Julia coaxed gently.

'No.'

'How well do you remember her? Brian hardly mentions her at all.' She was struck by the fact that she had considered Brian in the present tense.

'I remember she was always t-tired, and always sick, in

146

the end. And I remember her face in the coffin. She didn't look like herself. It's fu-funny, that, being able to see her face dead and not alive.' He dusted earth from his jeans. 'She didn't talk much,' he added.

'I guess she was too tired,' Julia said drily. She nodded toward the kitchen, meaning Jeremiah. 'What sort of relationship did they have?' She knew it was the wrong word to use when Edward pulled his mouth down at the corners. He shrugged, speechless for a moment at the thought of his father and mother having a relationship.

'I don't think they had one of those,' he smiled.

Julia had to smile too. Brian had told her once that his parents called one another 'Mr' and 'Mrs'. The formality of it, and babies popping every which way. Edward was still grinning as if he could read her mind. Julia rose and gazed down the fields. The sky was a garish white, hanging low over a pewter sea with its teased fretwork of ivory sails.

'Fancy a walk?' she asked.

'Sure.'

They walked in companionable silence for a while, then Edward stopped suddenly, a frown creasing his forehead. 'I'd like to remember her b-better,' he said. 'Sometimes, I kind of wonder if she was ever really there at all. It's like my memories of her are – I don't know, sort of m-misty or something. Like she was just a shadow.'

'Well, I'd imagine she was in Jeremiah's shadow to a great degree,' Julia offered reasonably. She observed the way Edward's face darkened again at the mention of his father's name. For a moment, she hesitated, wondering if she should tell Edward about his mother's journal. Maybe it would offer him some insight into the woman which had so far eluded

147

her. It might even offer him some connection with the memory of her. Julia opened her mouth to tell him, then closed it again. She knew that she was being selfish, but that little chink of illumination she had been offered earlier on, when reading about Noel's tears, was entirely addictive. She didn't want to share just yet.

'Brian used to say that she had a special fondness for Noel,' she lied. 'Does that sound right to you?'

Edward considered for a moment. 'Yeah. I reckon that would be . . .' He shook his head in frustration. 'It's all so f-foggy now.' The long white fingers flexed back and forth as though he were trying to summon the past. He stopped again suddenly. 'I think, if I remember right, she was even q-quieter after Noel's accident. Hardly spoke at all. Then she was sick f-for a long time. It's like she just sort of – d-drained away . . .' He visibly shook himself. 'At least th-that's what it feels like now.'

They headed down toward the cliff's edge. Skeins of barbed wire trussed around posts was the only protection on offer to the sheep who, instinctively perhaps, did their wandering to the north of the house in any case. Every now and then, one turned up in the back seat of a neighbour's car, looking like some frightened bolting bride.

Below, the sea was black and broiling where it surged into a little narrow cove to the right. A few small fishing boats worked at mussel rafts further out. It was raining on the distant peninsula.

'We can go down here, if you like.' Edward indicated a gulley-like crack in the cliff. He lifted the barbed wire so that she could worm through on her back. The way down had to be negotiated by shunting forward on the buttocks, clutching at wild, stubby trees on either side. Julia instinctively reached for a clump of sea-pinks and shoved them down the front of her blouse for later.

When they reached the bottom, she looked back up at the cliff: it loomed higher than she had expected. The rock face was almost black and scored more deeply toward the top. The smoother lower half was encrusted with barnacles and green algae.

Edward followed the line of her eye. 'Mostly sandstone and grit – the b-bedding planes,' he explained. 'And look here.' He pushed his spectacles further up and stabbed excitedly at a dark crystalline coarse layer almost by the shoreline. 'Granite. Granite's an igneous rock, you see, comes from the centre in a mo-molten state.' He quickly checked to see if she was yawning yet, but her intent gaze encouraged him to go on. 'Uplift,' he said, his eyes raking the cliff in wonderment. 'You see, all the decay and erosion can be reversed. All the layers restored by the f-forces of elevation.'

'So all the various bands of rock that are worn away by rain or sea –'

'And wind,' he interposed, nodding eagerly.

'And wind, can be pushed up again. The same, only . . .' She pulled a face, looking for the correct wording.

'The same, only different.' Edward beamed, the oxymoron posing no problem for him.

His expression gave nothing away but she wondered if, in his own peculiar way, Edward was trying to say something to her. And there was something vaguely comforting about the concept of endless recycling. She thought she might ask to borrow a few of his geology books later, to add to her collection.

The sea was snarling at their ankles, almost full tide. The white foam reminded her of some frangible lace crochet where it touched their shoes. Her feet crunched down on smooth oval stones. She reached down and picked one up. It was a delicate shade of green, tinged with copper and a few concentric circles of white marble. She swung her arm until her shoulder ached and tossed the stone as far out into the charcoal sea as she could. It sank, and she wondered how many millions of years would pass before it reached the shore again. And how many millions of years it had waited for someone to throw it. She sighed deeply and turned to Edward. 'Were you there' – she indicated the top of the cliff – 'the day Noel fell over?'

He bent on his haunches to lift a stone which had caught his eye, studying it with that childlike intensity which was steadily growing on her. 'No,' he said, 'just Jeremiah, Cathal and Br-Brian. I'm not sure if Ma saw it or not.'

'What happened exactly?'

He rose and cast the stone into the water. 'I d-don't know for sure. It was never talked about.' She could sense his deep unease. 'A stake gave way, I think.'

'I can't believe that Jeremiah would allow himself to be so careless,' she said, pinning him with her eyes. 'I have to know, Edward, was it Brian's fault?' The thought had only just occurred to her but somehow, from the extent of his agitation, she felt that she was on to something. She grabbed his arm. 'Edward, please . . . ? I have to know. I have the darkest thoughts about Brian – I wish him dead, I wish really bad things to happen to him.' She was babbling now, but she couldn't stop. 'I'm trying to make sense of what happened to Sam. Yesterday, I tried to visit his grave, but I couldn't. I just couldn't. Sometimes, I feel like I hate Brian so much that I can't even grieve for Sam. Does that sound terrible?' She released his arm abruptly, hands falling uselessly by her sides.

'I'm sorry, Edward,' she continued, mumbling, 'this isn't fair to you. I know how you feel about Brian, but I should have protected Sam from him.' She shrugged hopelessly. 'I just didn't know how damaged Brian . . . How could I know? That smile –' She broke off and cast him a final pleading glance. 'Please, Edward, tell me. Was it Brian's fault?'

'I – I d-don't think so,' Edward faltered. 'As far as I know, it was Noel's turn to check the stakes . . .'

Julia nodded. Her fists bunched. 'Hell of a job for a seven-year-old,' she said flatly.

Edward sighed his agreement. She followed his gaze out to where a soft, grey mantle of cloud obscured the horizon. Rain was not far away. 'I do remember how we all had to look for B-Brian after the accident.'

'How do you mean?'

'Well, he ran off.' Edward's forehead creased deeply. 'Jeremiah went down after the body. I came running out of the kitchen when I heard the screams – M-Ma's, I think, she was halfway down the f-fields and I remember seeing B-Brian passing her. He had his mouth opened wide, but he wasn't making a sound . . . It was later, after they'd laid Noel out and the priest was there and everything, someone asked where was Brian? We all went looking for him. All over the p-place.' He stopped to wipe his glasses again. A blue vein throbbed at the side of his temple.

'And . . . ?' Julia coaxed gently.

'He was f-found, two days later, behind a bale of hay in Cathal's place. I think it was Cathal who found him. He was in a f-fever. I remember them carrying him back, all hot and sweaty with a sort of – I don't know – a glassy look about his eyes or something . . .'

Julia started. She understood exactly the look to which

Edward referred. Had seen it herself on occasion when she had wondered what was going through his head as he stared so blankly ahead.

'After that,' Edward continued, 'he was put to b-bed for a while, and Noel was never mentioned again.'

'Never?'

Edward shook his head. He shrugged. 'Just in prayers and the like.'

'But in God's name why?' Julia exclaimed.

'Jeremiah.'

'Jeremiah forbade it? Was it because he didn't want to upset Brian or your mother further, do you think? Was that it?'

Edward cast her a dry look. 'My own thought is that he saw g-grief as a sign of weakness.' His mouth twisted bitterly to the side. 'And weakness interferes with "the work". Christ alone knows, n-nothing must ever interfere with that.' His expression softened and he cast Julia a watery smile. 'I don't know if it helps at all,' Edward added as an afterthought, 'b-but Brian was always the one to protect the rest of us.'

'From what? From whom?' Julia asked, an image of Brian as a young boy, locked into such a formidable silence, crossing her mind.

Edward jerked his head, signalling beyond the cliff, back over the fields. 'From him,' he said quietly. 'Brian never said a word against him, never, b-but me? I used to plan how I'd cut the bastard's throat in his sleep.'

Julia blinked, absorbing the degree of venom in his voice. She could understand that life was hard around the farm, money was scarce, the weather inclement, but she couldn't form a picture in her mind of a Jeremiah warranting such uncharacteristic acid on Edward's part. Perhaps the man had

152

mellowed over the years. Certainly, he cut a harsh figure, but she was still grateful for his silent hospitality. It seemed to her, at that moment, that she knew Jeremiah far better than she had ever known her husband.

They began to climb up the gulley again, Edward extending a hand for Julia's when there were no trees to cling on to. She was panting when they reached the top. 'Brian and Noel,' she gasped. 'How did they get –'

'Oh, grand,' he interrupted, wiping mist from his glasses. 'They had their f-fights – you know, just brother stuff . . .' His eyes clouded over as they caught sight of Jeremiah heading for an outhouse up above. 'He was always p-pitting them against each other. I've often thought about that . . . Sometimes I think he was making sure which one was the strongest – to see who g-got the land.'

'But Cathal's father got it in the end anyway, didn't he?' Julia struggled to keep up with his long strides. 'Anne told me about it.'

'Yeah. Corny got it. And s-sold a rake of it' – he pointed eastward – 'over there by the shoreline. To an Englishman, I think it was. For a riding school or some such. B-before that he sold another parcel to a German. Cathal's got the remainder now.'

Julia gazed up at her nascent shrubbery, longing to get back to it. Her fingers itched to hold the trowel. She smiled at the thin striding creature before her and broke into a run again, to keep abreast.

Cathal was above now too, loping around the outhouses in that peculiar bent-forward way he had, as if his eyes were constantly scouring the ground for something. He followed Jeremiah through a doorway, both of them holding ends of a ladder, gliding forward in precise harmony.

153

Julia was struck by something, and she lightly tapped Edward's elbow. 'Funny, isn't it,' she said casually, 'looking at Jeremiah and Cathal together like that – a stranger might think that they were father and son.'

Edward pulled at his nose. He cast Julia a wry, lopsided smile. 'It has been rumoured,' he said.

# NINE

# Fair Play

The children went to bed immediately after school on the Thursday, so that they could glean a few hours' sleep before departure at around seven later that evening. At the age of twelve Brian had long since had to forgo his hours of rest because he had to load the cart with cages of outraged chickens and sacks of whatever vegetables were in season, mainly cabbages and potatoes. Jeremiah fed and watered the sheep, then penned them near the house, ready for the journey. Occasionally, they had a heifer or two as well which meant that Brian would have to walk most of the fifteen miles to the fair in town, because his father herded the sheep.

At around six o'clock, Jeremiah ran through his check list, his teeth clenched tightly around the stalk of his pipe as his eyes surveyed the yard. He checked the ropes which fastened the churns of buttermilk and butter to the shafts of the cart, nodding in silent approval at Brian's secure knots. A rifling through the cabbage heads until he was satisfied that the best lay on top; a final cursory glance at the horse's hooves; then a quick sideways quizzical look to his wife to confirm that she had the food and blankets ready. When she nodded, he went upstairs and carried the sleeping children down, one by one, and placed them on a bed of hay at the back of the cart. Two collies sat on their haunches by the sheep pen, watching with their ears pricked up, awaiting their signal.

The cart trundled up to the main road with the animals in front, flanked on either side by the dogs, with Brian slightly to the rear of his father, sticking fast to the heifers, because they could be skittish. Sometimes, if he had more than two beasts to drive, Edward would have to help. On fine summer evenings with good light until past eleven at their backs, they could make town by the early hours of the morning.

Brian wished for one of those evenings, as he trudged forward in the soot-black night, following the lambent glow of his father's paraffin lamp ahead in the distance. It had rained all day and most of yesterday. His boots already held pools of water. Beneath the covering drape of Jeremiah's old oilskin, which slapped against every rut on the road, his body felt swollen with fatigue. Mercifully, after a while, a certain mindless state usually descended: just one foot in front of the other, one foot in front of the other, an occasional twitch of his stick toward the weary beasts beside him. But there was no release tonight, because the rack of his mother's cough from the front of the cart was bothering him. She was wrapped in a shawl, baby Teresa asleep in the curve of one arm, while her free hand held the reins. Brian ran back to see if she was all right – her face looked harried and drawn, a bit frightening, in the light from the lamp on the seat beside her.

Recently, it seemed to Brian, her face was always set in a grimace of pain. There had been a lot of whisperings in the house between neighbouring women since she came back from the hospital a few months ago with a hole in her chest where her left breast used to be, and when the coughing started, the whisper grew even more subdued. Sometimes,

Brian caught Edward's eye when she was stooped over her stewpot on the kitchen fire; she was thin as a bird with little sticks for legs, but they were sure that she would get better. Jeremiah could pray her better, Brian thought.

Now, with the white protruding knuckles of her hand holding the reins, she cast him a crooked smile, motioning him back to his place by the heifers. The twins and Cormac shifted uncomfortably on the rain-soaked hay. Brian thought of the squirming rats under the sheep pelts in the outhouse.

A thin watery light managed to break through the clouds just as they made their approach to town. Brian could just make out the looming shapes of fishing trawlers coming into the pier on his left, the smell of their catch drifting toward him on the wet air coated in seagulls. He could no longer feel his legs; his arms clung to his sides like stiffened clay. He could not lift his head from a tiredness which felt so real, so tangible, that he could eat it. Already, the buyers were out on the road, pushing back their caps and leaning on their sticks as they watched the weary processions of carts and beasts pass by, indicating their interest with a grunt or a raised forefinger from time to time. The dogs had to work flat out now, to keep the flocks separate and, more importantly, on their feet. Past-exhaustion sheep straggled by the roadsides, and Jeremiah twitched and manoeuvred with renewed energy on the final approach toward the square which was already full to capacity with carts and animals and local shopkeepers sluicing their doorsteps in a vain attempt to remove steaming green pats.

Jeremiah headed for the lower left-hand corner of the Square, his usual site. The fair was held on the first Friday of every month; Jeremiah attended maybe six months of the year but he always got his traditional corner which had been passed on from his own father. Thus Brian, in spite of his weariness, was more than a little shocked to find the site occupied by Corny and his heifers. A glance passed between the men; Brian waited for his father to voice his complaint but Jeremiah signalled to him to move around the back instead. They jostled for space with the dogs standing sentry over the sheep and Corny's fine heifers thrust out on display in front of them. But Brian was too tired to ask any questions. He nodded to Cathal who had come by truck and slipped back to join the others for a quick kip in the back of the cart before the selling began in earnest. The rain let up for a few hours and he buried his nose in hay and snored immediately.

When he awoke, his mother had broth simmering on a primus stove on the ground. The others had eaten. She handed him a hunk of white bread and he stuffed it into his mouth, his teeth barely making contact. She passed him a tin can of thin brown gruel, sediment clinging to the bottom, he felt his innards warm as it worked its way down, having scalded his lips and tongue. He dangled the can over the side of the cart for another ladleful.

The twins and Cormac took up their positions beside their mother, selling the produce. Later, when her sacks and churns were emptied, she would do the rounds herself, buying salted cod and ling from the local fish-hawkers and bastible cakes from the bakery. Jeremiah, Brian and Edward handled the beasts and fowl, Brian watching his father's profile keenly as he stared out to where the sea met the Square in a horseshoe inlet, for all the world as if he had better places to be, more important things to be doing, than standing there taking insultingly low bids from timewasters. Brian was relieved when the sheep went quickly, otherwise he might have to help drive them home again.

He herded them up to a train wagon in time for the first pull-out of the morning – one single engine pulling and another pushing from behind. If the track was wet, the wagons could not negotiate the sharp curve and had to return to the station for a fresh start. Local children threw rocks on to the tracks to hamper the train's departure further and Brian always envied them their indolent pleasure, while at once feeling intense irritation because they were also hindering his own day's work. His head was spinning from tiredness still, but he felt a sense of excitement too, leaning against a siding watching the resigned sheep practically crawl up the ramp into the wagon. The noise and stench from pigs and sheep and heifers was intense and above his head a sea of sticks was thrust into the air, poking or prodding or just raised for the hell of it. And everywhere Brian gazed there was a sense of transaction, of commerce, and then a sense of closure: the sideways roll of the wagon door, signalling completion. The long days of endless work were for something, after all. He liked that feeling and always stayed up at the station for longer than was necessary.

When he returned, Jeremiah was cinching a loose elastic band around a wad of notes which he stuffed inside his coat pocket. The fowl-crates and churns were empty, his mother lightly pressing her hair inside a scarf in preparation for her own shopping expedition. She looked pleased and made a little purse of her lips to Brian, indicating that she had done well. Only the heifers were left and would remain so until Corny had sold his own prime beef in front. Brian was conscious of the sleekness of their flanks overwintered on crisp hay instead of rank mangolds and beets. They looked fresh and alert in comparison to the sorry wilting beasts he had driven through the night.

159

Smells of frying bacon and freshly baked soda bread were drifting across the Square from all directions now, as the pubs and eating houses heaved with bodies. Corny left Cathal in charge and headed for a pint; Jeremiah remained by his heifers and Brian stared down at his boots, wondering if he would be granted leave of absence for any duration today. His head jerked up at a signal from his father. As if they too had been waiting, watching from different vantage points along the Square, the twins and Cormac came running with outstretched hands. Jeremiah always made a fuss of looking for the coins. He jingled his hand in one pocket, turning down his mouth at the corners as if to indicate that there wasn't enough. Then the other pocket, followed by a little shake of his head. By then Cormac was dancing in anticipation. Edward never held his hand out until the money was proffered first. The coins were found in a small plastic bank bag, somewhere around Jeremiah's torso. He extracted a threepenny bit each for the youngest, the same plus a copper penny for Edward and, finally, a silver sixpence for Brian, catching it between his teeth first before he handed it over.

'What do ye say?'

But the twins were gone already. Cormac stopped in mid-run and turned to offer a shy thanks. Jeremiah made a chuckling sound and motioned him on. Brian had waited for that sound – it was by far the best bit of fair day. He kept a serious expression on his own face and jerked his head at the heifers, silently enquiring if Jeremiah would be all right on his own. A hand waved him on after Edward. Brian ran to catch up.

With rectitude and some aforethought, a stash from the sweetshop could be made to last a month. But first, Brian and Edward had to run the gauntlet of the local corner boys, teenage lads with Brylcreemed hair, drainpipe trousers, even cigarettes sometimes. The twins and Cormac could just run past them unheeded, but Brian and Edward were forced by age and instinct to saunter. They strolled around the corner with their hands buried deep in their pockets, mentally plucking loose wisps of hay from their shoulders, every hole in their clothing suddenly a canyon. Occasionally, they managed to pass by without raising a murmur, if they got lucky and some fellow was leaning on his elbow out the window of a car, talking to the corner boys and blocking up all the traffic. Brian's heart sank as they rounded the bend. They hadn't got lucky. The lads looked bored. 'Head down, don't mind them,' he hissed under his breath to Edward. Edward nodded.

At first it looked as if they were going to wing by with just an accompanying snigger. But then a foot snaked out and caught Edward unawares. He went sprawling. The three-penny bit rolled out of his hand and did a pirouette for a moment on the edge of the footpath. His hand scrabbled for it but the foot got there first, slamming down to bring the dance to an abrupt end. Edward looked up. 'That's m-mine,' he cried.

Brian winced and reached down to help his brother to his feet. They were in trouble now. Loose change *and* a stutter. Already he was doing mental arithmetic, his stash halved by one fell swoop.

'What's yours?' a voice was saying.

Brian glanced across at the leader of the pack with the extended foot covering Edward's money. The sneer on his lean, pockmarked face reminded him of Corny. He was looking at Edward as if he were some strange bacteria let loose on his town. Edward was flushed and catching at the blockage in

161

his throat, determined to regain his coin. But nerves and outrage got the better of him and he could only gag soundlessly as the lads laughed.

'Cuu-cuu-cuu,' the leader mimicked. The laugh increased.

Edward tried to lever the foot sideways with the side of his own boot. That sent them into hysterics. One of them spluttered on cigarette smoke.

Brian weighed up the odds, two of them, younger by far, against six of the town's finest. He shrugged to himself, what the hell, they were going to take a pounding in any case. 'Get your foot off of it,' he said calmly.

There was an unearthly little pause. He felt a tremor of satisfaction that he had surprised them at least.

'What's that you said?'

'Give him back his thre'pence,' Brian responded. Edward shuddered beside him.

A pair of little black crow eyes squinted at Brian: initial surprise developing into something seedy and nasty. The thin mouth was sneering so much now, it looked as if it had set into a rictus.

'What thre'pence?'

'The one under your foot,' Brian sighed. His fists clenched instinctively to shield his face.

'Oh, you mean that thre'pence there?' The foot swung to the side.

Edward quickly hunkered down but the foot swung again and crushed his hand against concrete. 'Get off m-m-m . . .'

'Mu-mu-mu,' a chorus resounded. Edward could only peer upwards helplessly at Brian.

Brian thought: Ah shite, here we go. He put his head down and drove like a bullock into the bony ribcage of their tormentor. There was a shocked howl for a moment, then a frenzy of arms and legs meshing together to get at him. Edward did his best to help him, working his knees up and down, digging into every groin he could reach. Brian flailed all his limbs wildly; he managed to make contact several times before a crushing kick got him in the gut and he collapsed backwards forgetting to shield himself for a moment and he saw a flash of white light when the foot made contact with his balls. He felt every breath he had ever taken issue in one long guttural groan from his body. Another kick to the side of his head turned the white light black for an instant.

'Lev him, lev him,' someone said, a note of panic to his voice.

'Filthy fucking culshie.' The leader slammed a foot into his ribs with every word. 'What are you?' Brian was hauled to his feet and forced to peer directly into the black eyes. He saw his own reflection in the pupils before his head went limp again. He figured he must still be conscious because he was wondering why this stranger hated him so much.

'Bleddy culshies,' one of them said, spitting to the side to diffuse the situation.

'We don't want trouble,' Brian managed to mumble, 'we only want the thre'pence.'

'Who says it's yours?'

Ah blast and bloody and shite, Brian thought. He wanted to cough blood to frighten them. But his ribs were aching so badly he couldn't even manage that. Edward was nursing his own testicles, trying to tell him with his eyes about the better part of valour. As the mean little pupils of the leader held his own, Brian was in a quandary. He wondered what Jeremiah would do in the same situation. Fight to the death most probably. Brian considered the possibility for a moment, then he saw Cormac come out of the sweetshop glued to a blackjack bar and he reconsidered. 'Keep it so,' he said.

His magnanimity caught them by surprise. The glittering pupils hooded behind a series of blinks. Without actually meaning to, Brian had initiated a stand-off. This was a difficult situation for the corner boys now. They could keep the money as he had intimated, but doing so now would acknowledge that it was within his remit to offer it to them. The alternative was simply to claim that the threepence was rightfully theirs. They looked at one another; a pack of Carroll's was passed around. But the box of matches was empty.

'Have you a light?' one of them asked Brian. He shook his head slightly, the collar of his coat still constrained by two hands. More than anything in the world, he wished that he smoked, that he had matches, that he could end this with a strike of a wooden stick against a bar of brown and he knew instinctively that they were wishing the same. Everyone was left with no way out.

'I'll get th-th-them,' Edward said, running toward the store beside the sweetshop.

He returned in seconds, rattling a box of matches. Brian felt the hands around his collar relax for a moment. He staggered back against the wall. Then he wondered how Edward had managed to buy the matches without his threepenny bit. But his attention was diverted to the sucks of nicotine all around. The corner boys were acting as if their very lives had been saved by the rush of smoke to their lungs. He could go now. The question of the money could be overlooked. All might be acquitted with some measure of dignity, provided he chose to overlook as well. Brian shrugged. 'Give him back his money,' he said.

'B-Brian . . .' Edward muttered.

The leader's eyes were squinched up behind a gauze of smoke. He gave a little weary shake to his head. 'What are we going to do with you at all?' A prolonged note of sadness, before he stubbed the cigarette into the ground, then a lightning flick of his elbow to the side of Brian's head. Brian went down on his knees but managed to scramble up again quickly. 'You're calling me a thief – is that what you're calling me?' the leader was saying in a pained voice. He had to save face now.

'Yeah.' Brian nodded.

There was a little gasp at his bald effrontery but he could detect a few gleams of admiration too. He waited for the blows but the leader had to ask a few questions before he could launch right in again to finish the job. 'What's the name?'

'Donovan. Brian.'

'From where?'

Brian indicated west with a nod. 'Out along,' he said.

'Father?'

'Jeremiah.'

A gleam of recognition. The thin lips set maliciously. Brian had given him his way out. 'Ah, now we know who we have, lads.' He turned to the others, then peered at Brian again. 'You're the twin . . . Remember, lads? The other one went woosht over the cliff?'

Brian flushed and clenched his fists. They were murmuring and sniggering amongst themselves. The leader put on a little performance for them, pretending to lift lids off pots on the dinner table. Turning his mouth down at the corners, shaking his head sadly at the meagre quantities. Whether they understood his mime or not, his cohorts cackled appreciatively.

'Grub enough for the one of ye only today, lads,' he

mimicked an older man's voice. 'Run down the fields there
let ye, and whichever one of ye runs back again can have
it.'

They were holding their sides at that. Brian could hardly
breathe for shame. He wanted to kill the bony creature with
the black eyes. Edward studied the pavement, paralysed by
the humiliation he knew his brother must be feeling. It was
one thing to be beaten up just because they were from the
country, they were used to that, but direct reference to their
poverty and the implication that their lives were worth nothing, not even to their own father, was quite unbearable. The
slow flush began at Brian's toes and worked its way up to
his scalp.

'That's not funny,' he said.

The black eyes closed in on him, the mouth opening to
continue the torment. 'Why're they all laughing so?' it asked.

'Because ye're fecking stupid,' Brian shouted and launched
himself head down at the leader again. But this time Brian's
crown connected with a soft spot just under the chest cage,
seriously winding his opponent and before he could gasp for
air, or call for help, Brian floored him with a leap forward,
pressing his knees down against arms, pinioning them, as he
worked his balled fists back and forth across the acned cheeks
and jawline. He managed to break the leader's nose before
they pulled him off.

'He broke my bleddy dose,' the boy cried. Blood erupted
from his nostrils in a very satisfactory fashion. Brian stood
trembling, his fists still clenched. He was throbbing with
adrenalin now. Wanted to take them all on. He glared around
him. Saw several pairs of eyes lower, they were making a
fuss of trying to staunch the flow of blood.

Edward pulled at his sleeve. This was their chance.

'C'mon,' he muttered. 'C'mon . . .' He dragged Brian across the road to the sweetshop.

The twins smiled at him. They had been watching from the shop doorway. Brian shrugged casually but his knees knocked together, now that it dawned on him what he'd managed to pull off. 'What age would you say he is?' he asked Edward, indicating the bleeding figure by the corner who was blubbing into his coat sleeve now. Very satisfactory.

'Fourteen at l-least,' Edward beamed. His blue eyes crackled with delight and pride.

Brian nodded, peered over the sweetshop counter. There was still the matter of the stash. He pulled out his sixpence. 'Half and half,' he said to Edward.

A slow grin cracked across Edward's cheeks. He signalled for Brian to look down at his hand as he slowly unfurled the clenched palm to reveal a selection of coppers and a shilling piece. Brian's eyes rounded. Then he chuckled and looked out at the corner boys who were moving off to pastures new.

'One of them d-dropped a florin in the scrap,' Edward said.

Brian roared with laughter, then had to stop because of the pain in his ribs. They spread the coins along the counter and ordered enough slab toffee for everyone, which was picked off with a little hammer by the sweetlady, then the serious stuff: blackjack bars, gobstoppers, a bag of bullseyes for their mother, a quarter of cloves for their father, two extra long chews for Brian and Edward and, most coveted of all, a half-pound bag of rum and butter toffees which Cathal had offered them a taste of once. They had envied him those more than the telly. With a roll of gums each which could be made to last nearly a week by themselves, they had enough for two months and still money left over for a comic which they would pass around according to age.

They ran back to the square with the twins skipping, holding hands behind them. But Brian's heart sank when he returned to their site. The day's ructions were not over yet. His father was still staring out to sea but he had his lower lip thrust up, covering the top lip. Always a bad sign. Corny was back from the pub, his soft round face suffused with ire and large ones. Evidently, he had accused Jeremiah of something. A little group of onlookers had started to amass around them, licking their lips in anticipation. Brian could see Cathal scratching the inside of his ear with a pained expression on his face. The heifers were gone.

'What's going on?' Brian whispered to Cathal.

'The heifers bolted,' Cathal said uncomfortably.

'Which way did they go?' Brian asked, looking around. He kept his blackjack bar in the corner of his mouth; his tongue was black.

'Dunno,' Cathal shrugged, 'I wasn't looking.'

'You wasn't looking?' Brian was incredulous.

Cathal shifted uneasily on his feet. 'I had to go for a shite if you must know.' He kept his head down, knowing full well that Brian would shit in his pants if necessary rather than leave the beasts for a moment.

Brian took a long suck on the bar. He didn't mean to feel so glad it was Cathal and not himself but the feeling was there anyway so he decided just to enjoy it. 'God Almighty,' he said. Another slurp. 'D'you want a rum and butter?' This was turning out to be some day – Cathal in trouble and Brian in a position to offer him a rum and butter.

'No, thanks,' Cathal said dolefully. 'The trouble is, himself' – he indicated Jeremiah with his head – 'is getting blemt. Da says he left the heifers go on purpose, like.'

Brian stopped mid-slurp. He looked at Edward. Their eyes

stood out on stalks. Of all the dumb things Corny had ever done, this was by far the dumbest. You couldn't go around accusing a man of deliberately letting your beasts go. Brian pushed Cathal out of the way and edged closer so that he could hear whatever Corny was saying, which was obviously a lot because his mouth was working constantly and he had his stick raised in the air as if to punctuate his words.

Jeremiah continued to stare flintily across the horseshoe harbour. Brian wished that the corner boys were in his line of vision again; he'd finish them off, one by one. He wanted to run up to Corny, catch his fat sweaty neck between his bare hands and squeeze until the eyeballs popped from their sockets. He had thought that he could swallow any insult, every wounding slight – fair price for a look at a telly, the odd rum and butter – but he could not swallow the grim set of his father's face, forced to stand there, listening to the drunken, rambling accusations of a small plump man who was not fit to breathe the same air as Jeremiah. Brian felt a piercing sense of shame for his father, similar to the feeling when the corner boys had mocked their poverty and dishonoured Noel. He thought the world was wrong. It had got everything upside down and back to front. All you had to have was money or land, which was in effect the same thing. And good men, like his father, didn't count; they had to stand there and take whatever was thrown at them, because they had not accumulated wealth which, in turn, accumulated respect. And Brian was seething, because somehow it just didn't seem fair. There was something in the equation he simply could not fathom. It seemed as if they were destined to be pitted forever against an enemy they could not understand because when you were at the bottom of the heap, there was nowhere to look but up. And up there was where you could never be, because of the tiredness, and the fallow acres, and the thing that should have been done yesterday. And the bad luck of having two sets of twins when there were only sons like Cathal around with doting fat fuckers of fathers and the things that went with them. He thought at that moment that the whole world needed to look down on someone, and there was nowhere lower to look than his own family.

'I'll say it the once more,' his father was saying through gritted teeth, 'and that's all I'll say it. So hush up now and listen.' Corny had to stop for breath anyhow; he looked moments from a coronary. Jeremiah continued in his low voice, making heads strain forward all around. 'I turned around, like this.' He motioned with his back. 'I bent down like so' – he hunkered down, raising the horse's rear hoof – 'to make up my mind once and f'rall if she needed shoeing to the back left leg or if we'd make next fair day out of her. I looked for, oh, maybe half a minute, then I decided to lev her be and while I was deciding, I heard a commotion.' He rose slowly, gazed over to where the heifers should be. 'I rose up. The whitehead was acting headstrong. I looked around for Cathal' – he motioned again – 'but he wasn't where he should be. Before I could get across, the whitehead set loose and the others were away off after her, heading down toward the strand.' He put a match to the bowl of his pipe, exhaled a stream from the side of his mouth. 'If you've a mind to look, that's where you'll find them.'

Brian thrilled at the implied coda that Corny was more interested in causing trouble than looking for his animals, a fact which had got him into this mess in the first place. Several heads nodded knowingly around them. Brian saw a

170

young lad about his own age giving the ground his fixed attention. Impressed, no doubt, by the way Jeremiah was managing to put the fat man down with such quiet but ruthless determination. He took an extra long slurp. God what a sweet day. He promised himself that he would really concentrate on the Holy Rosary during the long ride home. He would never allow his mind to wander again but would remain with his father, throughout every decade, even if it *was* the Sorrowful Mysteries which demanded the most attention.

Corny was signalling impatiently for Cathal to head for the strand to round up the heifers. He hawked and spat to the side, a hand pulling and pushing at the peak of his cap. His colour had settled into a uniform salmon pink. Several coughs lubricated his throat enough so that he could mutter the painful words: 'My apologies to you, and all belong to you. You'll understand how it . . . I was a bit distracted in myself when I seen them missing.'

He extended a stiff hand, which Jeremiah gazed at first before he enveloped it with his own large palm. A look passed between both men for a fraction of an instant. Brian's eyes widened – he had always known that there was no love lost there, but the depth of their mutual hatred came as a shock to him. It was as if there was a wild animal stalking between their locked eyes. Edward nudged him; he had caught the look too.

While Cathal was away, Jeremiah struck a deal on his own beasts and the luck money was settled with a pat to Brian's head. Even Brian's mother was grinning from ear to ear as they loaded up the cart about four o'clock in preparation for the haul home. This time they could all travel in the wagon together. Brian sprinted up to the paper shop to buy his

171

comic which Edward could read over his shoulder from their nest in the hay.

As he walked back toward the square, chuckling already at the size of Desperate Dan's cow pie, he knocked against the young lad he'd seen earlier watching the fracas with Corny. Brian beamed knowingly at him. The boy stopped and pulled at Brian's sleeve. 'He left them go,' he said quietly. 'I seen him.'

'What're you on about?' Brian asked, drawing his sleeve back.

'The heifers. I seen him standing there. Just looking at them. They was fretting a bit, and he hupped them with his stick. I seen it. Your old fella's a liar.'

Brian closed his eyes tightly. He counted to ten under his breath. If he laid into the young lad now, he knew for certain that he would leave him for dead. When he opened his eyes again, the boy was about to say something else but decided against it when he saw the white-hot gleam in Brian's stare. Brian took a step forward and the boy spat to the side, shrugged, and ambled on.

Brian was still shaking his head in dismay as they pulled out of the square. What was the matter with people at all? He doubled his vow to pay close attention to the Rosary which his father would begin any minute now. Suddenly, the memory of the night Noel had yawned into his father's face during the Sorrowfuls made him wince. He would pray for Noel too, something he hadn't done for the longest time. He bit his lip hard and winced again, recollecting that the night Noel yawned had been his last Rosary ever.

As the cart trundled out past the harbour, the distant horizon crackled with rods of lightning. Black clouds collided overhead, sounding like the end of the world. This was a strange, forbidding world, Brian thought as he peered up from his drenched comic to study his father's unyielding profile, that would take everything from a man, even his unquestionable integrity.

# TEN

# The Sorrowful Mysteries

Julia stretched out on her cot for hours, the dark a feeble blanket around her. Some time after midnight, the August rain had ceased and a sallow, veined moon slid into the sky. With her head resting on the upturned cradle of her arms, she gazed through the window as huge, inky clouds like slow-gaited dinosaurs dragged themselves across the moon's surface. Out in the distance, dashes of yellow light broke up the sea. A corncrake sounded hoarsely somewhere down by the cliff's edge. Julia passed the back of her hand over her face. She could not read tonight. Her thoughts were consumed by Brian. No matter how hard she tried to remain fastened to her rage, she could not entirely deny the pity she felt for him when she considered what he must be going through, if only because she was going through it too, and human suffering looked for its own level in others.

A part of her desperately wanted to see him. She had questions. She wanted to know if he knew about the rumour that Cathal was Jeremiah's son. Edward was here again – doubtless at Jennifer's behest, because he so rarely came of his own volition, that much was perfectly clear. She had yet to hear a word, never mind a civil word, pass between father and son. But although she had walked for hours these last few days with Edward, enjoying his easy companionship while they collected rocks in a wicker creel, the subject of Brian's past was not brought up again. She wanted to know how the seemingly fearless, hard-working young Brian – the portrait Edward had painted – had turned into the easygoing, diffident character she had married. She had questions about Noel, which she felt still remained unanswered. But mostly, in the stillest moments of the early hours, as now, when she permitted herself an honesty untenable by daylight, she yearned for the sound of Brian's slow, easy breathing in the bed beside her. His sleepy morning greeting. The way he slept with his arms wrapped tightly around her body, still there, still shielding her, in spite of every blow she had rained on him throughout the course of the evening. He was constant in a way her own mother had never been once Carol had entered the arena. And she felt a pang of pity for Jennifer now too, denied as she was any opportunity to offer her daughter comfort, which would go some way to alleviating her own grief, and guilt for all the years of inconstancy.

Slowly, she crept from the room, about to go downstairs to start her chores ahead of the day, when she turned left instead, and slipped into Jeremiah's old room. She was taking too many chances these days. Jeremiah had nearly caught her last Sunday, when he returned early from mass. But she was finding it more and more difficult to resist the soothing, almost trance-inducing quality of the woman's words. Having found that one curiously subjective passage about Noel, a couple of months back, she had since experienced an irrational desire to find something similar.

Quite what Jeremiah would say or do if he found her, she had no idea. She only understood that it was a given, that he would not want her trawling through his wife's things. Perhaps he would demand her immediate departure and the

175

thought of that made her close the door behind her with extra care. She had placed a torch under the bed now, so that she wouldn't draw attention in the middle of the night with the overhead light. She groped around in the dark until she found the torch and flicked it on.

Edward's rumbled snores sounded from next door, her old room. She pulled the drawer open, conscious of every creak in the old furniture. Edward had been unwell – a bit chesty. But Margaret wasn't worried about that because Cathal up the road had suffered the same thing a couple of years back and it passed in good time. There were reports of an outbreak of foot-and-mouth in a nearby farm, and that concerned her greatly. Jeremiah was checking the cattle almost by the hour for any signs. But nothing so far. Thank God.

Julia smiled, grinding her buttocks against the floor – settling in. Margaret said 'thank God' for practically everything. Sold all the chickens at the fair, a pair of goslings too. Thank God. Julia felt as if she could read between the lines now. An occasional, almost incidental reference to some member of the family – such as Edward's chestiness – amid the litany of lists, was helping Julia to form a more defined picture of the woman now. She wondered how she had not picked up on the little messages before. The almost tongue-in-cheek codes: 'Thre'pence halfpenny for the wholemeal sack. Four shillings and fourpence for a good two set of flannel sheets. Jeremiah said too much. I brang them back.' Julia nestled against the bed. The key word in Margaret's list was 'good'. She had thought the sheets were a fair price.

There was not one reference to being tired, throughout all the years Julia had skimmed through, even though it was clear at certain times, during the saving of the hay for instance, that Margaret must have put in close to a twenty-

176

four-hour day. Everything to do with the children, apart from religious instruction, fell to her. If a baby was fretful, it was Margaret who walked the kitchen floor, all night if necessary, so that Jeremiah's sleep would not be interrupted. Such nights were recorded without a trace of self-pity, just something to add to the list of the day's chores. Babies, on the whole, did not constitute part of the 'work'. Until they grew to an age to be of some assistance, they had to be kept from interfering with their father's labours. An almost reverential tone entered the text, every time Margaret mentioned Jeremiah. But Julia was beginning to glean a little something more than that too – by now, she was pretty sure that Margaret was terrified of her own husband. Julia figured that maybe that was just the way of things in those days. She was becoming a little uneasy with the dark portrait emerging of Jeremiah.

The hopeless chronicling of Margaret's attempt at a garden saddened Julia more than anything. Again, not a trace of self-pity, but the dogged efforts, every failure valiantly recounted, touched a chord with Julia. With just a bit of assistance, Margaret might have acquired the colour in her life that she seemed to desire so fervently. In a way, the garden appeared to be Margaret's one and only stand against the wishes of her husband. Once, Julia came across a rather curious reference to some rose bushes which had belonged to Cathal's mother before she died. Evidently, Margaret coveted them.

Julia quickly backtracked over the years, searching for anything else, but there was only a note on the woman's death. As if neighbours died every day during childbirth. A healthy boy though. Thank God. Julia sighed, flicking the pages forward again.

Something about the next entry caught her eye. She had been yawning her way through the by now familiar Sorrowful Mysteries of the Rosary. Thinking: one more 'agony in the garden' and she'd finish the job herself. Why Margaret felt compelled to list each decade nightly was beyond Julia. The woman was obsessed with detail. But then, there was a reference to Noel. He had transgressed in some fashion, Julia surmised; quite how, she could not figure out, but it had something to do with the Rosary and Jeremiah had been furious. At least, reading between the lines, it seemed that way. Margaret was not one for straightforward narration. Julia screwed her eyes up and shone the torch directly on the tightly compacted text. Margaret had gone to bed, but she knew that Noel was out by some shed or other. It looked as if he might have to spend the rest of the night there as a punishment. Julia was transfixed. For what? What sin could a young boy have committed to merit such harshness?

She was about to turn the page when the door opened. Julia rammed the journal back into the drawer and quickly flicked the torch off. Too late, of course, she realized, but her actions were instinctive. She almost swooned sideways with relief when she saw an outline of a sleepy, yawning Edward framed in the doorway.

'Julia,' he said, 'I thought I heard something. J-Jesus, for a second there, I thought maybe a g-ghost. What are you up to at all?'

'Shh,' Julia remonstrated. 'You'll wake your father. I was, ah . . . I was looking for photographs of Brian – as a boy.'

He moved eagerly into the room. 'Did you find anything? God, I thought this room was locked long since . . .'

Julia hesitated. She wanted to know about Noel. The night by the shed. She stood to block his path to the chest of drawers. Edward stepped back. She could sense his unease. It was the fact that she was in her nightie, she realized. Albeit a quite opaque length of white cotton, but he was embarrassed none the less. She pounced on her advantage. 'Go back to bed, Edward. There's nothing there worth look-ing at,' she added in a whisper as he took a backward step.

'No photos then?'

She covered her mouth and mumbled something. A sound. Anything to make him retreat further. He obliged. Outside in the landing, she could barely make out his features in the gloomy light.

'Can't you sleep?' he asked.

'Not really,' she responded, glad to be truthful for a moment. 'Please, go back to bed . . . I'll just make a cup of tea or something. Then I'll try to sleep again. Go on . . .' she urged, indicating his door, when he hesitated.

'Are you sure you don't want me to sit up with you?'

'I'm sure. But thank you.'

He turned reluctantly. Julia motioned toward his door again.

'G'night then,' he said.

'Night night.'

Downstairs in the kitchen, which was blanched by flat, white moonlight, she spied Jeremiah's black bible by his chair. She picked it up, idly flicking through the pages to see if he had underlined any passages. Perhaps she would be able to see beyond the resolutely impassive features; but more probably, she figured, she would only see if anything vaguely pertinent or soothing struck her eye. There was nothing. Just well-thumbed pages and grimy fingerprints. She had a fleeting impression of a man to whom the saying of the words meant everything while the content meant nothing at all. She carried the book outside, pressing the cool leather against her thigh.

The wind on her face had a warming gulf-stream layer to it. The dog brushed by her knees. He gazed up at her curiously. She began to pick her way down through the fields and, as if to guide her progress, he remained by her side. She had to stop and start several times, dependent on the fluctuating light of the moon. When she came to the gulley by the cliff, she slid on to her buttocks, lifting the barbed wire for the dog. Several times, on the way down, she scraped her back on jagged rocks, but she managed to sustain her grip on the bible.

A full tide nearly covered the inlet. She edged forward, watching the lace fretwork break and reform around her ankles. The water was freezing but there was a film of sweat on her brow. The dog danced in and out of the small shore waves. Way out in the distance, huge, sinuous sweeps of ocean curved toward her but lost their potency long before they made it to the pebbled cliff line. The sea was black and gold beneath the moon's cast. She stood still for so long, the dog began to whine. He circled her ankles, over and over again, preventing her from moving forward or backwards, as if he knew what she longed to do. She sighed and reached down to pat his head. He crept away again after that reassurance.

'Let's go,' she said, waving him back toward the gulley.

By the time they reached the yard, Julia was feeling sufficiently tired for sleep. She had her thumb on the door latch when she heard a deep, thrumming growl behind, followed by one high-pitched yap; the collie shot past her through the opened doorway, his hindquarters dripping with fresh blood. Slowly, Julia turned around and found herself staring into the tawny eyes of the predatory animal once more. This time he did not growl but held her gaze in a brazen fashion.

'Go home,' she hissed. 'Go on – get away . . .'

He did not move, just a tiny ear flick to signal that he had registered her voice. When she took a step toward him with her hand raised high, she saw the battalion of hairs stand to attention in rings around his neck as before. Then the low, deep-bellied rumble. 'Shoo,' she said feebly.

His ears had pricked up higher, slowly, his skin was pulled back into ridges along his snout, the sharpest fangs dripped with some sort of syrupy, salivary liquid. He reminded her of a cartoon werewolf. She almost smiled when suddenly she realized that he was about to go for her and she remembered the bible still clutched in her upraised hand. Before he could move, she swung her arm in a wide arc, throwing the book at him with as much strength as she could muster. It hit the long groove which bisected his brow with a force that momentarily stunned him. She seized on his second of confusion, bent down for a rock and hurled it with the same force. It hit the same spot between his eyes. He yelped and leaped backwards. He was shaking then, but she could not discern if from pain or outrage. He emitted one furious howl, fixed her with a final yellowy glare and headed up the path, swaying slightly from side to side as he went.

Julia slumped against the doorframe for a moment. Then she went inside to see how the collie was faring. He had licked his wounds and fallen asleep, curled up in a ball by the legs of Jeremiah's chair. She stared down at him curiously. It didn't seem to matter how cruel Jeremiah appeared toward him, the dog kept coming back for more. She thought of Brian again, and wondered if he had felt like that toward her. There were times she had treated him like a dog – no, that wasn't entirely true either, more like a persistently recalcitrant child; and like a child, he had kept coming back for more. And for one strange moment, she understood how much Brian had loved her. Because the fiercest love is the love of a child for an abusive parent.

She crept upstairs to her cot just as the first streaks of a pearly dawn washed across the eastern sky. The cockerel croaked out one long throaty ululation, then silence again. A line of turquoise settled along the horizon. The moon was a transparent penny as her eyelids finally battened down for a couple of hours' sleep.

She awoke later than usual to the sound of fat drops crackling against window panes. The sky was low and formidably dark. A double flash of lightning blanched the room, followed by thunder almost directly overhead – huge wooden barrels rumbling down from a great height. She sat up and watched the flicks of rain turn into great sweeping waterfalls pouring down the glass, blurring her vision of the gnarled hawthorns outside, and the long stretch of rocky peninsula sliding into the angry sea.

Jeremiah was out when she went downstairs. He had left a boiled egg and chunks of bread on a plate for her. She picked at the food and jumped as every thunder-barrel rolled over the roof. The image of a womb dilating came into her mind. No sign of Edward.

The door opened and Jeremiah entered, head first, shaking his hair loose of rain. He stared across at her and Julia sat up rigid in her chair. She had never seen that expression in his eyes before. He was livid. His mouth worked back and forth from side to side, as though he could not trust himself to speak. The pale blue eyes were detonating with little charges, all aimed in her direction. 'What? What . . . ?' Julia mumbled.

She noticed his fists had clenched at the sound of her voice. And for an instant, she could see the man that Edward had sketched so inarticulately. A man brimming over with rage, seconds from self-implosion. The steely gaze swept past her to his chair by the fireside. She turned and saw the bible, sodden with rain, leaves stuck together, perhaps for ever.

'I'm so sorry –' she began.

'Lev it,' he barked in response.

Edward shuffled downstairs at that moment, stifling a yawn with the back of his hand. 'What's going on?' he asked Julia.

Jeremiah swivelled in his direction. 'You! Stop out of it!'

'I threw his – Jeremiah's bible at the dog that keeps –'

'I thought it was s-something serious, from the sound of ye,' Edward said, directing his words at Julia again. But she understood that he was directing the intended rebuke at Jeremiah.

She felt uncomfortably caught in the middle, as if in another moment an entirely new agenda, between father and son, might rear its ugly head. She tried to stave off the moment. 'Please,' she protested to Jeremiah, desperate to explain but also to save him face, while a sickening voice in her head remarked on the slight whining quality her voice had acquired. 'It was that dog again . . . I'm afraid I threw it at him, and then I forgot to pick it up,' she added in a whisper. 'I really am so very sorry.'

He stood there glaring, as if aware of her usurpation of his house for the first time.

'Look, maybe there's a book restorer or something in

Cork,' Julia faltered, realizing too late how strange those words would sound to him.

His mouth curled and he spat sideways. Letting her know in no uncertain terms that there were things you could not 'restore'. She waited for him to tell her that she must go. Her eyes closed for a fraction of an instant and she held her breath. She had had no idea until this very moment just how important it was to her to remain here, with the dog, the goat, the shrubbery, Anne's etiolated smiles up the road, the loping entry of Cathal through the door each evening, Edward's pained and fleeting visits, and finally Jeremiah himself, as hard a honing stone as she could find, because the last thing she wanted was pity. Pity made Sam dead. And would make her fully cognizant of that cold fact's irreversibility. She searched her mind for something to say, the words to prevent him saying his words.

'Please don't ask me to go,' she heard herself utter in that strangely submissive whine again.

He appeared to be making his mind up. He stamped his dripping wellingtons against the flagstones. His shoulders hitched. 'Suit yourself,' he muttered.

The ensuing moments grew stranger. She wanted to scream at him that she would do anything to make him approve of her presence – desire it, even. She cast him a look from under the curl of her eyelashes and wondered how a man like Jeremiah could have that effect.

'I accept your apology,' he said stiffly.

Julia nodded, breathing a sigh of relief. She felt reprieved. And then realized why she yearned so greatly for his approbation. It was because you could never really be certain of his approval, and human nature invariably decreed that approval be sought or offered, albeit in disproportionate measures most of the time. Thus Jeremiah offered an almost insurmountable challenge: a man in perfect communion with himself. The ultimate hubrist.

He was half smiling, as if he could read her thoughts. As if he understood the potency of his own being. And for another strange moment, that thought disturbed her greatly.

She glanced up at Edward. She thought that he was look-ing embarrassed on her behalf. She gave a slight, confused shrug of her shoulders toward him, but he was already head-ing for the door. He stopped with his thumb on the latch.

'D'you feel like a walk?'

Julia inhaled. She should say yes. She did want to walk. For miles and miles. But she caught the way that Jeremiah's mouth pursed, and the way he studied his splayed fingers.

'Not just now,' she said. 'In a while. Maybe.'

'Suit yourself,' Edward said.

He slammed the door after him, letting in a whirl of warm post-storm air. Julia felt that she had let him down in some way. But she turned for the milk bucket when Jeremiah gestured toward it with a nod of his head.

'What's the programme for today?' she asked.


Noel was so tired, Brian could feel his body list against his, as if in a way he needed to touch Brian to draw strength from him in order to stop his buttocks from collapsing back on to his ankles. They were kneeling with the others by the empty hearth, following with their eyes the movement of Jeremiah's fingers as they deftly moved from bead to bead. The third Sorrowful Mystery of the Rosary, the Crowning with Thorns: three Our Fathers, thirty Hail Marys and three Glory be to the Fathers, before Christ dies on the Cross.

185

Brian was feeling fairly exhausted himself. It had been a particularly arduous day for all of them, as they had begun the saving of the hay, working their scythes back and forth since the first crow of the yard rooster. The kneeling upright after supper for the Rosary was a back-breaking experience. Brian wanted to swoon into his mattress but he reminded himself again that he had to check the stakes down by the cliff, before dawnbreak, because it was Noel's turn and Noel was scared of heights. Brian would have to steal out before his father rose, to do it for his brother. A yawn bubbled inside his mouth. He didn't mean to wish Christ dead but he did wish that He didn't have to take so long. It was his turn to start the Hail Marys and the others were looking to him.

'Hail Mary full of grace, the Lord is with thee, Blessed art thou amongst women . . .' He droned on, twenty-nine to go, alternating first and second half with his father, an implicit agreement having been reached that he would act as the elder son, even if it was only by minutes. Noel was sagging. Brian frowned at him. His brother was all but asleep on his knees. Brian's initial impatience softened when he saw the light downy hair on the back of Noel's neck, and the tiny beads of sweat which grouped around his collar. There was a giant boulder in Brian's throat; he couldn't understand why it was, but Noel made that happen sometimes. It happened when Noel turned to him on occasion, fixing him with those big blue eyes that he knew must mirror his own. There was a helplessness in Noel, a lack of comprehension. Try as he might, he could not keep alongside of Brian, who felt at once glad that he was stronger, more able, and sad too for the part of him that had, in deference to nature, to be part of his twin. Often he wondered if he was strange, or if everyone felt that rock in their throats for the weaklings in the family. Were they born so weak, or was it just that all around were stronger? Brian felt guilty. He couldn't be sure of the reasons. He just knew that something about the cut of his twin's downcast head, the smell of his frailty, made him feel that peculiar mixture of sad and glad. Sometimes, he felt as if his head would explode from all the sadness and gladness, when all he really wanted to do was feel Noel in the bed beside him, smell the sweat from his neck, and place his arms around him securely, offering his protection and, yes, his love. So fierce was that feeling of love when Noel squeezed his hand, pressing it into the mattress between them, that Brian sometimes wanted to cry through the night.

Noel yawned. He couldn't help it. Not a yawn he could quickly turn into a cough either, but a full-mouthed jaw-slackener. Brian winced and experienced that strange mixture of fear, irritation and helpless love again.

'Holy Mary, mother of God, pray for us sinners, now and at the hour of our death. Amen.' Jeremiah's eyes flicked over Noel. 'You, boy. Outside. Stand by the shed and start at the first Sorrowful Mystery and work your way through the Joyful and the Glorious. Don't let up till I tell you let up.'

Noel rose slowly. Brian could see the tired tremble of his skinny legs which would have to support his weight for hours yet – until after midnight at the very least. He was looking at one hundred and fifty Hail Marys, fifteen Our Fathers and fifteen Glory be's. Jeremiah continued with the fourth Sorrowful Mystery, the Carrying of the Cross. Edward began to cough repeatedly, he had been chesty for the last few months. Jeremiah signalled with his eyes that his wife might take Edward upstairs and put him to bed. She moved slowly, creaking herself up from her chair by the fire, which was permitted her when she was nearly full term as she was now.

Brian could not take his mind off Noel outside in the yard. When the Rosary was over, he gave his father a little sideways glance to check if he was ready to relent yet but Jeremiah just gave him a black stare and pointed him upstairs to bed. Brian couldn't sleep in any case with Edward's persistent coughing, so he set up a vigil by the window, waiting for Noel's release.

He could just about make out the thin little figure leaning back against the shed wall down below. Noel had his palms pressed together, head down, deep in prayer, or deeply asleep on his feet, Brian figured. Then a movement indicated that he was awake after all. Noel glanced up, saw Brian and curled a limp hand in his direction. Brian returned the wave. He kept his eyes fixed firmly on his brother. Willing him to stay awake. Praying through every decade with him. Jeremiah's head peered around the bedroom door for his nightly check. Brian was concentrating so hard he didn't glance up. Jeremiah crept over to him so as not to disturb Edward's fitful sleep.

'What're you doing?' Jeremiah asked.

'Praying.' Brian kept his eyes on Noel.

Jeremiah cleared his throat. He stood beside Brian for a moment, gazing down upon his other twin son. Then the strangest thing happened – Brian had never experienced anything like it before – he felt the huge girth of his father's palm lightly graze the top of his head. Just a whisper of a touch and Brian's eyes filled with tears. He didn't dare look up.

'I'll fetch him in,' Jeremiah said and left the room.

Noel clung steadfastly to Brian throughout the night. Brian could hear him sucking his thumb in his sleep. He reached out and laid his hand on the top of his twin's head, just as his father had done to him earlier. And his heart swelled with that burning love for Noel, the love that made him sad and glad and all mixed up inside. His last thought before he fell into a black coma was of the stakes. But he had forgotten that Jeremiah rose before dawnbreak during hay-saving time and he awoke to the clanking sound of the bucket his father carried to milk the cows.

'Is that you awake now, Brian?' A soft female voice drifted over him.

'Carol?'

She perched on the edge of Sam's bed beside him. 'I hope I didn't startle you,' she said with concern. 'I let myself in with Julia's keys. I've been here for hours. At first I thought there was something wrong with you – it was the strangest thing, you were asleep but your eyes were open. At least I figured you were asleep. I stood by the door there and you never saw me. Are you all right?'

'Grand, grand.' He tried to lend conviction to the lie by propping himself up eagerly on his elbow, but it gave way and he slumped back on to the pillow again. He ran a hand along his stubbled jawline. He had no idea how long he had been lying there; it might have been hours, for all he knew, it might have been days. His stomach was so empty it felt as if the lining was touching his spinal cord.

Carol was staring intently at him. She was so like Julia, blonde hair with cobalt eyes, but there was something infinitely softer, more rounded about Carol. She had a fresh, delicate smile, reminding him of primroses for some reason. 'Brian, you're unwell,' she was saying with that little

189

Canadian fleck to her accent. 'You look terrible. When did you last eat?'

He shrugged. A part of him wanted to tell her that he had just eaten, prior to the Rosary, but he stopped himself in time, realizing how crazy that would sound. 'When did you arrive?' he asked.

'A couple of days ago. I think Mum was hoping that I'd try and get Julia back, but I don't think that's such a good idea.' She stopped and gave him a wan smile. 'They said you visited back in June. They were hoping you'd come again soon?'

The latter was a question, he realized too late. He sat up and wrapped his arms around his knees. 'I kept meaning to . . .' he said, then allowed his voice to trail off. But she motioned for him to continue. He took a deep breath. Except for the estate agent every now and then, he had not really engaged in conversation since that visit to Jennifer and Richard two months ago. The answering machine had run out of tape. Edward had written, telling him that he would like to come and see him; he mentioned that he had spent some time with Julia and that she was doing OK. She was helping around the farm and trying to get their mother's old shrubbery patch to flower. Brian had smiled on reading that – the idea of Julia up to her neck in wellingtons and fertilizer seemed so incongruous. He had thought of his mother on her knees by that patch, the wind whistling through the braids in her hair, her exasperated little smile as she dug in deeper and deeper, rain falling, filling her holes in an instant. He had written back to Edward, asking that he didn't come just yet, he was very busy with the sale of the house and so on; he would write again soon.

Now he looked at Carol and realized he was still holding

his breath in preparation for speech, but there was nothing to say so he just cast her a shadow of a smile to beg her indulgence.

'Oh, Brian.'

'I can't make sense of anything, Carol.'

'Yes, I'm sure you can't,' Carol said softly after a while. She gazed around the room at Sam in the photographs, reaching out to press one to her chest. 'Come on,' she said, 'let's go downstairs. I'll fix us something to eat. It won't help but it will give us something to do.'

Something to do like Julia and her shrubbery, he thought. Sometimes he was sure that he could feel the gales of her hate and anger gusting toward him across the Irish Sea, and he wondered if her anger was as great as his guilt, both of them keeping full grief at bay for another while at least.

Carol could only find a can of baked beans in the kitchen so she fixed them beans on toast. She made a pot of tea and they sat in the living-room, Carol still clutching her picture of Sam. Twin washes of liquid poised tremulously on the rims of her lozenge eyes. She picked at the beans, then pushed the plate away. 'Actually, I'm not very hungry,' she confessed. Her mouth opened to say something but she sealed it shut again quickly.

'It's all right,' he said, 'you can talk if you like. I won't . . . well . . .' he added with a shrug.

'It's horrible feeling so useless all the time,' she faltered.

'I know.'

'I mean I'd fly over to Ireland right now, this minute, if I thought it would be of any help to Julia.' She made ringlets in her hair with a finger. 'But she would just freeze me out. I know she would.'

'You're probably right.'

191

Little chips of ice refracted against blue irises. Then her face did a little twist, just like her sister's. 'Sometimes, I really hated her, you know, when we were children.' She shuddered, remembering. 'God, she could say the meanest things – really take your legs from under you and then she'd act so sorry that I would end up feeling sorry for her.'

'I know the feeling.' Brian smiled ruefully. He thought of his father and that little inarticulate pat to his head the night before Noel died. Julia's expressions of remorse were not dissimilar. He had watched her with Sam after she had been particularly abrasive with him. It was as if she hovered around him, without touching, breathing silent apologies into the space he occupied. When he walked to the fridge, she slipped by him on her way to the sink. When his chin drooped on to his chest, she bent down to remove a speck from the floor. As if she were trying in a way to protect him from her own sharp edges by emitting an invisible force field with which to surround him.

'Do you still love her?' Carol gazed at him shrewdly.

'Yes.' He didn't hesitate and that seemed to please her.

'I don't know why that makes me feel glad in a way,' she said. 'I always found her very difficult to love . . . and to be honest, I think our mother found – it – a problem too . . .' She allowed her voice to trail off. Perhaps it was the first time she had made that admission to herself.

Brian sipped his tea. He felt that a mystery was unravelling inside his mind. Perhaps the clues had always been there but he had never really questioned his feelings for Julia before. They met, they married, she was his wife, he loved her most of the time and if not exactly hated, certainly resented her some of the time. End of story. Too much analysis only created problems, he had always believed. Now, he wondered if it was because she was so determined to appear unlovable from the outset that he had felt compelled into offering more and more, until eventually a loose seam might be found in her straitjacket, allowing him to slip stealthily in. And from inside, next to her skin, he could see things which had bypassed her own family. He understood that she was profoundly shy, though no one would ever guess that. He knew too that she was almost hopelessly insecure behind her screen of irony, sharp little asides, wisecracks. Whipping her tongue across rooms to stop anyone getting next to her, unaware that Brian was there all the time, so close she couldn't feel him. He had given her Sam, a conduit for a love she was able to express openly and nakedly for the first time in her life. And then he had taken him away again. Just as he had taken Noel away. That thought struck him so forcefully he collapsed forward, his hands trying to clasp his head, sending the plate of beans crashing to the ground.

'Brian?' Carol jumped up.

'No – don't touch me,' his muffled voice called up to her. 'Please, Carol. I'll be fine in a minute.'

# ELEVEN

# Growing Things

Two weeks after Edward's rather silent and hurried departure, Julia surveyed her shrubbery with a mixture of pride
and triumph. It would have blended in anonymously in her
father's manicured acre, of course, but here amidst the dung
heaps, cabbage heads and drills of potatoes, it shone like a
jewel. Edward's permeable windshield had managed to stand
fast and the battalions of escallonia and buckthorn took the
brunt of salt spray so that there was only a delicate mist of
fresh morning dew on the flower heads in front. She picked
an assortment of dahlias, chrysanthemums and Michaelmas
daisies for Anne to make into one of her dried-flower
arrangements. The delicate white fronds of the daisies around
their butter-yellow hearts reminded her of little girls in tutus.

She had finished all her morning chores so she went inside
to see if Jeremiah needed her for anything immediate. The
dog brushed against her ankles, following her into the
kitchen. He got a swift kick up the ass from Jeremiah, who
was about to pass them on his way out, which sent the dog
yelping back into the yard.

'I was thinking of bringing some flowers to Anne,' Julia
said, ignoring the disgusted curl of his top lip. Sometimes
she got a kick out of saying something deliberately 'girly'
just to see that lip curl. He almost always obliged. The fact

that she had been successful with the old barren patch went completely unremarked by him. Julia felt that it was a little victory for Margaret. 'Did you want me for anything in particular?' she asked casually, fixing the flowers in a basket to let him know that she intended going anyway.

'What time'll you be back?' he responded indirectly.

Julia felt that this was almost becoming some sort of game between them. She would tell him what she intended to do, then he would tell her what he wanted her to do, but always in an indirect way – so that on the surface it might appear as though she had an element of choice, while in reality Jeremiah got his way.

'Oh, in the afternoon – sometime,' she said airily.

'I'll be doing the gates and the shed roofs roundabout then.'

'Oh.' She tried to leave it at that, but her voice carried on regardless. 'Do you want me to help?'

He hitched his shoulders. Julia silently mouthed 'suit yourself' as he said it. He turned in the yard. 'Get Cathal to give you a can of that old stuff he has for the rust. He'll have it waiting for you,' he added, moving on.

Julia pulled a wry face. So she would have been sent up to Cathal's this morning in any case.

She headed up toward the main road with the flowers in a wicker basket draped over her arm. She thought that she must look like something from a nursery rhyme with her sunhat and long paisley skirt, an image instantly dispelled when she remembered that she was still wearing her muddy wellingtons. Her heart felt strangely lighter: perhaps it was the scent from the blossoms, or the way the liquefied sun draped along the cusp of the hill to her right. Maybe it was just that she'd managed to put colour in a barren, forgotten tract of scrub. The day ahead promised warmth and, more importantly, dryness. She decided that it was the simplest of things that could make a person most happy, or unhappy, according to the particular moment.

She had stopped reading Margaret's journal for a while. In deference to Edward really. She still felt guilty that she hadn't told him about the photographs and his mother's book. She should have shared them with him, but he had left so abruptly, she never got a chance. Now, she wondered if he would visit again – her submissiveness toward his father had sickened him greatly. The prospect of not seeing Edward again soon dampened her spirits a little. Only the dog for company now, on her long walks.

Anne's 'closed' sign dangled in the door. The curtains were still drawn but Julia knew that Cathal would be up checking his livestock. She walked around the vanilla house, past the various dry-stone outhouses until she spied him halfway up the hill, moving his cattle from one field to another, a sedate black-and-white matutinal procession, nose to tail, tremulous-legged calves with eyes like small ponds bringing up the rear. Cathal saw her and raised his stick into the air. She called a greeting to him. Anne's curlered head stuck out from a top window.

'Julia, c'min, c'min. I'll be down in a sec.'

Julia stepped through the back door directly into the parlour. She absently studied photographs on the gleaming dresser while waiting for Anne, holding one of Cathal's father up to the light of the window to see if the resemblance was striking or not. They were both stocky, but in truth that was about it. A fat, florid face beamed out at her: there was nothing resonant even in the smile, which had a somewhat cruel aspect, Julia considered. Turning the photograph this way and that, any resemblance grew even less apparent; Cathal's gentle almost apologetic quality was wholly absent. Corny looked like the sort of man who might blow smiling kisses at your baby while one hand rummaged through the contents of your handbag. She wondered if he had had any political aspirations.

'Morning.' Anne stepped in. She was dressed in jeans and sweatshirt, a line of pink accentuating the thinness of her lips, the curlers still in place with sparse sections of yellow hair wrapped around them. 'Are those for me?' She indicated the basket of flowers.

Julia nodded, presenting them to her. She felt inordinately proud of her achievement. Anne had her head to the side, pulling a face at Julia's wellingtons.

'What's this?' she asked. 'Are you developing a rubber fetish or what?'

Julia looked down, shrugging. 'This *is* the country after all, Anne.'

'We do wear shoes in the country too, Julia – outside of the farm. I'd watch out if I were you ... Next thing you know, you'll be washing your smalls in rainwater or some such old wives' tale, to make them –' She cackled when she saw the slow flush creep up Julia's cheeks. 'You've been doing that, haven't you?'

Julia nodded. She had been emptying a rainwater tank by the side of the house since she read Margaret's note on the subject. 'Margaret always washed the children's nappies in rainwater,' she said.

'"Margaret", is it? Oh, very cosy. You can't mean that Jeremiah's been telling you fond memories of his wife – can you?' she asked, her mouth dropping open.

Julia decided to come clean. 'I found a journal she kept.'

197

'Go 'way.' Anne's mouth opened further. 'She never struck me as the writing type – not that I knew the woman from Adam. What did she put in it anyway?'

'Mostly lists,' Julia said drily. 'You know: jobs around the farm, shopping lists, and so on. Pretty boring stuff to be honest. But sometimes . . . I kind of like the sound of her.' She gestured toward the flowers. 'I grew those on her patch – only she couldn't get anything to, because of the wind.'

'Well, I –' Anne broke off, shaking her head. 'Margaret's journal, huh?' The grey eyes gleamed mischievously. 'So what's next? You'll be shagging Jeremiah and having his babies?'

'Have wellingtons will shag?' Julia roared with laughter.

'Well, you do every other blessed thing for him,' Anne slyly shot in.

'There are limits,' Julia responded, deflecting the little dig.

'I certainly hope so . . .' Anne stopped mid-sentence to place two china cups with saucers on the coffee table. 'Because if you don't watch out he'll be calling you "Mrs" before you know it. "Here Mrs",' she mimicked, thrusting her groin out. '"Brace yourself, woman."'

They both fell on to the sofa laughing at the image of Jeremiah's lovemaking technique.

'My own mother used to call it "the agony in the garden",' Anne exploded.

'"The agony in the garden"? That's one of the Sorrowful Mysteries, isn't it?' Julia asked.

'Margaret again?' Anne said.

Julia nodded.

'All agony, no garden,' Anne laughed, pointing to the flowers.

198

Julia wiped streaming tears from her cheeks. She hadn't felt this good in the longest time.

Anne made a pot of coffee and they sat chatting for a while, both of them revelling in a closeness between them which hovered in the air like a palpable presence. As if somehow, growing friendships moved up another stratum on shared tears, or shared laughter.

Julia spoke of the shrubbery, how she had never understood before the pleasure to be had from watching something take shape from nothing. How her father had spent hours every evening, leaning hands and chin on a rake, saying things like 'we're being taken over by the blues, we need some pinks here'. How every petal bore her own personal insignia; the strange tenderness she felt toward every flower.

'And a sort of gratitude too,' she went on, to Anne's encouraging nods, 'towards everything which grew itself – for me. When I'm doing something else, my mind is always on the shrubbery, wondering, you know, what's happening now? Oh, I must sound half crazy . . .'

Anne jumped up, arranging the bouquet this way and that for her dried-flower arrangement. Julia sipped her coffee, making shapes with her hands to convey opinions which Anne seemed immediately to understand, all the while rearranging deftly with her eyebrows raised for approval.

'This way, I think,' Anne said, pulling the daisies toward the centre.

'Mmm. I like that. Try a couple of ferns around the . . . Oh yes, much better.'

Julia was struck by what they were doing. It occurred to her that they were having a conversation. So this was how it was done. Someone said something, you said something back. It didn't have to be of monumental importance, it didn't have to lead anywhere in particular. Just two people, or more, passing time together. Yet a whole slew of quietly ingested information was brought to bear within the circle of communication. Taking in subjects to avoid and things which remained unspoken but understood nevertheless. Unconsciously making judgements all the time, so that when your interlocutor said 'it doesn't matter to me in the slightest', you knew that it mattered hugely. Idly talking, while keenly watching for eye flickers, or shadows drawing down features, to check if the last thing you said was coherent, or appropriate, or too incursive. Wondering if it revealed too much or if you should reveal more, or if you revealed more, would you regret it later? And all this computation silently going on, as kettles boiled and cups settled on to saucers with little chinking sounds. Julia was amazed. Twenty years of trying to teach people to speak, when all the speaking done in conversations was in the silences.

Cathal came in, shunting out of his wellingtons at a glance from Anne. He cast Julia a crooked smile on his way to the kitchen.

He joined them for a moment, munching on a heel of bread and butter.

'D'you want a fry?' Anne asked, rising.

'No, no,' he assured her, motioning for her to sit again. He looked at Julia. 'Jeremiah didn't give you any messages for me, did he?'

Julia noticed the grim set of Anne's lips. She scratched the back of her neck. 'Just about some stuff for the rust . . . ?'

'I've it all ready,' he nodded. 'You can take it away with you when you're going, or lev it and I'll bring it with me later, when I go down to give him a hand.'

'I'll do the sheds with him, Cathal, there's no need for you . . .' Julia's voice trailed away. She could tell from a passing shadow in his eyes that she was saying the wrong thing. On several occasions lately, when he turned up to do something on the farm and found Julia had already completed the job, she had seen that shadow. The last thing in the world she wanted to do was to hurt this gentle man, so she quickly added: '. . . On second thoughts, maybe you'd better do it with him. I hate ladders.'

Cathal slurped back his tea and rose to leave. 'I'll be down so tell him.'

'Tell me, Cathal,' Julia blurted out, 'why do you worry about Jeremiah so much?'

Anne inhaled quickly. Cathal looked pained. He did not care for things to be put so nakedly, requiring answers from him on subjects that were best accepted and never questioned. He brushed crumbs with one hand into the waiting scoop of the other. Not wishing to appear impolite, he shrugged in response to her question, so that it might appear that he did respond. He opened the back door, bidding them goodbye with his customary backhanded salute.

'You've heard the rumour, haven't you?' Anne's eyes bored through Julia.

'Edward told me. Is it true?'

'I asked Cathal once. He said he didn't know, but it felt like it. That's what he said. We've never discussed it since.' Anne twisted her mouth to the side.

'Tell me about Cathal's mother.'

'I only know what I heard from my own mother, she was dead before I was born . . . a haemorrhage during the birth.' Anne refilled her coffee cup, running a tissue around the lower rim to prevent straying drips. 'Good-looking by all accounts, plus near on a hundred acres going with her. I told you before – Jeremiah was courting her. Maybe she decided she didn't want or need to marry such a cold bastard. I don't know. She married Corny. Maybe she still carried a torch for the cold one, who knows?'

Julia was entranced for a moment at the prospect of Jeremiah, rosary beads and bible cast aside for a quick roll in the hay. It seemed inconceivable. Anne must have read her thoughts because she broke into a broad grin.

'Don't get carried away,' she said. 'My own feeling, if it is true at all, is that he always kept an eye on the business at hand . . . Keeping one son at least on the land. Didn't much matter to him how that came about or which son it was to be. D'you follow me?'

Julia nodded. That made more sense.

'My reckoning is that Corny knew. Leastways, he had a pretty good idea. There were enough whispers.' She gazed through the window. 'And I reckon Cathal knows too – deep inside. Always has. But he was torn between two fathers. Then when Corny died ten years back, he went over to Jeremiah's side altogether. The same year we married,' she added, with a tinge of bitterness. 'Hot drop?' She held the cafetière aloft.

'No thanks.'

'Between you and me, I hadn't much time for Corny either. Always struck me as a bit of a snake. You know, one eye looking at you, the other behind you, checking what was there. Cathal's a bit of an eedjit that way – believing in people too much. I like to think I'm that bit sharper.'

'You are.'

'Now, you look sharp,' Anne said, smiling. 'A person would take one look at you, everything so quick and all, they'd say that one has a sharp look to her, a sharp tongue. But if you don't mind me saying . . .'

'I'm a bit stupid?'

'No-oo. I wouldn't say that at all at all. It's just that . . . Well, that . . .'

'Dense. That's the word you're looking for, isn't it?'

Anne made a singsong movement with her head. 'That wouldn't be fair to you either. No, it's more of a . . . a sort of stunned look you have to you. Like everything is a bit of a surprise. D'you mind me saying that?'

'No, I don't mind you saying that.' Julia smiled.

Anne placed the glass and chrome jug on its ersatz silver settle. Her razor palms pressed together. Don't ask, Julia thought.

'My turn.' Anne smiled knowingly. 'You and Brian – what was the attraction? I hope you don't mind me asking, but I always wondered when you first started coming here with him.'

It was a fair enough question. One that Julia had asked of herself so many times before. There was nothing immediate to cite as proof of instant attraction, or subsequent love for that matter. She had convinced herself that she liked his easygoing manner, his smile, the way he addressed everyone with the same deference. Then there was the fact that she was single at the time, and secretly worried. Now she saw that she had spent ten years of married life trying to fall out of love with her husband. Because the plain truth of it was that she had never considered him worthy of her love in the first place. He was a compromise. And she had never allowed him to forget that fact. But Anne had not meant it that way, Julia understood. To Anne, like his siblings, Brian was that most worthy specimen: a steadfast man.

203

'I'm sorry, I shouldn't have asked.' Anne pressed her hand contritely. 'It's just that – that – the two of you seemed so different . . . Sorry,' she added again.

'It's OK,' Julia said. Her fingers picked at loose threads along the hem of the paisley skirt. 'It's funny how you just amble along, day after day, pretty much confident that there is a pattern to your life. At least, you *think* you understand what that is. Then something . . . something' – she shrugged, at a loss for a word sufficiently big enough – 'happens, and suddenly you don't know anything any more. All that's left are emotions. Feelings.' She tried a downturned smile. 'And – I was never very good at those.'

'And Brian . . . ?' Anne said softly. 'Do you still hate him as much as when you arrived first?'

Julia considered for a moment. 'Yes,' she responded truthfully. 'Yes, I do. But – love – too. It's complicated . . .' Her voice trailed off.

'Strange, isn't it?' Anne looked thoughtful. 'Sometimes I think that Cathal feels that way about Jeremiah. I asked him – well, begged him, to get shut of the acres by the water his father bought off Jeremiah. Just those acres, I said, knowing that a German – or maybe it was a Frenchman – was looking for a place for a language school or some such. Anyway, I wanted to get rid of them. Yeah, sure, for the money, but mostly, I just wanted all that "stuff" between Corny and Jeremiah to come to an end. Land like that is bad luck.'

'What did Cathal say?'

'Nothing.' Anne rolled her eyes. 'But his look said "you've two chances".'

'In other words . . . ?'

'No. Being the short and tall of it. Cathal would never do that to Jeremiah. He'd feel he was letting him down.'

204

A shaft of sunlight pierced the window panes and lingered on their faces. Julia shielded her eyes and looked up toward the hilltop. A tall, slender figure strolled toward the west. 'Edward,' Julia said, surprised by the gladness welling up inside her. So he hadn't decided to keep away for good, after all.

Anne was studying her under clogged mascara spires, a knowing little smile playing on her lips. Julia felt a flush creeping up from her neck to suffuse her cheeks.

'We're not . . . There isn't anything . . .'

'Oh, I know. I know.' Anne stuck her tongue in her cheek. 'Like you said, things're complicated.' She scraped back her chair and began to stack the used cups. Her head jerked sideways, indicating the hill. 'Go on let you. Get a walk in while the day's still fine.'

Julia was breathless by the time she reached the top. By now, Edward was almost at the point to the west where he would begin his descent. She called to him but he couldn't hear. She stopped for a moment to gather her breath, bending forward with her hands on her hips, eyes straining to take in the great sweep of view so that she might always remember it like this. Streaks of yellow spiny furze pushed up between outcrops of speckled rock. Horizontal bands of rust and ochre ropy grasses, and scabby, misshapen fields – or what passed for fields – bordered by dry-stacked walls sloped down to the grape sea. A layer of clingfilm over a bowl of still grape juice, darts of mercury sketched across the limpid surface. Shifting pockets of light and shade on the distant shore, where the mountains played with the light – momentarily seizing, then passing it on. Subtle movement everywhere, it seemed, catching the periphery of her vision, then stillness again when she concentrated on one spot.

A solitary mass of cloud, like a giant charcoal paw, suspended above the centre of the comatose sea. She watched two Friesians lope down the length of Cathal's best field, one black where the other was white, white where the other was black, a curious mirror image. The grass, eerily green on the fertilized fields, appeared silken where a touch of wind revealed its shiny underside. She thought of rich sweet lamb, grazed on such a pure diet.

There was no sign of Edward when she looked to the west again, and she felt a little stone of disappointment fall inside her chest. She decided to walk home that way in any case, crunching through the dry grass which reached up to her thighs in places. A few sheep clung to rocks nearby, as if affixed by glue. They effected the little obligatory fleeing movements as she passed, but in truth her presence was hardly registered. She had never before been conscious of being so contentedly alone. Quite dissimilar to the estranged loneliness of her childhood eyrie, when she had gazed down at her family, happily together in the garden below.

But she was not entirely alone, she realized as she rounded a large black rock and saw two long limbs stretched out over a sweep of hay. Edward was fast asleep, his head lying back on the cradle of his arms, the little round spectacles placed carefully on the scoop of his belly. Julia approached quietly, not wishing to startle him. She gazed down at the spidery eyelashes, thrashing together in a series of little tics, signalling deep sleep and dreams. She held her breath and fell to her knees beside him. He appeared so vulnerable – she recalled the many nights she had observed Brian, wondering at that quality of innocence he possessed in sleep.

She leaned forward to breathe in his scent, which was at once comfortingly familiar and strangely alien. Her lips brushed over his cheek; he moaned and shifted slightly. Julia listened to the warning voice inside her head then bent to press her mouth against his anyway. His eyes opened instantly. Julia caught her breath, not knowing what she would do if he rejected her. There were no ground rules for behaviour like this. Her own recklessness terrified and exhilarated her; she wanted to stop, if only to stave off possible humiliation, but her hand continued to caress his cheek, fingers fanning down his neck, toward his chest.

He did not react at first. The startled blue gaze took in the sky and the twisted branches of a solitary holm oak above them, before his face creased into a shy smile as he reached out and drew her body lengthways on top of him. Julia buried her head in the curve of his neck and sighed. It felt good to be holding on to something, someone, again. She kissed him gently on the mouth, her lips barely touching his, allowing him a way out still, if he wanted one. Their eyes locked; Julia raised her eyebrows questioningly but he responded by tightening his embrace. She remembered the wellingtons and flushed. How to get out of them with any measure of dignity? In the movies, women were always unhooking bras, or stepping out in high stilettos from frothy little circlets of lacey camisoles on the ground. She had yet to see a scene where a shitty boot was slung devil-may-care over a shoulder. As if he understood her quandary, he chuckled and placed his spectacles to the side, letting her know that he had had his own little moment of panic.

She reached for him then, quickly, shunting her legs from the passion boots, her skirt splaying over his groin as she began to unbuckle his belt. He was already half erect – perhaps from a dream. The blue gaze stared past her for a moment, a fleeting look of panic again, then wonderment, before they wrapped around one another in a frantic, frenzied meshing of limbs, both shedding their skins of mutual loneliness for what seemed like the first time in their lives.

Edward made love like a man drowning. At once inarticulate, flailing madly about for a rock to cling on to; at once quietly, desperately, forestalling the void. Julia pressed down on him, moving her pelvis back and forth, delicately tipping him against her pubic bone while her arms followed the outline of his chest and shoulders through his T-shirt. He shuddered. She caught his head in the vice of her hands, forcing his mouth wider and wider until her tongue could extract the essence of him. She felt his fear, his delicious terror, his lust and guilt, and squeezed herself around him until he sighed in complete submission and rolled from under her to utter a cry into the long spires of grass beside her head. 'God, I'm so sorry,' he moaned.

Julia lightly grazed the back of his neck with her lips. 'Don't be, it was me ... Thank you,' she whispered, not knowing if he would understand or not.

He turned to look at her, conflicting emotions racing over his features. 'I have to know,' he said, 'I have to know ... Revenge ... ?'

Julia lay back. She stroked his trembling back. There were no words linguistically evolved to tell him that he was good and pure and innocent like her husband. That she had needed to taste that innocence again. That she was sorry, because she had used him so ruthlessly. But no, it was not revenge. If she used the word ... substitution, she might hurt him further. So she gently forced his head around to kiss his lips reassuringly.

He was about to offer more regrets when she placed a finger to his mouth. 'Shh, there's no need. I know how bad you feel because Brian is your brother. My husband. But it's happened. Maybe we both just needed something – something special in our lives right now.' She smiled, running her finger along his cheek. 'I know I should feel bad too, but I don't. And I never will. I promise you that, Edward. It was just something we shared for all sorts of reasons. So let's forget about guilt for now. I feel . . .' She sat up, hugging her knees. 'No, I won't say happy – but contented.' She turned to him. 'Yes. Contented. I thought I'd never . . . Thank you . . .' she said again, because he had no idea what he had given her.

Edward smiled, but there was a note of sadness in his eyes too, as he reached out to stroke her hair, his long fingers lifting handfuls of blonde streaked with grey, allowing each handful to fall back against her cheek. Julia rocked on her side, gazing at him. For a moment his face blurred and she saw Brian lying there and she wanted to cry. They embraced awkwardly. In-laws again.

Julia lay back, enjoying the sun on her face, remembering Edward's little dissertation on the intrusive qualities of granite. 'The same only different', he'd said of the resultant uplift. Now, she understood fully.

She thought of all the changes brought about to so many lives, not least her own, all the tears shed, because of the loss of one little boy. The sudden absence of his presence, so unutterably senseless; the presence in the first place, senseless because of the sudden absence. Then she wondered if, ultimately, the sense to any life lay with the survivors, in their memories. In their tears.

Edward was standing, cinching the belt on his jeans. He reached a hand down, drawing her up. They stood for a while, Julia resting her head against his shoulder. She understood instinctively that Edward would not visit again

209

for a very long time. He would feel obliged to offer Brian that much at least. She would miss him terribly but she knew that it would happen again and then he would be hurt. Because he could only ever be a substitute.

She was struck again by the vagaries, the consequences of death that were visited on the survivors. If she had ever thought of being unfaithful to Brian, the last person on earth she would have conjured up was Edward. She had always considered that she was perfectly unhappily married, and intended to stay that way, thank you very much, should anyone have asked.

They held hands walking down the slope, breaking apart when they reached the main road. Suddenly Edward laughed. He caught her waist, swinging her around to face him. His cheeks were flushed, a look of wild, infectious exhilaration in the blue eyes.

'What?' Julia laughed.

'You d-didn't realize, did you?' He beamed. 'You're the only p-person I can tell . . . That was my first –' He broke off and nodded toward the top of the hill.

'Edward, you're nearly forty-two years old.'

'I know, I know.'

'So how come? I mean you must have had . . .'

'Chances?'

'Well, yes . . . Sorry, I don't mean to sound . . .'

'No, it's OK, really. Of course, it's a wee bit s-strange . . . But –' He broke off, looking around him for a feasible explanation. 'I can't explain it properly – it's j-just that I thought it was a sin . . . Don't laugh now. I know it sounds ridiculous in this day and age. But I just could never . . . you know, do it. Until . . .' His mouth curled down at the edges. 'Hell of a j-jump,' he added, 'from no sin, to – to my own brother's wife.'

210

'God, if I'd known, I'd have . . .'

'What? You'd have what?'

'I don't know. Tried to make it more special or something.'

His face creased into a smile. 'B-but it was special. To me. Not t-to you?'

'You'll never know,' she smiled in response to allay his fears but also because it was the truth. Conversations again – she felt that she was getting good at this.

Then, on impulse, she hugged him to her, conscious of the little ripples of delight coursing through his slender frame. Despite his guilt, he was relieved beyond measure too, and proud of himself.

'I'm so glad. There'll be no stopping you now,' she said with a wry smile.

'B-bloody right,' he chuckled hoarsely. He reached for her hand, kissing her fingertips, saying goodbye with his eyes. He would leave tomorrow. 'You're a good woman, Julia,' he said.

'Am I?' She was confounded by the compliment, good being the last adjective she would ever have used to describe herself. Carol was good.

'Made you b-blush,' Edward teased.

They walked on in companionable silence, stopping occasionally to watch the sea changing colour. Jeremiah approached on his bicycle. Julia opened her mouth to greet him, but he cast them a baleful stare and rode on. She stared back at his receding figure, that stiff spine erect in spite of the road's upward slope. Head up, the long legs pumping mechanically in perfect rhythm. Her gaze turned to the forty-year-old erstwhile virgin beside her. She thought of Brian and those long, blank, inscrutable stares of his, and she wondered just how great was the damage wreaked by one solitary figure on a bicycle.

# TWELVE

# Falling

Brian's mouth felt so dry, he thought he would never again prise his tongue down from the roof where it clung like a thong of dried leather. He stopped for a moment to purse a bottle of warm milk against his cracked lips. His back reluctantly straightened from its crouched forward position, and even when the spine formed into a line again, he could still feel his body swaying from side to side, as if he had been at sea, instead of scything hay since dawn.

Noel was turning yesterday's hay with a pitchfork in the field ahead of him. Beyond Noel, Jeremiah worked the horse and mower through the longer tracts to the west. Further west still, sloping down to the Atlantic, already cocked hay stood up like golden helmets along a shorn undercarpet. A week of intense, hazy heat and they were working flat out before the break forecasted in a couple of days.

Cathal joined them about ten o'clock, hay already tucked away safely in barns around his house with the aid of modern machinery. The white of his eye, against tanned skin, made Brian think of the underbelly of a fish, lying in a mound of pink prawns. He signalled to Cathal to pass him the honing stone and ran the curved blade back and forth until he saw sparks. Cathal sharpened another scythe and worked alongside him, their bodies picking out an unconscious swaying rhythm. Although only Edward's age, at nearly six, Cathal could cut for nearly as long as Brian or Noel, because of the bullish strength in his stocky frame.

Brian's mother interrupted her own cutting to bring them slices of brown cake smeared with lard, wrapped in muslin. She poured lukewarm milky tea from an enamel jug. Jeremiah waved her away as she approached. He turned the horse up the field again.

Noel wolfed his bread then curled up under a hawthorn for a brief nap. Brian and Cathal stood. Cathal because he was still reasonably fresh, Brian because he knew that if he hunkered down, even for a moment, he would never rise again. He had been unable to sleep on, once he'd heard the clank of his father's bucket in the early hours, and he was still worried about those stakes. His gaze carried down, mentally checking them. They looked safe enough. A slight list to a couple at the furthest end perhaps, but not sufficient to catch Jeremiah's eye. He would have to make himself stay awake tonight until he could be certain that Jeremiah was asleep. Then he would steal down and give them a few quick smites with the mallet. He had already placed it under brambles down there, in readiness.

His mother picked up her scythe again; she worked the patch up by the house. Brian had given Noel the job of turning the hay, because he knew that he was still exhausted from the hours on his feet the night before, when he'd prayed nearly every decade by the shed wall. Cathal wiped the back of his hand along his mouth and motioned that he was about to make a start again, when Brian noticed that Noel was snoring.

He gave him a little prod with his bare foot. 'Get up,' he hissed.

Noel snored again, a scum of dried-in spittle along the corners of his mouth making Brian feel sad for some reason. He wished that Noel didn't make him feel so sad all the time. Brian could see Jeremiah, shading his eyes, looking across at them. He quickly tried to shield Noel from his line of vision by spreading out a mat of straw-like grass beside him. His eyes narrowed as he saw the long legs in the western fields begin to make a hesitant approach. A few strides, then a pause to peer from under the canopy of his raised hand again. As if Jeremiah could not make up his mind whether or not they were all back scything and turning as they should be.

Brian lashed back with his leg, this time making a rough connection with Noel's unprotected stomach. Noel hollered. He was still only half awake when he staggered to his feet like a raging lunatic. His eyes barely registered Brian as his fists instinctively flailed out to beat back whatever had attacked him in his sleep. Brian felt a thunk to the side of his head; he reeled as a burning pain erupted across his cheek and ear. His own fist swung in a wide arc, smashing against Noel's chin.

They were on each other then, fisting, gouging, biting. Too tired and crabby to stop and make sense of it. Edward and Cathal came running, shouting, 'Scrap! Scrap!'

But Edward's thin legs tripped over a pitchfork and he had to watch from his sprawled position. By now, Cathal could see that the fight had developed a frightening earnestness to it. He called to them to let go of each other. Noel was attached by a vampire's bite to a soft fold of skin around Brian's neck. Brian screamed. He brought his knee up quickly, shoving it into Noel's groin. Noel went down and Brian jumped on top of him.

They were heaving and grunting, nails clawing at faces which twisted with hate. Physical exhaustion cast aside, as that hate and adrenalin and an inflexible desire to be final victor carried them through every punch and kick. Brian had only one thought, he wanted to kill his brother. He wanted to rid himself of the endless pity, the covering up, the stupid, demented love which choked him every night before they fell asleep. He wanted to rid himself of that painful lump in his throat, once and for all.

Noel screamed obscenities as Brian's fist crunched into his jaw over and over again. Their mother had dropped her scythe and was now running across the fields to fetch Jeremiah. Edward, no longer enjoying the scrap, bawled at them to stop, then ran in terror toward the house. Cathal locked on to Brian's forearm, drawing him back momentarily. 'That's . . . That'll do now, lads . . . Ah stop, let ye,' he grunted as Brian tried to shrug him off.

Brian's belly was exposed by Cathal's hold, and Noel took quick advantage, stamping his foot out sideways into unprotected flesh. Brian howled, more from outrage than from pain, which would come later. He managed to break free of Cathal and hurled himself headfirst at Noel, sending them both rolling down over the fresh-cut hay, locked together, limb to limb, cheek to cheek, as they fell away from a now blubbering, beseeching Cathal.

Jeremiah had left his wife standing in the western field. He vaulted over a ditch and broke into a run toward Brian and Noel who were almost at the cliff's edge, one body, as they tumbled ever closer. Cathal ran down after Jeremiah, muttering incoherent entreaties to their father to put an end to it. 'Ah, ah make them stop,' he cried breathlessly.

Jeremiah came to a halt beside his sons. Brian managed

to look up for an instant. Expecting severing hands to pull them apart any moment now. But Jeremiah's eyes had a trance-like gleam. His head was nodding, sending them mental commandments. Grab hold of him there, dig in, twist with your backs. Brian could feel that first flush of strength ebb from Noel's body. He was sagging against him now, still desperately locking on, but more from a fear of exposing himself than anything else.

'Stand up, let ye,' Jeremiah shouted. Enraged that it should end so impotently just as he had got there.

Brian shook his head slightly, all that he could manage: No, it was over. They were spent now. Noel's exhausted whimper sounded in his ear. Brian felt his own back pressed up against a stake. It felt solid. He surged a last burst of energy through his arms, forcing Noel to break his grip, forcing him to roll to his feet, sending him teetering back toward Jeremiah. Brian clawed away from the stakes on all fours. Noel staggered sideways. Brian's head began to spin. His opened mouth let loose a stream of clotted blood. Little white beads of light danced at the corners of his eyes. It sounded as if there was a waterfall in his head. He saw Noel's trembling legs approach.

'Go on, go on,' Jeremiah urged, sensing Noel's advantage.

No, Brian thought. This can't be. Him on all fours, his body refusing to take instruction while Noel effected a staggering approach, vigour renewed because he finally had the advantage. Because his father had said so. Because he was still standing. His mouth opened wide and he screamed as his legs first buckled, then straightened, to carry him across the short distance to his crouching dazed twin.

Brian waited for the final kick or blow that would finish it. Noel was feet from him when he stopped suddenly.

Jeremiah was closing in on both of them. Brian managed to raise his head. He could see from one eye only. The other had closed behind a cushion of swollen skin. He saw the confusion on Noel's face, even now looking to Brian for direction. One leg raised hesitantly in mid-air. Brian felt that spear of love and pity. He wanted to shout at him to get it over with. Kick him hard – he would go down for a while. It would be over. Noel would be victorious. Vindicated at last, in sight of his father.

'Go on, boy,' Jeremiah urged through clenched teeth.

Noel closed his eyes. He covered the last few feet at a gallop, running blindly with his arms stretched out in front of him. Feeling for Brian. For where Brian should be.


He reached out too late. The box containing Julia's best dinner service clattered to the ground, narrowly missing Brian's toes. He slumped against stacked wooden crates for a moment, staring down at the fallen box, loath to hear its rattle when touched. The contents of every room, except for Sam's, were systematically packed and labelled in the crates. He had chosen to do it that way because it didn't really matter if everything was mixed up. The crates would have to be placed in storage in any case. Possibly for ever, as far as Brian was concerned. He never wanted to see any of it again.

Completion date on the sale of the house was four weeks hence, but packing gave him something to do. Finding a home for the crates was relatively easy; a home for himself was entirely another matter. He had thought that he would look for a flat to rent. Or if needs must, a room. Then he had wondered where. The where was of no importance because it wouldn't be dictated by any of the usual influences: work, transport – family. So he figured that when the time came, he would simply call a list of numbers from a newspaper and settle on whatever was available and affordable, wherever. Whatever, wherever, whenever: the new vocabulary of his life. His existence, the manner of it, was now only singular in the degree of its unimportance – most of all to himself.

Sundays were the worst. Dragging by, each minute seeming separate and endless in itself. With Noel shadowing him constantly, following him from room to room, slipping in between the sheets beside him. He had tried blocking him out with a combination of whiskey and sleeping pills, but even in a drugged stupor, just before his eyelids finally surrendered, that familiar scent of his twin drifted up from the pillow.

Brian understood where Noel was taking him – and he did not want to go there. But the memories were so vivid now: he could smell the sea beyond the cliff's edge, and sometimes he could reach out and touch the contours of his brother's face . . .

No. It was still a box. Just a box which had fallen. Brian stood again, withdrawing his outstretched, quivering fingers. He ran to the front door, grabbing at car keys on the hall table. A sheen of sweat along his brow. As he turned the car in the middle of the road, he wondered why he was turning. Did the car know where it was going? He wished that he had spent every waking moment of his adult life revelling in the absence of pain, when he had had the chance. Just as he used to do when he suffered toothache as a child.

The car was going to Golders Green. Brian decided to go with it. There would be people there on a Sunday, shops open, signs of life on the streets. An illusion of normality he might enjoy for a few hours.

He parked up and bought a newspaper because he figured that might look good in the act. He ordered a cream cheese bagel and black coffee and passed a couple of hours quite adequately until the café owner began to cast him dirty looks as bodies milled in for lunch. Brian paid the bill and left. He wandered up the high street, then back down again, until he found another café with a window seat where he ordered more coffee, and watched bodies pass by over the rim of his unread newspaper. But the sense of reality he had hoped for, of himself, somewhere, doing something, eluded him. He gazed out through the eyes of a stranger. Said 'sorry' to the table leg when his foot jarred against it. 'Sorry' to the spoon which shook in his hand scattering grains of sugar on the ground. Caffeine jitters.

By late afternoon, he was ready to give up on the experiment. Time to go home. Noel would be waiting for him. He wandered for another while, standing by shop windows with his eyes widened and unblinking. Bodies brushed against him. He knew that they knew. A couple of times he thought he could hear them whispering. They were probably pointing at him, behind his back. 'Yes?' He turned and stared defiantly at an elderly Jewish woman who had stopped to look at something in the shop's other window. She remained nonplussed, just a shrug of her shoulders and she walked on.

On his way back to the car, he passed a shop selling bathroom fixtures. He went inside. And passed another half-hour staring at bidets and sinks, toilet bowls and baths. An assistant persisted in offering help. He did not require help, he tried to get through to her, he was just looking. For now. Thanks anyway. She stood in the corner, having a word with her boss.

Noel laughed. He tugged at Brian's hand. 'C'mon, come o'on,' he said. Urging Brian out into the schoolyard for first play.

'I'll be there in a sec,' Brian called after him.

'We'll be right here, if you need us,' the assistant's boss said.

'That's an amazing display you've got,' Brian said, wandering past one wall of the shop which was entirely devoted to flush handles. Wood, brass, wrought iron, ceramic numbers with flower motifs – if you couldn't find a flush handle to suit here, Brian thought, you wouldn't find it anywhere.

'Thank you,' the boss replied. Brian turned to look at him. For what? he thought.

In the very back of the shop was the Taj Mahal of bathroom suites: cream glazed with faux crackling and a cascade of small, blue, perfectly rendered flowers descending down the funnel of the toilet bowl. Brian was transfixed. It seemed to him that he had never seen a blue quite so – blue – before. The colour fizzed before his eyes. This was no ordinary urinal, this was a shrine. He placed an order at the front desk, giving his name and address and a date for delivery. The assistant looked to her boss again. He mouthed something and she asked for a deposit, tapping a pencil against her pursed mouth as she watched Brian go through his pockets looking for his wallet. But he had only a handful of coins and a five-pound note on him. He apologized profusely and offered the fiver. The boss carefully furled the note into a tight scroll, placed it inside Brian's pocket and showed him to the door.

'Not like that, ya eedjit,' Brian said, grabbing Cathal's

hurley from Noel. 'Give it a fierce swing with your shoulders ... like this ... like this ... Are you watching ...?'

The car headed home, taking Brian with it. Noel and Cathal argued the whole time in the back, about whether or not Cathal had told Noel that he could have a loan of the hurley for one full day or just the morning. Noel had sobs in his voice and that maddened Brian.

'Stop it, the pair of ye. Noel, give him back his ould hurley ... D'you hear me?'

Brian stretched out on Sam's bed. A soft August wind breathed through the window, drying the sweat on his temples. He longed for a cool white hand on his forehead, remembering a scorch-aired afternoon when he lay martyred to chicken pox, glassy pustules itching so badly that he had wanted to rip the skin open with his fingernails. His mother's crenellated forehead hovering just above him, her hot, liquefied stare under weary triangular eyeflaps, the curve of her back, stooped from her morning's labours, yet no urgency in the cooling to and fro of her hand as it swept over his sticky brow. Her generously given time, a commodity she possessed in scant amount. Nothing to make him feel guilty. She had held his hand then and urged him to sleep and he had closed his eyes, to please her, but his nostrils had flared, breathing her in, before she had left the room. So that all day, throughout the heat and the unconscionable itching, the scent of her had remained with him.

'Come on, come o-on,' Noel shouted.

Sam smiled down from the photographs all around. The years ticked off by gaps in his teeth. Brian had held him before Julia even. She was turned to the side puking into a basin when they had delivered this enraged, wrinkled thing, vomited forth quite literally into his waiting arms. Brian's

221

eyes had travelled the world in eighty seconds of fingertips, dark matted hair, gossamer toenails – until they had lifted the squalling creature from his embrace.

Not love; no, not that word instantly – more a recondite, half-formed wish that a bull elephant would storm the delivery room so that Brian might fell him with one judicious blow. Not love – but a heady, dazzling precognition of the love that was to come. Then, Julia's hands were flapping in front of her body retches. She had wanted her son.

He swigged from the bottle of whiskey in the bathroom. Gulped down the first handful. Kept on swigging, kept on gulping. Evening shadow along his jaw as if his face had been dipped in ashes. Loose bags of crepuscular flesh under his eyes. He wondered if he should leave a note for Julia. Or someone. Saying what, though? Sorry and goodbye . . . Goodbye and sorry . . . The tune of his life. He felt that he was a cold comfort acquaintance of eternity already: the beaded, intransigent hours of a Sunday afternoon. What odds – a change of scenery. The face in the mirror looked like some battered nomadic tent. Thought: I could do with the sleep anyway.

It took longer than he would have expected, that first blurring of the edges. Time enough for Noel to get to him. He saw the outstretched hands, the closed eyes, the tremble in the thin legs as they made for that place where his twin was crouching. Cathal was calling something to their father. Jeremiah's long shadow draped over both sons, encompassing them both in its cast. Brian shut his own eyes. Waiting for the kick.

'Put out the leg. Put out the leg,' Jeremiah urged.

A final, fleeting touch of toes stubbing against his extended calf. The last time he would feel his brother's skin next to his own. Head down in the grass, ears burning with Noel's scream as he crashed through the loosened stakes. Barbed wire whipping freely in the air. The aftersilence like a death. Until Cathal lifted him to his feet, making little gagging sounds at the back of his throat. Brian turned. He was swaying. Jeremiah stood rock-still gazing over the cliff's edge. Then he raised his head and turned his profile to the distant horizon. Brian waited for him to say that it was all right. Noel was alive. Injured but alive. But when Jeremiah finally turned to face them, Brian moaned and fell to his knees. He was sure that he could see the image of Noel dashed out on the rocks still etched on his father's black pupils.

He staggered from the bathroom, managing to make it to Sam's bed. 'Put out the leg' ringing in his ears like a childhood air, only half forgotten, half submerged – a key note of the refrain remembered and the rest followed, the words falling into place. But adulthood gave sinister meanings to simple nursery rhymes. Ring-a-ring-a-rosary was about the plague – we all fall down – not families huddled together praying around the fire hearth as Brian had discovered. Just as his father had meant for Noel to put out the leg, not him. The moment had been Noel's, and that was the least that Brian had taken from him. A tinny laugh. Fundamentally apposite really, that it should have been blue flowers in a toilet bowl that had done for himself in the end.

'How can you live?' Julia's words, the last time they were together. But even then, when she'd turned to him with such horror in her eyes, Brian had felt the memory of love between them. Perhaps they would have parted in the years to come, in any case. Certainly that would have been at Julia's instigation, not his. For now, he could only harbour the remotest hope that when he left, he would take some of her pain with him.

223

He felt Noel's hand wrap around his. The gentle persuasiveness of his touch. He felt the great weight of his father's forgiveness wing by – beyond his reach to the bitter end. He wondered vaguely if there were words he should be uttering, something profound he should be saying as he bade his leave of the world. But none came to mind. His eyelids sagged heavily. He thought of Julia again and remembered the only word, the only word in his life worth saying. A last look up at Sam's glow-in-the-dark stars pinned to the ceiling. Pink and green. So he said 'sorry' to them instead. Then closed his eyes and hovered above himself for a moment, real at last, as his lips curved into a smile.

# THIRTEEN

# The Boy in the Moon

Jeremiah had cycled to Sunday morning mass. Before she heard the definitive slam of the door behind him, Julia had listened to the grunts downstairs between father and son which passed for conversation. She was reluctant to face Edward, the passage of a night having erected a barrier of acute embarrassment that she knew he must be experiencing too. She had heard the zip of his bag earlier, in preparation for departure, and she understood that he was waiting downstairs to say goodbye. A shaft of sunlight surrounded the spaceship in the corner, holding it in a halo for several moments. Julia's eyes had clouded over, but she was smiling – a hand flying up to check her lips. Yes. She saw his tousled head bent over the box, panting with impatience as he pulled at string and cardboard. The prolonged 'co-ool' when he lifted the spaceship up, immediately rifling through the box for instructions to see what it could 'do'. Sam liked things to do something. Fire a missile, make a noise, flash a light – otherwise it was just a toy. There had to be bits: bits you could add and bits you could take away. The spaceship had lots of them. She had raised her eyebrows then, wanting a little more than 'cool'. He understood, giving her the thumbs up. 'Well cool,' he'd said. The ultimate accolade. They had spent the rest of the afternoon stretched out on the living-room floor together, adding bits, taking them away, as she stroked his hair and wondered at his wonder.

She sat up, leaning forward on the side of the bed, catching her face in her hands with a groan. If Edward left without saying goodbye, she would feel wretched. If she had to endure another goodbye in her life, she would feel equally wretched. Her hand was on the doorknob when Edward knocked lightly.

He was standing there, studying his shoes, when she opened it with a reluctant grimace. Twenty-four hours earlier, they had clung to one another so intimately; now they could barely sustain a look.

'I wondered if you were all right. It's n-not like you to be so late,' he said shyly.

'I was just – I was just about to . . .' Julia's voice trailed off. She shrugged helplessly. She thought if the word 'sheep-ish' had not been invented, it would be invented now, to describe their expressions, their stilted body language. 'Oh God,' she cried, laughing suddenly at the preposterousness of it all.

Edward bit his lower lip. He looked as if he were about to crack some joke, then thought better of it. 'Look – I'll be going . . .' He moved toward her, head craning forward to kiss her cheek, one hand extended as if to shake hers – not knowing quite what was appropriate. Julia grabbed his hand and pulled him into the room.

'Please, won't you sit for a second, Edward.' She indicated the bed. 'I want to tell you something.'

'If you're w-worried about . . . about . . .'

'Yesterday?' She sat down beside him, reaching for his hand. 'No. I'm not going to deliver some spiel about guilt and my state of mind at the time and so on . . .'

He looked relieved.

'I'm not sorry,' she continued firmly, 'and I'm not going to be sorry in the future either. Maybe you will . . . ?'

'No,' he lied.

Julia squeezed his hand. 'Look, I don't know if this is inappropriate or not, but all night, I just lay there – thinking . . .'

'Me too.'

'And – Oh, I'm not sure if this is the right time . . .'

'G-go on.'

'Edward.' A pause. Would he understand? Deep breath. 'Edward – I miss Brian in my life.' She waited, holding the breath, to see if he interpreted her words as hurtful but he was motioning her on, something in his eyes making her think that she might be saying the right thing, or something like it. 'In some respects it feels as if I've lost both of them. And yes, in the beginning I did wish Brian dead too. But I feel like I owe – like I owe Sam more than this. The least he deserves is his parents' honest grief.' She looked away, clamping her lips together for a moment before continuing. 'And I can't do that until I resolve things in some way between Brian and myself. Yesterday . . . It was as if . . . I mean . . . What I mean is . . . Oh, I don't know what I mean –' She broke off and studied her twisting fingers.

'Yes, you do,' he said quietly. 'S-say it.'

'I don't know if I'll ever forgive him.' She stopped to reflect. 'No, that's not true either – I know that I won't ever forgive him. Part of me will always have this rage – this incredible hate toward him. But yesterday I realized that a part of me will always love him too. The part of him that made Sam. You gave me that . . . So, last night, lying there, I decided . . .'

'T-take him back, Julia.'

227

Her mouth opened in surprise. 'You think that too?' she asked. So ineffably simple, the way he said it.

A sad, crooked smile played on his lips. He nodded. 'F-for a moment there, yesterday, I'll admit . . .' He turned away, ashamed. 'I'll admit that I w-was playing out a little scene in my head: you and me, you know? B-but I knew straight away. I knew what was happening. I might st-stutter but I'm not a fool, Julia . . .' The long fingers trailed down her cheek. 'You love him. P-people can't always explain the reasons why they love. They just do. That's all. Christ, Brian always loved the old m-man and look where that got him . . .'

'How do you mean?'

'I'm not sure what I m-mean,' he said soberly, 'just – that's the way it is. We can't always explain . . . Friends, right?' He extended a formal hand like a schoolboy. She felt a cheat, shaking the hand, a fixed grin on her face like a gargoyle. Because he had just told her that he loved her. She wondered for how long.

'Edward . . . ?'

'No. There's n-no need, really,' he said, a finger pushing back his spectacles. His gaze was deadly earnest when he looked at her. 'I want you to – you know – you and B-Brian . . . I want you to be together. For Sam too,' he added. And she believed him.

Julia exhaled a huge sigh of relief. The complicated stuff of adulthood, so simply handled by children. I wuv you. I wuv you too. Night night. She would call Brian from Anne and Cathal's shop, not tomorrow perhaps, but later in the week. The prospect of hearing his voice at the other end of a mouthpiece, a sea in between, sending a thrill rushing through her veins. Yesterday, something to hold on to; today, something to look forward to.

Edward was about to leave when she remembered something else she had meant to say to him. 'Edward, I lied to you that night when you caught me in your mother's room. I'm sorry. There *are* photographs of your family, and a journal she kept too.'

Edward frowned, trying to remember. 'A journal you say?'

'Yes.' She led him by the hand toward the room. 'You should have it.'

Edward followed her through, his eyes gazing trance-like around the room. 'Hard to b-believe really,' he said, 'but I haven't stood in this room since the day they buried her. I d-doubt if any of us . . . except for himself maybe.'

'Did he actually forbid it?'

'Nah.' He pulled a face, smoothing a hand over the threadbare candlewick bedcover. 'Not in so many words. We j-just knew.'

Julia nodded. She had seen for herself how Jeremiah could make it perfectly clear what he wanted and what he did not want, without ever having to use the words to convey his message. 'Didn't you ever wonder why he' – a thought struck her – 'or was that the custom at the time – to vacate the marital bed?'

'Not a c-custom I've ever heard of.' He smiled wryly at her choice of phrase. 'That was j-just Jeremiah for you – hard as granite, making the big show when she was dead, like he d-didn't half kill her from the work in the f-first place. I don't remember any big gestures when she was alive, though. Nor ever a kind word. She had a miserable enough old life, the p-poor bitch,' he exclaimed angrily. 'I'm glad you got something to grow in her bit of garden. I'm really g-glad about that.'

'So am I,' Julia said quietly.

She pulled at the bottom drawer in the chest, offering him the shoebox of photographs. Edward eagerly wiped his spectacles and sat cross-legged to study them, a broad smile on his face as he held each one up to the light.

'Me,' he said, entranced by his own skinny image. 'God, I haven't changed that much.'

'Look,' Julia said, 'she's written all your names on the back.'

Edward turned them over, one by one. 'Such neat handwriting,' he wondered aloud.

'Wait until you read her journal.' Julia reached for it, flicking through the pages with her thumb. 'You won't believe how meticulous she was.'

He looked reverentially at the book, almost as though he were afraid to touch it. Julia automatically flicked to the last page she'd read, over a fortnight ago.

'Look,' she said, 'see how she lists everything, even every – what do you call it – of the rosary?'

'Decade,' he said softly.

Julia frowned. She was just about to hand it over when the passage about Noel's punishing night by the shed wall caught her eye. She still didn't know what heinous crime he had committed, so she read on, the frown deepening on her forehead.

'What is it?' Edward asked.

'Just a sec . . . Just a . . . She goes on here about saving the hay – and some dreadful fight between Brian and Noel.'

'That would be the day that Noel . . . Here, show me.' He reached for the book but something else caught his attention and he held a photograph up to the light of the window, as Julia rapidly read on, her eyes squinting at the tiny text.

She didn't want to stop, but Edward thrust the photograph

230

on top of the page. It was the strange tableau of Jeremiah, Brian, Cathal and Noel. The one which had troubled her for some reason before.

'Look at that,' Edward said. His eyes held a peculiar gleam.

'Yes, I know,' Julia said, 'I thought there was something funny about that one too, but I couldn't quite put my finger on it.'

'Turn it over.' He stabbed excitedly at the inscription.

Julia read. Her mouth opened. She wondered how it had slipped by her before. 'She's written "Jeremiah and *sons*".' She eagerly turned the photograph around again. There was something vaguely proprietorial in the way Jeremiah's hand lightly grazed the top of Cathal's shoulder. 'Jeremiah and sons,' she repeated to herself, her gaze returning to the journal again. 'You didn't miss a trick after all, did you, Margaret?'

Edward emitted a low whistle. 'Oh, she knew all right,' he said with a hint of triumph. 'And that was her way of telling him that she knew . . . Christ he'd have hated that.' He looked curiously at Julia. She was reading at a furious pace, her mouth working silently, unconsciously repeating the text. 'What is it? What's the matter?'

She raised a hand for a moment, to stay him as she read the last few lines. Her head lifted slowly. Her mouth opened but she couldn't speak. Edward followed her horrified gaze down to the page again. 'Oh, my God.' Her hands were trembling as she tried to signal him toward a passage. Edward craned forward. But he didn't get a chance to read.

They heard the first creak on the stairs too late to shove the boxes back into the drawer. Julia felt Edward's body stiffen into a poker, sensed the rising of the tiny hairs on the back of his neck. She couldn't move herself; her body listed sideways in shock. Edward scrambled to his feet just as Jeremiah filled the doorway. Julia began to cram the photographs into the drawer, but they spilled from her hands and scattered all over the floor.

Jeremiah was quivering with indignation. His outraged gaze encompassing both trespassers. His lower lip was flecked with spittle, he could hardly speak. 'Get out!' he roared. The sound ricocheting around the small room, filling Julia's ears – she had time to wonder at the terror that sound must have instilled in the small ears of children – before Jeremiah advanced on Edward with his fist raised.

'Don't you da-are . . .' Edward warned, taking a step back.

Jeremiah's reddened face twisted with fury at the sound of Edward's voice. His jaw clenched. The fist made a wide arc before slamming into Edward's cheek, sending his spectacles flying across the room. The glass splintered into tiny shards by the wall. Julia cried out and jumped up to get between them but it was too late. Edward's fury matched his father's. He caught Jeremiah by the collar, pinning him against the doorframe. Their faces pushed together.

'You'll never lay a hand on me again,' Edward hissed.

'I told ye keep out of this room,' Jeremiah spat back, undaunted by his son's outrage. 'You have no respect, boy. No respect for your mother's memory . . . Going through her belongings like that, with a stranger.' He managed to swing another fist into Edward's cheek but their closeness rendered it impotent.

'I gave you fair warning,' Edward said, his voice dangerously calm.

'Edward . . .' Julia reached toward the hands restraining Jeremiah.

As if the sound of her voice ejected him from another time,

Edward took a deep breath, visibly trying to calm himself. He released Jeremiah's collar, casting him a final look of untempered hatred as he made to go through the doorway. Jeremiah snarled, a dreadful, primal sound as he thrust out his leg, forcing Edward into a trip, but he just managed to right himself on the top steps. Turning quickly, he hurled himself at Jeremiah in a blind fury. Julia realized there was no interceding now; she stumbled backwards, out of their way. Edward had waited a lifetime for this moment.

He had his hands in a tight vice around Jeremiah's neck. Squeezing so hard, Jeremiah's eyes were beginning to bulge. Julia could hear the wheeze of his breath, what he could catch of it. The years of pent-up anger and frustration were so clearly etched on Edward's transformed features, she thought he must be fighting for every one of his siblings. He released Jeremiah's throat, smashing his fist into the side of his head which hit against the wall with a sickening crack.

'You fucking hypocrite . . . You're a sick, sick bastard . . .' Edward was punctuating every expletive with another crunch of his fist into the side of Jeremiah's head.

'Jesus,' Julia whispered. She thought that Edward would almost certainly kill his father. But she couldn't get near them. It was as if their rage had formed an invisible barrier around them; like two dogs fighting, there was nowhere safe to place a restraining hand.

She heard Cathal's voice calling up the stairs. 'Cathal,' she screamed, just as Edward and Jeremiah tore at one another's throats in the doorway again. Nails gouging red rivers along their necks. Their eyes clashed together in a locked battle which could not end until one of them was bested. For the first time, Julia saw the man his children knew, and it was a frightening vision. Still full of his own righteousness, his incredible sense of self, but older now and weaker, and as enraged by that weakness as he was by Edward's flailing fists. She saw too, the man whom Margaret had known, and obeyed, and hated.

'Jesus Christ Almighty.' She could hear Cathal halfway up the stairs, just as Edward managed to get a full swing at Jeremiah's left temple, forcing him to stagger backwards until his feet teetered on the first step. There was something almost comical about the rigid set of the outthrust jaw, hands clawing air madly in front of him, determined to get at Edward, instead of reaching for the wall to steady himself. Jeremiah went down with one head over heels just by Cathal's feet, a thrust of his shoulders sending the banister rail crashing with him.

Edward stood, legs trembling, in the landing. He bawled after Jeremiah. Julia crept up behind him with her hand to her mouth. Edward and Cathal's eyes were locked together for a moment. Cathal's ashen face, slowly turning to review the collapsed heap of Jeremiah's body. 'Jesus Christ, you've him killt,' he said.

Edward was shaking so badly, Julia could hear the chatter of his teeth. 'I hope so,' he managed.

Cathal jumped down, checking Jeremiah for signs of life. Julia was struck by the way he cradled the big head in his hands.

'He's breathing,' he shouted.

'Oh, he'll live all right,' Edward said, descending slowly, his hand feeling the wall for support. 'His own venom will keep him alive.'

Jeremiah was groaning now. Trying to lift his head from the cradle of Cathal's hands. He flexed his limbs, as if checking them in turn. Julia saw that Edward was right, for albeit

234

bruised and shaken, with maybe a broken bone or two, the malicious cast of his father's eyes at Edward's approach, signalled life yet. Jeremiah would survive.

'Are you mental?' Cathal reached for Edward's leg. 'Your own father?'

Edward stopped on the last stair tread. He held Cathal's upturned gaze. 'Better to you than he ever was to any of us, maybe,' he enunciated slowly. Julia sat on the top step, her hands clutching her face to stop the shaking of her head. Edward slowly turned to look up at her. 'K-keeping you here, Julia – it's not kindness that makes him do it. He's scared. That's what it is. He's trying to make amends n-now that he knows he's mortal after all . . . Just one word of regret or remorse in all these years, and I'd . . .' He turned to Cathal. 'I waited. I k-kept coming here, in the hope . . .' His mouth curled down as he looked at Jeremiah who remained in his supine position, staring balefully back at his son. 'That just the once, one time, you'd say sorry, for all the beatings, all the humiliations.' Edward was addressing him directly. He shook his head sadly. 'But no. You'll be a liar and a hypocrite to the b-bitter end, won't you?' He looked at Cathal again, a mixture of anger and exasperated fondness in his eyes. 'And you'll still b-be here, Cathal, making a big man of him, c-covering up for him.' He bent down to whisper loudly in Jeremiah's ear. 'You never so much as let us grieve our own b-brother . . . her son . . . because you were even b-bigger than that, weren't you?'

Julia's eye was caught by the way Cathal's face had crumpled at the allusion to Noel. He bit into his lower lip, turning from Jeremiah, his glittering eyes travelling up the wall until they rested momentarily on Julia's face. Then he hastily lowered his gaze again, murmuring to Jeremiah, but not before she'd seen some ghostly spectre residing in the pupils. His shoulders quivered now almost femininely – an absurd contrast to his stocky bulk. As if his body was buckling under the weight of some dark secret, undivulged even to himself. He pressed Jeremiah's head closer to his chest, rocking gently – perhaps rocking his own disturbed thoughts away.

'Cathal . . . ?' she whispered hoarsely.

He ignored her. Edward was rising, the back of his hand smearing a long streak of blood along his cheek. Jeremiah glared defiantly up at him. 'Get out,' he choked.

'Whisht now, don't –' Cathal intervened.

'You were always – useless. Look at you. You can't even talk.' Jeremiah spat up at Edward, trying to manoeuvre his body upright, but he collapsed again, a long groan tearing reluctantly from his bloodied lips. He swallowed and spat to the side. 'Useless,' he added bitterly.

Edward hunkered down again, his eyes flashing with tiny electrical sparks. 'Like Noel was useless,' he hissed. Jeremiah pursed his lips and held the gaze. Edward's face twisted. 'Who couldn't keep his land, hmm? The next time you talk about useless, you th-think about that.'

Jeremiah opened his mouth to respond, thought better of it and motioned to Cathal to help him up. Edward reached for his bag by the door. 'I hope you rot in hell, you miserable bastard,' he said over his shoulder. The slam of the door cut into the ensuing silence.

Julia drew her hands down along her face. She felt as if the walls around her were bleeding violence. The stench of it, rank in her nostrils. It felt as if some already crumbling plaster had been clawed away from those walls, to reveal a brooding, malevolent presence in this house. As if Edward had ripped up floorboards, torn down the screens which kept the thing itself at bay, and now it trickled in making an insidious approach. She could see that Cathal was likewise aware that something had changed irrevocably. She watched him half drag, half lift Jeremiah toward his sterile, holy cot in the back kitchen, his face contorting with that silent, hopeless love of tormented children, more anxious to love than to be loved. Because above all else, children wanted adults to be right – it lay somewhere in their simple view of the symmetry of things. Maybe Sam too had joined their ghostly ranks in the kitchen.

Her arms stretched out, as if he were this very moment falling from her. Finally permitting herself that most dreaded speculation: what were his final thoughts? Did he really understand what was happening or was his mind a blur of fear and confusion? Was there time to blame them as he hurtled backwards? Those shocked, unblinking eyes, holding hers – saying goodbye perhaps, or wondering if his turn had come round to be the screaming boy in the moon.

She ran down the stairs, clutching blindly at the wall for support. Edward was revving the car engine in the yard, fixing his spare set of spectacles into place. He tried a watery smile. She stumbled toward him and reached out to embrace his shoulders through the open car window. 'I'm sorry,' she gasped, 'that was all my fault. I should never have –'

'Oh, that was a long t-time coming.' He smiled, then a frown creased his forehead.

'Edward, I –'

'Julia,' he interrupted firmly, 'I don't want to know what you read up there. If B-Brian was responsible for –' He broke off with a shrug. 'Well, I just d-don't want to know, is all. You keep her book. It's yours now.'

'But . . .' Julia began, then she allowed her voice to trail away. Perhaps Edward was right in some respects, but he was wrong about the book. It should belong to Brian now. Her fingers tightened on his arm.

'Call Brian,' he said tersely, his fingers gently loosening her grip.

'Oh, Edward . . .'

'And get out of there,' he urged, 'you've b-been hurt enough by this – this' – he stopped to look around him, encompassing the house and its history with a sweep of his hand – 'madness. That's what I see, when I look at him.' He indicated Jeremiah within. 'He's – Well, let's just say he's left a fair few scars.' A little sad smile played on his lips at Julia's confusion. He tapped her hand. 'B-Because you can't always be right, unless you g-go a little mad . . .' His hand turned the ignition. Eyes already fixed on the distance ahead. Julia leaned forward and kissed the top of his head.

'You won't . . . ?'

'Not until he's in a b-box.' His eyes crinkled mischievously. 'The sooner the b-better . . . And Julia . . . ?'

She was stepping back from the car. 'What?'

'I wish – you know, you and Brian . . . I have hopes for the both of ye . . .'

Julia nodded. Her hand curled into a limp wave as he drove away. Leaving his own ghosts behind him perhaps. She fervently hoped so. Hers had yet to be faced, because now she fully understood that she could not meet Brian without saying goodbye to Sam. And her heart ached to be with Brian, to rest her head on his shoulder for just one brief, silent moment – before they had to speak the useless words – when she could feel part of a family once more.

Because that was what he had given her, she realized: an end to the isolation years.

Cathal's pinched face loomed in the doorway.

'How is he?' she asked.

'Not too good.' He avoided her eyes. She wanted to question him about that look on his face earlier but she let it pass. A hand raked through his hair. 'I'd better get a doctor to him,' he said, striding past her up the road.

Julia broke into a run after him, about to offer her car. He understood, but waved her back. 'No, no.' He looked distracted. 'Just go and sit with him. I'll be along soon. Just sit with him . . .'

Julia acceded to the pleading quality in his voice. She turned and stepped inside. As she moved across the kitchen, she could feel the violent past still pulsing along the walls. A thought struck her forcefully – perhaps without Sam to glue them together, it might be Brian who had no need of *her* any more.

She stood outside the door to the back kitchen. Loath to go in, wanting to remember Jeremiah as the harsh sanctuary she had run toward. The man who had asked no questions when she had needed that. Instead her mind could only conjure visions of his face twisting with a rabid hatred as he tried to send Edward tumbling down the stairs instead of himself. She wondered how many times Brian had had to endure the weight of that look. And a faint smile curved on her lips at the memory of Brian's vague, easygoing smile. The one which had incensed her above all else. She longed to see it now. The smile on her own lips quickly faded as a faint cough from the other side of the door brought her back to the present. For a moment she wished so fervently that the man within would die right now, right this minute, that she half expected to see a corpse when she pushed the door through. But he was alive all right, blue eyes glinting accusingly as she stepped in.

'Fetch me water,' he rasped.

'Sure,' she said in as equable a voice as she could muster. 'But first – I have something to show you.'

# FOURTEEN

# The Unfit

Dog burst through the kitchen door, rubbing against her heels, when she came downstairs clutching Margaret's journal to her chest. She noticed the telltale marks on his hind legs – he had been attacked in the middle of the night again.

'Here, boy,' she called, stroking his head. 'Sorry, I didn't hear a thing.'

Jeremiah had fallen into a fitful sleep when she returned to him. Aftershock, she supposed. Her hand tightened around the diary. It would have to wait. He moaned aloud. She filled a tin mug with water and reached down to lift his head, putting the rim to his lips. The water trickled from the corners of his mouth. She feared that he was unconscious and stepped back to wait for Cathal and the doctor.

She was deeply engrossed in Margaret's words, rehashing the same lines over and over again in her mind, when they arrived. She hastily shoved the book into her pocket. Cathal paced uneasily in the kitchen while the elderly doctor checked on Jeremiah within. Try as she might, Julia could not get Cathal to make eye contact with her. She opened her mouth to say something but the doctor came out to them.

Cathal ran over. 'What's the story, doctor?' he asked.

'Fractured hip, I'd say, cuts and bruises. He's a bit shocked in himself. What happened at all?'

'A fall,' Cathal said quickly. 'Down the stairs.'

'Oh now.' The man clicked his tongue. 'That's what does for us at our age.'

Julia had to suppress a smile. The doctor looked even older than Jeremiah. A small wizened creature with enormous protruding teeth and bi-focals giving his eyes an owlish quality.

'Hospital, d'you think?' Cathal was asking anxiously.

'Yerra – if he'll go,' the doctor said, turning to Julia. 'Is that water? I'll have a sup if you don't mind.'

She handed him the mug.

'Should he go?' Cathal insisted. He received another shrug for his pains.

'I suppose he should . . . But I can tell you now that he won't.'

'Did you ask him?' Cathal was shifting from foot to foot impatiently.

'Sure how could I ask him, when he's not conscious?' A hint of rebuke in the voice.

Julia understood then, what Cathal patently could not. Jeremiah was dying. And he would not thank them for removing him to the sterile confines of a hospital.

'Cathal . . . ?' she said quietly, trying to force him to look at her, but he was pinching the bridge of his nose, eyes firmly pinned to the ground.

'Haven't you something we could give him?' Cathal demanded.

The doctor rummaged around in his black valise. 'A couple of aspirins so, if it makes yourself feel better.' He headed for the door. 'Won't do him any harm. I'll drop in again later tonight.'

When he had gone, the ticking of the grandfather clock

cut into the silence. Cathal hung his head for a while. Julia approached, about to extend her hand when he swung around quickly. 'I'd better do the bleddy cow for him,' he said, marching out to the yard, shoulders up around his ears.

Julia stared helplessly after him. They both knew that Jeremiah would have milked the cow long since. She opened the door to the back kitchen, looking down at the supine figure, twisted at what seemed an awkward angle along the mat. His face was a white mask; she thought she could hear the gums grinding together. Ting ting, time's up. Come in, Jeremiah. Maybe he had thought that he could live for ever.

'She never forgave you,' she said softly.

He slipped in and out of consciousness for the remainder of the day. Eyelids flickering as both Cathal and Julia took it in turns to put the mug to his lips. Once, his eyes opened fully and Julia thought that he could see her, but he was staring over her shoulder, and then the lids battened down again.

The doctor returned later that night and helped Cathal to change Jeremiah's soiled underclothes. He quietly told Julia that he thought Jeremiah might have suffered a stroke, but if he passed through the night, he might just linger on for a while yet.

Cathal insisted on spending the night by his side. Julia could not prevail on him to let her take a turn. Anne arrived some time before midnight. By then, Julia was practically asleep on her feet, hauling at pieces of the broken banister rail, trying to put them out of the way.

'Here, let me do that.' Anne firmly pushed her aside. 'How is he anyway?' She indicated the closed door.

'No change as far as I can make out,' Julia responded wearily. 'Cathal's in there with him.'

'Now tell me something I don't know.' Anne's mouth twisted to the side. She surveyed the wrecked banister with a low whistle. 'What in the name of God happened here? All I know is Cathal came thundering into the house earlier, called the doctor and ran off again . . . I had to do the cows and everything else myself – that's what took me so long.'

'Jeremiah and Edward had a fight. Jeremiah fell downstairs.' Julia could feel herself listing to the side. The events of the fraught afternoon were finally taking their toll.

'Are you all right?' Anne reached out. 'Jesus, you look shattered.' She grabbed at a chair. 'Here, sit down a minute. Draw your breath.' Another softly exhaled hiss as she flung a lump of wood into the empty hearth. 'Pssh – some fight, eh? What brought that on?'

Julia's head had lolled on to her chest. She tried to lift it to explain to Anne. But Anne gently pressed it forward again, she drew up another chair and placed Julia's legs on it. Then she draped one of the crocheted blankets over her. 'Shh, it's all right,' she urged. 'You can fill me in tomorrow. Sleep now. Go on.'

Julia wanted to tell Anne about the diary. She wanted to tell her that things didn't always make sense in the end, that justice didn't necessarily prevail, that remorse and forgiveness didn't have to go hand in hand. That love didn't conquer everything, that every silver lining had a cloud and that time didn't wound all heels. She wanted to say that the stars in the night sky might be there for no other reason than that they were there. As Sam had been there. Until one morning, suddenly, he was gone. Air closing around the space he had occupied. But sleep got in the way. All she could drowsily manage: 'I'm going back to Brian, Anne.' She just registered Anne's pleased response before the first rumbling snore.

She awoke at just past dawn. Staring blearily around for a second, trying to get her bearings. Then she remembered. Her body felt stiff, an ache deep within her bones. Bladder at bursting point, too. No sign of Anne. She tiptoed to the back kitchen. Cathal was curled up in a ball beside Jeremiah. For a moment she thought that Jeremiah was no longer breathing. She crouched down closer. But she could hear the grinding gums.

Cathal sat up suddenly. 'What? What?' He took a while to focus then turned to Jeremiah immediately. Julia could hear his sigh of relief.

'I have to use the . . .' She indicated the little cubicle toilet.

'Oh, right.' He jumped to his feet.

'You don't have to . . .' Julia began, but he was already through the door.

When she returned to the kitchen, Cathal was pacing again. 'He ought to be in a hospital,' he said.

'We could call an ambulance,' she suggested.

He stared blankly at her, digesting that. 'We could, aye,' he agreed. Then his face puckered up with worry. 'Would he be furious, d'you think?'

'Don't ask me,' Julia said, genuinely surprised. 'How the hell should I know?'

His long strides covered the room in seconds. Wall to wall, back again. 'I thought maybe you had some sort of, like – understanding, like. Of him, is what I mean. Or with him . . . I don't know what I'm saying.' He stopped and gave her a penetrating stare. 'Look it, should we be doing something?'

'Why should you think I had some sort of understanding with Jeremiah?' Julia persisted.

'I don't know.' He shrugged again. She knew that he was

trying to convey an intuitive feeling on his part, but that sort of language was alien to Cathal. She felt sorry for him, realizing for the first time how deeply he had felt supplanted. Moreover, she saw too that Jeremiah had enjoyed taunting him on occasion. 'She've it done already', when Cathal turned up to help with something. Not a whit of gratitude for all the years when there was only Cathal. She felt a bit guilty about that, for not seeing what was happening more clearly. She moved toward him, slowly, because he looked like he wanted to run for the nearest hill.

'For a while there, I admit,' she said softly, 'there was something – almost soothing about being his new "slave" . . .' She took another step when he flinched. 'But that's what it amounts to with Jeremiah, don't you see, Cathal? He doesn't really care about anybody. His wife knew that, but she didn't dare to –' She broke off, realizing that she had gone too far. Cathal wasn't ready to face the truth yet. He still needed someone to look up to, someone to do his thinking for him, so that his vulnerability could be exploited without his ever having to expose the fact that he was vulnerable in the first place. Not too dissimilar to herself, she thought.

He glared at her now with barely concealed animosity.

'Cathal . . . ?'

'I'll be back later. I have to check on things at home.' He turned on his heel, heading for the door. 'Keep an eye out for him,' he added, leaving. The door crashed shut behind him.

Julia sighed heavily. She checked on Jeremiah again. Still breathing, anyway. She stared down at him for a while. He mumbled something then tried to turn in his sleep, but the pain evidently prevented him. A little guttural exhalation.

Some tiny part of her felt sympathetic and she rushed outside to purge herself of that feeling.

She scattered grain for the disgruntled hens, put beets through the mangle and filled the troughs along the ditches with sheep nuts. She fed and milked the goat, leaving the cow for Cathal, swept the yard, plucked snails from the cabbage heads and then stood with her hands on her hips, the dog at her ankles, surveying the ocean below through swollen sleep-deprived eyes. The waters mirrored the placid green of the sky, seagulls circling over a darker patch out to the west. This was her favourite time of the day, when there was an intense stillness to everything, and the light was at its purest, giving the mountains on the other side of the bay a clear pop-up-card definition. She went inside to scour the flagstone floor on her hands and knees with a small bristle-loose brush, because it was her turn to make the butter, and she liked to have the floor clean beneath her feet.

The cream was congealed in a muslin-covered wooden pail – nearly a week old now, a day or two off turning completely. But Jeremiah had explained that it was best a little stale. The smell hummed but not in an acidic way yet.

She scoured a timber barrel and placed it on a wooden pedestal. Into the barrel she poured the glutinous liquid, remembering to add a palmful of salt, then she began the slow, grinding process of turning the handle at the side. She had only made butter three times in all, but already it was getting easier because the muscles around her shoulders and the tops of her arms were bunched and solid from all the beet-mangling.

Roughly half an hour of turning the deep yellow clots as fast as she could twist would do it. The faster the twist, the thicker the butter, Jeremiah had said. Another load of bollocks, she thought now, but she was sweating all the same. He coughed from behind the door; she stopped; but then he snored again, so she allowed him to sleep on.

The handle was beginning to resist her pressure. When most of the cream had solidified into a strong, golden butter, she poured the remaining translucent milk into a large enamel jug. It tasted bitter, but Jeremiah might ask for it later. She placed the golden lumps into flat pans and began to beat them into long rectangles with two wooden, ridged spades until she had a row of gleaming ingots. She scored a bar with her fingernail, tasting the butter – strong, salty, with an unexpected flavour of ground almonds against her tongue.

She went outside, placing the rectangles into the north-facing 'safe', a makeshift cupboard with a fine mesh door to keep flies out. Jeremiah would never keep the butter in the fridge. Then she realized that she was still trying to second-guess him. Still accommodating his every dictate, no matter how absurd. She quickly withdrew the yellow slabs and watched them drop one by one on to a pile of goat shit. The butter would have gone to Anne and Cathal anyway. To be sold, or, more truthfully, not sold in the shop, because everyone was into polyunsaturates these days, Anne had said.

Dog licked his hindquarters then slid between her ankles to enjoy the unexpected feast. She hunkered down to examine the fresh bite marks again. Jeremiah called aloud and she rushed inside.

He was still asleep when she peered through a crack in the door. Perhaps he had been dreaming. Of what? she wondered. There was a faint rattle to his breathing but the up-and-down motion of the chest was regular enough. The large head twisted to the side, his fingers made clawing movements along the stone floor. A line of spittle made a constant stream from the corner of his downturned mouth. No less granite-like in sleep, that fissured face, she thought, criss-cross lines along his cheeks like some parched landscape, eyelids falling in drapes along the sunken sockets. The blue eyes opened suddenly. A moment to focus on his surroundings – then he saw her at the door. Their eyes locked. He made a purse of his mouth, turning it into a grimace as he tried to push himself a little more upright. A hand flapped impatiently, summoning her to him. Julia remained still, with her arms folded, by the door. 'I'll fix you something to eat,' she said coldly, turning.

He called to her several times as she prepared a chicken broth. 'Woman', in a croaky, feeble voice. Maybe he was hallucinating and thought she was Margaret. She wrenched the door open.

'Do you know who I am?'

'I know who you are.' He looked at her the way he had looked at Edward yesterday. Hating her because she had seen that photograph. The one his own pride had forced him to keep. She wondered when he'd come across it himself, how long after Margaret's death – or had Margaret had the gall in the end, when she knew that she was dying, to just leave it casually around one day for him to see? Julia hoped so. 'Do you remember what happened?' she asked.

He tried to spit to the side but it clung to his jaw in a long drool. 'You'd no right,' he muttered.

Julia pulled the diary from her pocket. She waited to see if he would react – but he was staring blankly ahead. 'You never even read it,' she said incredulously. 'Never had the slightest – not one ounce of curiosity . . . She didn't even mean that much to you. Poor Margaret,' she added sadly, pressing the opened pages to her chest. 'She wanted you to know.'

He was looking through her. Not even hearing, Julia suspected. She was no longer of use. She wanted to read aloud to him then, but a deep sadness welled up inside her – almost excruciatingly pleasurable in a confusing way. The feeling was oddly comforting, as if she would be reinvented when it passed. As if she had another emergent self that she had yet to meet.

His eyelids were drawing down again, baggy folds over eyes that had always obeyed him. Seeing only what he wanted to see, reshaping history if needs must, to make the picture conform to his requirements. Looking at others no further than their usefulness. His only conscience to his land, because it was a manifestation of himself – the thing his children should have been. Now she understood those long blank stares of Brian's. It was the unformed part of him. The waiting child. A ghostly presence in his own adult history, because Jeremiah had decreed that his young eyes remain firmly shut to what really happened, one hot August afternoon – the date of which her thumb now covered on Margaret's book.

She read the date aloud, but then her throat constricted. So she left him again.

The broth was simmering on the stove top when she went outside for a breath of air. Her clothes clung rankly to her body, the book in her pocket felt like some sort of outgrowth she had acquired over the past twenty-four hours. The thought of spoonfeeding him sickened her. The intimacy of it. She hadn't heard Cathal's approach and jumped when he asked: 'Did he wake?'

She nodded without turning around.

'When?' Cathal asked quickly. 'Is he lucid?'

'Oh, he's lucid all right.' She headed for the shrubbery, calling over her shoulder, 'I made a chicken broth, if you want to . . .' But the slam of the door signalled that Cathal had already run inside. She spent the next few hours enjoying the calming effect of her garden as she deadheaded her flowers, planted and replanted various shrubs. Dog worked his way in and out through her ankles. She stopped from time to time, staring down past the long uncut grass, almost yellow now, to where the ocean made a narrow black line behind a passing trawler. She thought how she would miss this, the daily panorama – something different, every time she looked.

By late afternoon, Cathal was ready to check on his own place again. He had fed and changed Jeremiah. Julia made no attempt to hide the visible relief on her face. She went inside to have something to eat herself, but first she pressed an ear to his door. He was sleeping again.

She sipped at a bowlful of soup, but she wasn't really hungry. Hours passed as she thought about Brian. About Sam. This was the first time that she had allowed herself to sit so purposelessly since the day she'd arrived, back in May. No books, no chores – nothing to deflect the random thoughts and memories coursing through her head. She covered Sam's lifetime. Inconsequential things coming back to her, things she thought she had long forgotten. Brian carrying his sleeping son from the car, late at night. The flushed, cranky face whining to be let alone. A faint smile curved on her lips: Sam, inconsolable in the bathroom one night, refusing to come out, because Arsenal had lost. She could even see perfectly clearly, in her mind's eye, the text on the ticket to his first match. He had slept with it under

251

his pillow for weeks beforehand. She thought of the space-ship again. How she should have allowed him to take it. There was no reason not to really – she had just been exercising her control.

It was the 'neverness' of death that the mind tried to reject. The finality of his absence. Everything else could be brought back from the brink, so she found herself saying over and over again, no, it can't be true that I will never *ever* see him again. It almost seemed absurd. How could you live for such a short period? What was the point? Then she thought again about the air whooshing shut around his space, the space he should be filling. It would have to be different somehow, she figured, that air – once it had sealed around his shadow. It would have to be touched by him. She thought of Brian, and wished that he was sitting beside her so that they could remember Sam together, keep him alive for a little while longer, before they had to face that neverness. Brian was her last connection to Sam. She wanted to see him so badly she thought that she could close her eyes and conjure him from thin air. But Jeremiah's voice cut into the room instead. He was summoning her again.

'Do you want something for the pain?' she asked from the doorway.

He clicked his tongue impatiently at that, and demanded his rosary beads. She placed them between his fingers, large bead between thumb and forefinger as she had watched him do so many evenings. But now she viewed the performance as a wearied audience might: while the technique was still admirable, the act itself had grown hackneyed. His lips worked soundlessly. The beads clacked on. He dismissed her with his eyes but she lingered a while on the pretext of wiping his brow with a cold flannel. She had to steel herself to touch him. He blinked when she ran the cloth down over his eyes. The first chink – a look of fear when his eyes reopened having been closed against his will. He took a deep breath and prayed on, the jaw jutting out as ever. Julia had a feeling that Jeremiah could even pray God into submission.

In another time and place, Julia figured, Jeremiah might well have stridden in jackboots, past a chanting crowd paying homage to him. Because passionate will was a glamorous, enviable thing to the sometimes weak, who equated it with righteousness.

Out here on the edges of the Atlantic there was no one around to turn that will upon, except for sheep – and family. And behind every strutting peacock was a small brown hen with chicks, a Margaret, busily getting on with things, taking care not to interfere with the pavonine display. Julia wondered if Jeremiah had in truth felt some sense of remorse toward the wife he had literally worked to death. It would account for the fact that he had kept the diary in the first place. Then again, it would be just the sort of thing that Jeremiah would do, sticking her in a drawer like that. The ultimate dismissal – who could possibly want to read her words anyway?

She thought, oh, I'll nurse you all right. Just to read those words to him.

The backyard door crashed open, sounding louder than usual. Julia scrunched up the flannel and left Jeremiah's side to see who it was.

Cathal stood there. He leaned against the doorframe for a moment, to catch his breath, evidently having run the mile and a half.

'What is it?' Julia moved toward him, her head angled to the side, taking in his almost crazy appearance. Wearing his emotions on his face like that, twists and contortions – she almost giggled.

He took a step back, making a halting motion with his hand to indicate that he wished her to retreat also. But she followed him out into the yard. Anne was running down from the top of the road, gazelle legs kicking out at awkward angles.

'Cathal,' Julia demanded, loudly now. 'What?'

'I can't – I can't –' he gasped.

'Take a deep breath,' Julia commanded. She tried to place a hand on his arm but he shrugged her off. His head bent forward, hands resting on his knees as he tried to fill his lungs.

'Jesus, Cathal,' Julia half laughed. He looked so comical with his face on fire, glistening with sweat, and the heave of his breaths sounding like a cow lowing. 'What possessed you to run –'

'Why'd he do that?' he managed in one long moan.

Julia blinked. She stepped back.

'Julia!' Anne called, nearly pitching head over heels in her agitation to get to them.

Julia was seeing everything through a veil of muslin. She felt her shoulders draw up instinctively, preparing to bear. She thought, I won't hear it. If I don't hear it it won't be true.

Cathal was crying now, in big childish gulps, wide fat tears splatting over the tops of his wellingtons.

Julia could only stand there helplessly waiting. Already, she was standing in a place beyond herself, gauging her own reactions. Thinking, how can I make him not say it?

'I can't believe he . . .' Cathal choked.

'Jesus.' Julia listed sideways into Anne's waiting arms.

'Julia, listen now...' Anne panted. Dried-in streaks of mascara along her cheekbones. Curlers dangling off skeins of twisted hair. 'Listen to me...'

Julia crunched her forehead back and forth across Anne's bony shoulders, wanting to force her way inside Anne. If she could just get in there, she might be safe.

'If it's Brian,' she said hoarsely, 'don't let him tell me.'


Jennifer sat very still, hands on her lap, making and breaking upside-down steeples. She could see Richard in the gardens below, head craning forward, fingers entwined behind his back. Checking the flower borders. He bent to stroke some rare specimen. She felt a hot pang of pity for him, for the way their lives had turned out. For the things they obviously had not done, did not know how to do, that had resulted in this emptiness. She thought that later, when they were at home again, she would show him some kindness, some gentle gesture, because they were not bad people, it was just that bad things had happened to them. She thought that a person must still feel love, if they could feel pity, because it was the pity that made you see the other person as a human being, with needs and desires, and then the love kicked in while you watched those desires being thwarted. She remembered the day, not so long ago, when she had said to Brian that she was never sure if she had really loved Richard. And she felt a bit ashamed about that. Because she had been trying to hurt Brian, as if he had needed hurting. But the loss of Sam had made her wantonly cruel.

She compressed her lips, twisted her fingers in and out, and thought that the world was crueller than she could have imagined. A ridiculous thought, she knew, but there were so many unloved children out there. Sam had had love oozed into every pore from the day he was born. She would always remember him that way. A vessel for uncomplicated love, the kind of love which had grown equivocal, somehow tainted, between their adult selves. And in a strange way perhaps that was all the meaning that could be given to his brief span. She desperately wanted to say that to Julia. She wanted to tell her to stop looking for meanings, stop trying to make sense of the senseless, because the only thing that was irrefutable was that Sam had lived and had been loved. And denial of grief was a denial of that love. She wanted to hold her daughter to feel the baby that had once clapped hands and kicked her legs at the sight of her. She wanted to lavish her with that uncomplicated love that had somehow become estranged once Carol was born. Julia – the child who had done everything possible to be disagreeable because it was easier to be that way than to face up to the possibility that she was not loved.

If only people could behave according to textbook logic, Jennifer surmised, then they would strive to attain the thing that eluded them, or fight to conquer the thing that frightened them. Sometimes they did and sometimes it worked, but mostly there were Julias: people who placed the thing they wanted at some fixed point in the distance and then worked backwards from it. By the age of nine or ten, Julia would pretend to be asleep, or would pointedly turn her head to the wall to avoid her mother's goodnight kiss. Jennifer knew that she was meant to persist, but she was tired in the evenings, and irked by the irrational, nightly performance. And she had had strange, disturbed thoughts for a long time after Carol. They had a validating name for it now; back then, it was called 'throwing a wobbly'. She could almost laugh at that notion today – throwing a wobbly, when she snipped the tops off Richard's roses one rainy night; when the bread knife sang to her every morning, begging her to plunge it into her chest; when she had had to bunch her fists at bathtimes, to stop her hands from submerging that surly, uncooperative daughter's face.

She'd just stopped trying after a while, at first to punish Julia, and then because quite simply it was easier. It was always easier to love soft children like Carol, to bestow nightly kisses upon their peachy, willing cheeks. But she knew, even then, that it was the hard children who needed kissing. Parents always hoped for a time when they could play catch up. And their adult children, nursing childhood grievances, did their utmost to deny them that chance. To be fair to her daughter, Jennifer didn't think that she indulged in the cult of self-indulgence she saw everywhere today. It saddened her that she could not reverse time to get back to the child she had quite wilfully hurt at times, because she was less kissable.

Jennifer reached out and pressed her hand around Brian's limp fingers. The eyelids flickered, then opened abruptly. He cast her a crooked, sleepy smile. 'You're still here?'

'Yes. Richard too. He's walking the grounds.'

'How long have I . . . ?'

'A couple of hours now. They said you'd be very sleepy for a while, even after all the gunge was pumped out.'

'What . . . I've lost track of . . .'

'Monday morning.' She checked her watch. 'It's very early, but we couldn't sleep so we decided to come back to check on you . . . We stayed at the house last night. After . . .' Her voice trailed off.

'I suppose I should be thanking you,' he said, wincing.

'I suppose you should.' Jennifer smiled and squeezed his hand.

'I'm sorry.' He passed a trembling hand over his eyes. 'God, I'm tired of saying that word.'

'It's Carol you should be thanking really – if thanks come into it,' Jennifer said. 'She warned me to keep an eye on you after her last visit. She had a bad feeling, she said. I kept remembering her saying that all through yesterday morning. Normally, Richard would just tell me that I was being silly or something, but when I asked him to go up to London, he didn't say a word – just got in the car and drove us up.' She pinched the bridge of her nose. 'It's funny – when I saw you lying there, on Sam's bed, your arms were like this' – she wrapped her arms around her body – 'as if you were holding someone. I felt so calm. I knew that we were meant to get there in time. I just knew it. I held your hand while we waited for the ambulance, and I felt angry and relieved and incredibly happy all at the same time.' She frowned. 'You'd better tell me now – are you going to try this again?'

The crisp, starched sheet felt cool in the damp cleft between his chin and neck. How could he answer that? He was still contemplating a return to life since late last night, when his eyes had flickered open to white walls, fluorescent tubes along the ceiling, a cobweb in the far corner of the otherwise sterile room. And a pain in head and gut rushing at him like a deranged bull. Jennifer and Richard were bent over the bed, their heads locked together, only drawing apart when he had flapped them aside to drool a rancid green bile over the side. What way should he look at things now? Because, by definition, life after suicide – or suicide attempt, or bid, or however people chose to put it – must mean yet more failure. The upshot was – life. And he had sort of hoped to be done with that. He had to admit it: amongst other things, he felt a bit embarrassed.

'Because if you are,' Jennifer was saying, 'I'll do the job myself right now . . . What were you thinking of?' she added in a softer tone.

'Everything.' Brian turned his head away. 'Everyone . . . Sam . . . Noel, my brother.'

'Brian, you can't . . .'

He caught her eye then, so she wouldn't think that he was flunking it. 'I think . . . No, I know now that I killed him too.' He held on to the last word, fixing her with his eyes.

Jennifer opened her mouth, closed it again. A plump nurse whisked into the room, giving Jennifer a tight little smile as she wrote something on Brian's chart. The smile froze when she looked at Brian – another sentimental Irish drunk, taking up a bed and her precious time. 'How are we feeling? All right?'

Mullingar or thereabouts, Brian thought. Thick accent still but slightly tempered at the edges. Probably said 'cor' or 'what it is, is' after twenty years in England. Round, flat face with small dark eyes, like a half-baked bun.

'Fine thanks.' He shifted up on the bed. 'Umm, when could I leave, d'you think?'

'Soon as the doctor's taken a look at you, shouldn't be long more. She's verrry busy. Will you have a cup of tea now?'

'If it wouldn't be too much trouble.'

'Would you like one yourself?' she asked Jennifer, taking the grit out of her voice again.

Jennifer smiled and nodded. Brian had begun to shake all over. He clenched his teeth and gripped his hands together.

'That happens sometimes.' Mullingar was altogether softer

259

now. Probably had a brother, a priest, a drunk. 'The shakes'll pass in a minute. It's just the system settling into itself again.'

For a crazy moment, Brian wanted to say that actually he wasn't a drunk, he was a murderer. But he still wanted that cup of tea. The nurse left and Jennifer moved closer.

'What did you mean, Brian? About your brother?'

'We were fighting. I tripped him. The stakes came loose. I knew that I should have checked them. I've always known that. But I didn't remember – remember putting out my leg, until yesterday.'

He sank back into the pillow. The shaking stopped. He felt curiously relieved, to have uttered those words, to someone other than himself. The thing that had not been real was realized at last, no less terrible for that, but somehow, a little more bearable.

'Are you sure?' All that Jennifer could summon. He felt grateful to her for the honest shock in her eyes.

'I'm sure.'

She sat back with a deep sigh, steepled fingers tapping against her lips. The tea arrived and they sipped in silence for a long time. Richard's head craned around the door. 'Brian,' he said.

'Richard.'

It seemed to Brian that Richard was almost tiptoeing across the room to take up his chair by Jennifer. As if any sudden movements would plunge them all into chaos again.

'How are you – um – feeling?' Richard asked.

'Oh, fine. Fine.'

'That's good. They look after their garden here. I'll say that for them.'

'Do they? I haven't actually . . .'

'Oh, of course you haven't. Well, not yet I mean. Worth a look before you leave, though.'

'I will.'

There were conversations you didn't want to have, Brian thought. The post-suicide attempt must rank a certain ten out of ten. Richard looked just as uncomfortable, humming now as he tapped his knees.

'You must go to Ireland, Brian,' Jennifer suddenly interrupted the gloomy silence.

'I must?'

'You and Julia – neither of you can go on like this. None of us can.' She looked at him with steely determination. 'I've booked you a ticket. We'll take you to the airport once the doctor has . . .' She stopped to check if he intended arguing but he was gazing impassively up at the ceiling.

'Does she . . . ?'

Jennifer shook her head. 'Not yet. But I have a number to ring. Some friend of yours – I can't quite remember the . . .'

'Cathal.'

'Yes. That's it. I'll phone him later today.' She waved back Richard's interjection. 'No, no, Richard. This is the right thing to do. I'm sure of it. When Brian gets there, he'll realize it too. We have to . . . We have to –' She broke off, struggling for words.

Take our beating, Brian completed the sentence in his own mind. There was no getting away from it. Perhaps Jennifer was right. If there was nothing else he could offer them, he could at least bare his back so that Julia and, yes, his father too, might have something to strike against. He thought of all the years of silence his father had endured for his sake. And it was for his sake, he saw quite clearly now, that they had learned to behave as though Noel had never existed.

261

Because Jeremiah had always remembered what Brian had chosen to forget – had seen the extended leg, had advocated Noel's victory, then had been forced to watch as Noel sailed back on to the rocks in a defeat so final that there could never be another chance at triumph.

'My only fear is that I might upset her –' he began, breaking off at Jennifer's pointedly droll expression. 'Yes. I see what you mean,' he added with a grimace.

In some respects, he felt as if they had all been divested of superfluous garments, as if they now walked, nakedly, into a strange and unfamiliar landscape, where the usual platitudes and trite offers of apology and subsequent forgiveness did not exist. 'I'm sorry.' 'You're forgiven.' No, there were places where that simply would not work. So you took your punishment, by going on anyway.

'You'll go?' Jennifer bit her bottom lip.

'I'll go.'

He wondered if Julia were discovering the same thing. The family was a ruthless entity. And very often, contrary to belief, the rule of thumb was survival of the unfittest.

# FIFTEEN

# Perfect Truth

Julia couldn't hear another word of Anne's babbling. All she could fix on to was 'no, no, he's alive'. She felt as if she were in a dream as she gripped Cathal's still heaving shoulders. 'But it's all right, Cathal,' she was half laughing, half crying.

Cathal was in a similar state. Embarrassed to be crying so openly in front of them. He pawed at his cheeks, laughed, then snorted again. Anne hugged him. 'Ah, Cathal,' she said, winking at Julia. 'Come to Mamma. There now, shh shh.'

'Stop that,' Cathal said trying to brush her off.

' "What kind of a stunt is that to pull?" he says when he gets off the phone from your mother,' Anne laughed to Julia. 'And away down the road with him like a deranged bullock. Only letting me know in bits and pieces what your mother said, when he had to stop for a breath. Had to head for Jeremiah though, didn't you, pet?' Anne added, pinching his cheek with just the slightest edge to her voice. She turned to Julia again, her expression serious. 'Your mother said that Brian remembered – well – that he was responsible for Noel –'

'It was an accident,' Cathal shot in, looking directly into Julia's eyes for the first time since Jeremiah's fall. But he failed to hide his lack of conviction. Repeating the old line, the one he had been fed so often as a child that he had learned to regurgitate it without question. But she could see the doubt swelling even as she returned his gaze.

'He means Noel,' Anne interjected quickly, not realizing that Julia understood perfectly well. 'That's what –'

Julia cut across her with a frantic wave of her hand. She didn't want to hear any more. Cathal stiffened when they heard a cry from within. He moved automatically to the door. Anne tried to stop him. 'Lev him be a minute.'

'I can't,' he said simply.

Julia desperately wanted to get away from there then. She wanted to walk for miles and miles. An overwhelming desire for straightforward movement after all the circling, the stops and starts. Cathal was nearly past her when she pulled on the sleeve of his sweater. He turned and glanced at her vaguely, his body already with Jeremiah. She pulled the diary from her pocket, quickly riffling through with one hand until she found the page she wanted. She thrust it at him. 'No accident.'

He looked curiously at the book; she thought it seemed unfamiliar to him. 'Not here,' she urged softly, jerking her head toward Jeremiah's room. 'In there, with him.'

She left them then, the dog circling her ankles with excitement, Anne's plaintive cries following them all the way up to the top of the road. 'Julia! Julia, come back here. What's going . . . Are ye all gone mad or . . . *Jesus*!'

Julia turned once to wave down at her. Anne was still shaking her head, curlers flying in every direction. But she looked quite amused at the same time. She was about to follow Cathal inside when an afterthought struck her. She called up again but Julia couldn't hear. Julia supposed that Anne shared her own relief that she hadn't been the bearer of such terrible news after all. It was poor Cathal who remained most horrified of all, that Brian would even attempt such a thing. Had reached a place, unthinkable to Cathal, where he had been willing to consign his Catholic soul to everlasting oblivion. Julia laughed aloud. She only cared that Brian had managed to continue the tawdry pattern of his life – by being unsuccessful.

She felt that she could walk for a thousand miles. Her legs were on coiled springs, not a hint of fatigue even when she turned down off the main road following a narrow track she knew to be a good four miles from Jeremiah's place. Dog lagged behind at times, then, fortified by ditchwater, he broke into a loping run to catch up with her. She turned to encourage him. 'C'mon, c'mon, Dog, just another mile or two. I don't want to go back just yet.'

His tongue lolled sideways, limp as a long pink rasher. He reached her and thumped what was left of the tail against her legs. She bent down and buried her face in his matted crown. He keened softly with pleasure.

Now, he pranced ahead, energy renewed by her little caress. He wanted to please her. They were heading down toward the sea. Smoky tendrils of cloud gathering on the horizon. Rain in the air, making bushes quiver in anticipation. Ploughed white furrows cutting across the charcoal bay.

Dog hesitated. Then went on. Halfway down the track, he stopped again, put his nose in the air. He did not like the smell of it, turned and hobbled back to her ankles. He refused to budge another inch despite her entreaties. She looked back at him; he had hunkered down in the middle of the road, tail drumming a forlorn beat against the ground. She missed him.

A question mark of turf smoke in the distance. Unusual for the season. She had not seen that roof before. Something, a sound, maybe not a sound, a disturbance of air, in the blackberry bushes ahead. Julia stopped and waited. And knew instinctively what she was waiting for.

He stepped, or rather slunk out because it did not seem like a concise movement, more an insinuation. Unblinking yellow eyes took her measure, took one flicker sideways as if to check the area. She drew her hands down along her cheeks. A curious half-smile was etched on her lips. 'Ah, you,' she said.

The tail was up, the very tip of it, flicking from side to side, almost insolently. He was enjoying himself. Now, she could quite distinctly hear the low strum of his vocal chords. He advanced, but slowly, at his own pace. There was no need to hurry. There was nowhere for her to run. She stood motionless and waited. Nothing else to do. The rising up of the circlet of hair around his neck, then the slow, deliberate pulling back of skin around his mouth. Acerose fangs settling upon each other like old friends. His eyes had slitted. Julia took a step.

Her movement disturbed his composure for an instant. He had not anticipated resistance. The growl deepened. He moved quickly to the side then back again, legs quivering, just to let her know that he was in control. A lunge forward then back again. Tired of that game, he waited for her to make her move, maintaining the tension of the bow against the strings of his throat all the while. Julia knew that she should be doing something; at the very least thinking about a retreat. But she felt strangely listless. Watching him with more curiosity than fear.

He was crouched now, inching forward on his rear flank, belly scraping the ground. In daylight, he was even bigger than she had estimated. Standing to full height, his head would align with her waist. That head was grotesquely large too, a chiselled slab of black and tan markings, nostrils flaring on the black stub of nose. Malevolent, unblinking eyes holding her gaze.

Julia took a few steps backwards, toe to ankle, more to gauge his reaction than to effect a retreat. His ears pricked, a slight rise of the haunches, legs trembling in anticipation, the steady timbre of his snarl rising a decibel. She stopped still again, and wondered what part of her body he would eventually go for. A savaging of the ankles to bring her to the ground? Or would he go straight for the throat: rising on his hind legs, front paws pressing heavily on to her chest? Instinctively, a hand reached around her neck, although there was still that numbness within her anaesthetizing fear, a fear which would be healthy, necessary even, if she were to find some intuitive way to get away from this beast reasonably unscathed.

She took a step forward again and he half rose, startled by her unfathomable reactions. He could not smell her fear. She had heard once that it was through the palms of the hands and the soles of the feet than an animal could scent the victim's terror. She looked down and spread her palms, then rubbed them together. They were dry and calloused from the farm. No sweat. She could sense his confusion. He would be compelled into action soon, to quell his own rising doubts. A shadow flickered in the tawny gaze. The teeth clicked together. Then, a startled, furtive glance beyond her. The collie was moving slowly down the road toward them. He kept by the ditch side, brushing against bramble bushes. Although the hairs were up around his neck she could see the fear in his eyes. He took another step, paused with a hesitant paw in mid-air, then another step, another pause. The tail firmly tucked between his hind legs. 'Go back, Dog,' she hissed between clenched teeth. 'I'll think of something. Go on now, go back.'

The black and tan stood fully erect now, back slightly arched. He had the meanest eyes she had ever seen. Then she remembered the malevolence in Jeremiah's gaze when he fought with Edward. She slowly lowered herself on to her haunches, keeping her eyes pinned on him. Her hand snaked out for a rock. Fingers curled around cold, jagged granite – and he took her movement as the signal. He sprang forward so fast she could only see a dark blur from the corner of her eye before sharp, searing needles pierced her out-stretched wrist.

She lost her balance and fell backwards with her free hand covering her vulnerable, exposed throat. He concentrated on her captured wrist, snarling while his head heaved from side to side, a dog with a bone – a bone which would surely crack in another instant if she could not shake him off. Still, she waited for the fear to tell her what to do. But nothing, only pain which even in her prostrate position she found herself analysing in that curious, deadened way. His teeth moved up an inch. Blood dripped from her scored wrist. She managed to swing up on to her haunches again so that her face was mauling distance from him, their eyes locked. She saw the growing confusion in his glare. Dog was moving behind him, nipping at the massive hindquarters then darting back before another quick foray forward again. The pain in her arm was steaming by now. The animal gave a quick glance of irritation back at the collie, then his teeth moved up, snaring her elbow. In a brief moment, he would go for her face, she understood that perfectly well. The smell of his breath so close was rank, fouler than she could have imagined, the fangs yellowed and dripping. Her silence, the lack of a natural response was incensing him further but it had also gained her useless seconds. The head was so near now, she could see the reflection of her own deadpan mask in the black of his pupils. Sharp incisors ground against sinew; she could feel a tendon snap, sending a thrill of white pain up her arm. The collie was yelping, utterly frustrated in his efforts to help her. The monster's tail swatted back at him as though at an insistent fly. She saw a predatory gleam of triumph in the yellow eyes which rolled back in his head just as his teeth released her elbow and snapped together once, on their way to her cheek.

He moved quickly. Eyes skimming marble and grey. A small, white, insignificant cross cast a shadow over a mound of earth beside the headstone of his mother and brother, in the top left-hand corner. Two other siblings lay there too, of whom he had no memories. Brian stopped halfway across the graveyard to register the familiar names along the rows: neighbours; friends; to the right of him his old teacher, Cotter, alongside his wife and one son so far. The air itself here was spicily familiar in a way he had not experienced for the longest time. Further up, under shiny speckled granite, lay Cathal's father and mother, flowered perspex crosses keeping them company.

No perspex on Sam's rough grave though. Brian knelt to lift the little dried-flower bouquets, shielding his eyes from the tomb's inscription. Anne, he smiled sadly. She must have placed one every month. Little memorials to a boy she hardly knew. He felt intensely grateful to her, and sorry for his son who had to be remembered by a stranger. He raised his eyes and read 'Sam' . . . The rest blurred.

Above him, the sky sagged heavily with rain. It brooded around the small grey-stoned chapel. The birds were flying low, in anticipation of the coming storm. He recalled a night when he had sat in Sam's room until the early hours, the two of them waiting for the first flash of lightning. Sam gazing at the sea through sleepy eyes, tightening his grip on Brian's fingers when it arrived. Jumping a little in his skin when thunder rolled directly overhead. Brian had wondered then where the world would take his son. And when the time came, how far he himself would lag behind. They had curled up together on the narrow cot, Sam's curly head pressed back against Brian's chest. The scent of sweat rising from a gap in the pyjamas around his neck, vividly, achingly reminding Brian of his twin.

A few pregnant drops plashed across graves. Streaking grey stone with threads of black. Brian reached out his hands, stroking the mound, the white wooden cross, feeling the grooves of his son's name with his thumbs. Whatever destiny he had imagined for Sam, it was not this. Nature had been defied, the natural order of things turned upside down. Children were supposed to pray beside their parents' gravestones. And yet, kneeling there, feeling the increasing rain slant against his face, fingers clutching wooden slats, he felt a strange sense of peace rise within him. There was nowhere else to be, but here. He thought that there should be another language to describe such purity of emotion, when everything extraneous was whittled away, leaving only perfect truth. He craned forward, placing his lips against his son's name. In saying goodbye to Sam, he understood that he was finally saying goodbye to Noel too. Locking them together in the history of his heart; already carrying them with him into the future. A hope glowing like a hot little coal that the future might yet contain Julia.

The fangs snapped together, missing her cheek by a hair's breadth. Julia's head drew back; he lunged again, this time grazing her shoulder. In a reflex movement she threw herself on to her side, minute daggers piercing a circle in her lower back. She pulled away with a huge effort, tightening her eyes against the pain, just managing to stagger to her feet. The savaged arm dangled uselessly below the elbow. She still held the rock and transferred it to her good hand. He was stalking again, crouched down for the final spring. Her throat for certain this time. The collie whined mournfully, received one snapping half-hearted lunge for his troubles and in that second of freedom, Julia felt something happen inside her. Not the terror she had waited for, but the purest, most refined rage, exquisite in its white-hot flow through her veins.

A towering, glorious rage – it blurred her vision – caused her throat to issue one long guttural cry. His ears pricked at the sound after such a long silence. He sprang and she concentrated all her rage into a fireball of hatred hurled right back at him. He was up on hind legs, huge front paws pressing against her breastbone. She stood perfectly still, supporting both weights. Her good hand whipped up, a deliberate movement taken at lightning speed as the slavering jaw thrust forward at her face, and she plunged her curled fist between the gaping maw, forcing her wrist all the way through. He gagged and allowed his front quarters to slip a little but she thrust harder, feeling the contraction at the back of his throat. He moved his head from side to side, but she kept her arm straight, oblivious to the tearing teeth. She released the rock and quickly withdrew her arm. His eyes bulged. He put his head down and hacked, jaws open and dripping in an effort to expunge the stone. His front paws tore at his throat. He emitted sounds like a geyser stopped in mid-gush. Julia stepped back, every inch of her body coated in hot sweat.

'Come on, come o-on!' she screamed. Summoning him to her with flailing damaged arms. She lashed out with both legs, kicking the side of his head, her own teeth gritted into a snarl. The collie cowered, whimpered under a bush. She kicked again, desperate to hold on to the rage.

But the animal lay on the ground now. Trying to pant, legs taut and quivering, a series of strangled sobs issuing from its blocked throat. She kicked the base of his neck and the rock came spewing out. He wheezed with relief. Dumb, pain-filled, bloodshot eyes gazed up at her. He trembled. She turned on her heel and left him lying there, gasping.

Dog circled her stride, tail victoriously erect. She looked back once and saw a trail of blood on the path between her and the now erect animal, hobbling his shaky retreat down the track. She felt a rush of pure exhilaration. The pain in her arms and shoulder intensified. She had to stop for an instant; the road ahead cleaved into ten before her drunken vision. She gritted her teeth, carrying the useless arm in the cradle of the other. Feet barely skimming the road for the four miles back to the house.

She stood at the top of the road for a while, staring down at the whitewashed stone walls and the surrounding grey outhouses, sheds, lean-tos – a steady build-up over the years of sly additions. Just like deceit, so that now it was virtually impossible to tell where the original house began and the annexes ended. Rain patted her shoulders. She could hear it ricocheting off the iron roofs below. A couple of hens circled the yard, flapping useless wing feathers, fighting over a few remaining grains. Dog waited by her ankles. She felt incredibly tired all of a sudden. Almost too tired to face them – then Anne stepped into the yard and stopped stock-still when she saw Julia. She waited, motionless, as Julia approached, only taking a step forward when she saw Julia's bleeding arm. Julia thought that Anne's taut, pinched face must mirror her own.

'Jesus, what happened?'

Julia tried a tight smile to let her know that she was all right. 'I'll be fine, Anne. It looks worse than it is . . .'

But Anne had stepped back soundlessly to the kitchen, drawing Julia with her. Already grabbing for iodine and bandages so that she might be prepared at a signal from Julia who was grateful for her silence.

Cathal came through from Jeremiah's room. His face had the same pinched look as his wife's. Julia motioned impatiently that her hand was fine – they could deal with it later. He held the diary in one hand. The three of them were just standing there. Cathal shrugged. There was no need for words. His shocked, crumpled face told Julia everything she needed to know.

She ran upstairs, falling sideways against the wall on every second step. She allowed her damaged arm to swing uselessly as she pressed the spaceship to her chest with the other. Downstairs again, her exit was blocked momentarily by Anne who reached out, barely grazing her shoulder.

'Cathal's read it to me,' she whispered. She turned slowly, indicating Jeremiah's room. 'Read it to him too.' Julia saw her own hate reciprocated in Anne's grey eyes. She thought she saw a little gleam of triumph there too. 'We're selling that land, all of it,' Anne continued tersely. 'That may not be much comfort to you, Julia, but I'll sleep easier.'

Julia swallowed. She was about to leave when she turned on impulse and strode past Cathal to where Jeremiah still lay at an awkward angle, on his mat. His gaze was unfocused. Something had dulled in the blue irises. She craned down and curled his bony fingers around the beads of his rosary. He did not resist. 'Cathal's selling your land, Jeremiah,' she whispered. A few drops of blood from her arm splattered across his cheek, forcing him to blink. He caught her look. And she stumbled out of the room again, hoping that he would die with that look in his eyes.

Cathal kept his head lowered. He gently prised her fingers open around the spaceship and slid the diary into her grip also.

She felt a spear of pity for him, with his bowed head, his hands finally emptied of Jeremiah. She wondered how much he remembered or if, like Brian, he had managed to digest a rewritten history.

A pool of fresh blood lapped by her feet. She stepped over it, ignoring Anne's attempt to reach her with the cloths and iodine as she ran blindly out into the yard, legs weaving a path through the fields, down to the cliff's edge. Beads of rain clung to her face. She breathed in deep gusts of salt air. Placed the diary on the ground beside her and made an arc of her body, whizzing Sam's spaceship back to him. For a moment a fleeting illusion that it was flying. Then a fizz of white where the sea claimed it, regurgitating a small round, white vessel. She strained her eyes and watched it bobbing further and further out into the withdrawing tide. She smiled, wanting it to sail on for ever.

A slender figure caught her eye, making an approach down the fields. Edward, she thought. She shielded her eyes against rain with her good hand. Although as thin as Edward, the figure was shorter. Brian. She held her breath and waited.

It took him a while to reach her. His gait so hesitant she thought that he might turn at any moment to head back toward the house.

'Julia.'

Everything about him separate. A creature set apart, palpably alone. She understood only too well. Dark circles under his eyes, grooved cheekbones where there used to be flesh. The blue familiar gaze, just catching the edge of hers, uncertain if he dared to meet her eyes. A tiny muscle clenching and unclenching along his unshaven jawline.

Julia instinctively reached out to touch his arm but stroked air instead. Too soon for touch. Her hand recoiled, making python loops in empty space. He wanted to say something about the bleeding arm, she understood, but it seemed as though he were afraid to utter a solitary word in case he might lose whatever moment she might offer him of her company.

She looked past his downcast head, imagining Jeremiah standing by the window, seeing in her mind's eye the basilisk stare, the clamped outthrust jaw.

Her voice was flat and emotionless. 'You didn't kill your brother, Brian.'

He shuddered, eyes so far back in their sockets she thought they must be touching his mind.

'Jeremiah did,' she added softly.

He looked at her then. A growing confusion spreading over his face.

'It's all there, in your mother's journal.' She lifted the book and pressed it into his hand.

He turned it over. Vaguely smiling at the memory of it. 'Her recipe book?'

Julia nodded. 'She saw it, Brian. Maybe Cathal did too, but, like you, he was just a child and believed what Jeremiah told everyone. Just an accident . . .'

'But I . . .' Brian searched for words. 'I remembered putting out my leg. I remembered the touch of him . . .'

'Read it,' she said quietly, opening the pages for him because his hands were trembling too much. 'Jeremiah told you to put out your leg.'

'Me . . . ?'

'Yes, you. But you didn't. You stayed curled up in a ball. He was furious, so he showed you what he wanted you to do. It was his foot that you felt against yours, just before Noel . . .' Her voice drifted away. 'Margaret saw it. Noel tripped over your father's foot, Brian. And she had to live with that secret for the rest of her miserable life.' She tapped the journal. 'She had to get it out though – one way or the other. If only for herself.'

Brian followed her gaze down to where the sea washed over black rocks. She saw his eyes take in the spaceship, heaving up and down, almost out of sight already. 'I wanted to give it back to him,' she said hopelessly.

His eyes squeezed shut.

'You don't have to be entirely wrong for him to be entirely right, you know. Not always. Not for ever,' she said.

Tears slid down his cheeks. He shuddered so hard that she thought he might break.

'Thank you,' he said hoarsely. 'I don't deserve it. But thank you.'

276

She thought for a moment that in all the world there were only the two of them. Their memories – the last thing left to make sense of Sam's existence. An existence as inconsequential as a snowflake in the grand scale of things, as a speck of ash flying loosely into the cosmos from two colliding galaxies. And as inimitable. And if they could not grieve for him, for the loss of him, then who might? There was nothing else to offer. The last thing they could share, perhaps the only thing.

Julia felt her legs buckle. Brian caught her before she sank to the ground. He held on tightly. His eyes were dry as they stared grittily over the top of her shoulder.

'I loved him,' she cried out – surprised herself, by the simplicity of it. Perhaps all truths were simple in the end; it was the path to them that was complex.

He nodded, words of agreement catching in his throat. 'I think that I – went looking for Sam – and found Noel,' he said after a long while.

She thought there was something faintly comforting in that. An idea of Noel watching Sam for them formed in her mind. The only thing she understood with any certainty was that they should remain here. In this place. Where they could share in Sam's isolation.

She knew that the long serrated grief was yet to come. Nights when there would be no consolation in sight, only stars. There might be moments of forgiveness, and moments when that would be retracted again. Moments of bitter, acrid recriminations, but also moments when they might remember what had made them better than they were for such a brief time. Sam. A ghostly presence who would always hover between them.

Brian tightened his grip, squeezing the breath from her

body. She felt her deadened arm struggle to return the pressure. Her inarticulate cries echoed his as they clasped one another. For now, all they could do was cling and weep: for Sam, for Noel, for themselves, for the possibility of love enduring without forgiveness – and for the blind, trusting love of constantly betrayed children everywhere.